"Grandpop warned me Yankees were no better than dogs.

"You stood there, watching me undress, watching me bathe myself, and you have no remorse, no shame."

Lizzy struck him again and again, and Cody did nothing to block the blows. "You are mean. Cruel. Horrible."

Tears sprang to her eyes, and she felt ashamed that he should see her crying. But as she tried to turn away, he caught her by the wrists and held her.

"Don't cry, Lizzy."

"I am not crying." But at the denial, her tears flowed even harder, and she felt them stream, hot and wet, along her cheeks. She tried to yank her hands free, but he continued to hold her firmly by the wrists.

"You're laughing at me!" she cried.

"I'd never laugh at you." His tone hardened. "I'm sorry that I startled you. But I'm not sorry for what I saw."

Dear Reader,

As the holidays approach (at much too fast a pace for most of us) we, at Harlequin Historicals would like to take the time to wish our readers well.

This month, *Christmas Miracle* by Ruth Langan tells the story of a Southern family displaced by the Civil War. Though their lives would never be the same, Lizzie Spooner was determined to show them all that life was still worth living.

Impetuous Julia Masonet had always chafed under her guardian Richard's watchful eye, until she was faced with losing him. With *Tender Journey,* Sally Cheney has written a delightfully different story of a free spirit and the proper gentleman who has captured her heart.

China Blossom, Margaret Moore's second historical for Harlequin, offers the reader a glimpse of 19th-century England's elite society, and a young woman who dares to defy its strictest rules.

When a handsome drifter saves the life of an Irish-Mexican beauty, their love threatens to destroy them, in Elizabeth Lane's tale of the old West, *Moonfire.*

Also this month, keep an eye out for the HARLEQUIN HISTORICAL CHRISTMAS STORIES 1992 collection, wherever Harlequin Books are sold.

Thanks again for your continued support.

Sincerely,

Tracy Farrell
Senior Editor

Christmas Miracle

Ruth Langan

Harlequin Books

TORONTO • NEW YORK • LONDON
AMSTERDAM • PARIS • SYDNEY • HAMBURG
STOCKHOLM • ATHENS • TOKYO • MILAN
MADRID • WARSAW • BUDAPEST • AUCKLAND

Harlequin Historicals first edition November 1992

ISBN 0-373-28747-X

CHRISTMAS MIRACLE

Books by Ruth Langan

Harlequin Historicals

Mistress of the Seas #10
Texas Heart #31
*Highland Barbarian #41
*Highland Heather #65
*Highland Fire #91
*Highland Heart #111
Texas Healer #131
Christmas Miracle #147

Harlequin Books

Harlequin Historical Christmas Stories 1990
"Christmas at Bitter Creek"

*Highland Series

RUTH LANGAN

traces her ancestry to Scotland and Ireland. It is no surprise, then, that she feels a kinship with the characters in her historical novels.

Married to her childhood sweetheart, she has reared five children and lives in Michigan, the state where she was born and raised.

To: Haley Langan Bissonnette—
our Christmas gift,
And to her proud parents, Carol and Bryon,
and her big sister, Aubrey,
And as always to Tom,
whose proposal one Christmas Eve led me on the
adventure of a lifetime.

Chapter One

New Mexico Territory
Winter, 1866

"Doggone it, girl, stop dawdling and lean your shoulder into that wheel, or I'll never get this wagon rolling."

"I'm trying, Grandpop."

Lizzy Spooner felt her muscles protest as she heaved all her weight against the lever she had rigged from a pole and a boulder. Gradually the wagon tilted enough to allow her grandfather to replace the broken wheel.

While they worked, Lizzy's younger sister, Sara Jean, lay in the dried grass that dotted the hillside. Every few minutes she rolled from one side to the other, trying to find a comfortable position for her body, swollen with child.

A few yards away a boy of five was busy trying to capture a grasshopper.

"Maybe we ought to stop here in the shelter of these trees, Grandpop. I don't like the color of that sky."

Lizzy shivered and wished she'd pulled a blanket around her instead of the thin shawl she'd fished from the trunk. "You can feel the air growing colder."

"We're not stopping." Amos Spooner gave a last twist of the wheel, then wiped his hands on his ragged britches. "You can let up on that lever now and help your sister into the wagon."

As Lizzy opened her mouth to protest, the old man turned away and climbed onto the wagon. She'd learned years earlier that there was no use arguing with Grandpop once his mind was made up.

"Come on, Sara Jean." As gently as possible Lizzy helped her sister to her feet.

"I wish we could stay here for the night." Sara Jean pressed her hands to her lower back. "I swear I just can't take much more of this jarring."

"Maybe we'll find a town up ahead. James," Lizzy called to her little brother. "Time to climb aboard."

As he scrambled up onto the wagon seat, the boy wrapped his arms around his oldest sister's neck and received the expected hug.

With a creak of wagon wheels, they lurched ahead.

"Will we really be in California by Christmas?" James asked with a note of wonder.

"That's what Grandpop said." Lizzy fought to swallow the lump in her throat. She had spent every one of her eighteen years at the Willows, the beautiful old plantation that had been in her family since Grandpop's father had cleared the land nearly a hundred years ago. This would be their first Christmas ever spent away from their Georgia home.

"Do you think Christmas will come way out here in the wilderness, Lizzy?"

"Of course. Christmas comes every year."

The old man beside her shot her an angry look. "Stop humoring the boy, Lizzy. You know we got no time for such things anymore. It's enough just trying to survive."

The little boy lifted a pudgy hand to wipe at his eyes. It wouldn't do for Grandpop to see tears. "I guess it won't be the same as it was at home, will it?"

"Nothing's ever the same, boy," Amos said with a scowl. "Now stop acting like a baby."

The boy hid behind his sister's skirts and said softly, "Last Christmas Pa was off fighting the Yankees, and all Ma did was cry. And now Ma and Pa are both in heaven."

Lizzy thought about the crude marker they'd left on Ma's grave alongside the trail. Not much to show for a lifetime of love. But at least Ma had found a haven from a world gone mad.

It had broken her poor mother's heart to leave everything behind and seek a new life. Sweet Ma. She'd done the best she could. Sickly as a child, she'd been pampered by family and servants all her life. She had grown up to be a dreamy woman. Fragile, Pa had called her. His fragile little Jo Mae. Pa's death in a war she didn't understand had left her shattered. Leaving the Willows had been the final blow.

Lizzy glanced toward her sister. Sara Jean looked just like Ma. Pale yellow hair. Soft blue eyes. No wonder Pa couldn't help spoiling her. At fifteen, she was like a silly child in a grown woman's body. Except for the discomfort, the fact that she was carrying a baby had not registered in her mind at all. The baby's father, Ben, had been one month shy of his eighteenth birthday when he married Sara Jean and went off to fight in the war. They'd only had two days and nights together before he got himself killed by a Yankee's bullet. But that was long enough to leave her with Ben's baby.

And James. Poor little James. It was plain to see that Grandpop wanted him to be tough, to grow up as fast as possible and take Pa's place. As if anyone could ever take Pa's place. It hurt too much to think about the handsome, courtly gentleman who had called his first-born his little whirlwind because she was always in a hurry.

Lizzy could understand Grandpop's pain at the loss of his only son. But James had a lot of years to live before he'd catch up with manhood. Ma, on the other hand, had wanted James to remain her baby forever. Her little Jamie. No one had given a thought to what James wanted.

Lizzy drew the shawl tightly around her and clung to the wagon seat. As eldest, it was taken for granted that she would carry on as she always had. But now that their plantation was gone, and Pa and Ma were dead, she wasn't sure just what to do. Sometimes she missed Ma and Pa so much she wanted to bury her face in her hands and cry her heart out. But there wasn't time for even that. There'd been no time to grieve for Ma. The morning after they'd buried her, they were back on the trail. Heading west. For a new life. A new beginning.

She knew why Grandpop had insisted on bringing them all west. After the plantation was destroyed and the land sold for back taxes, it was his way of dealing with the loss of a way of life he had always known. With the land of his father gone, he needed a new challenge. In a new setting. Far away from all the memories. But was he really strong enough to start over and lead them to the promised land?

Lizzy was startled out of her thoughts by the sting of something wet and cold on her cheek. She brushed a hand to it, then stared in wonder.

"Look, Lizzy," James said, "the rain is frozen."

"Snow," Grandpop muttered. He cracked the whip, urging the horses into a trot. "We've got to find a town. Soon. James, you'd best crawl into the back and warn your sister to hang on. We'll be moving at a fast clip."

"But I never saw snow before, Grandpop."

"You heard me, boy. Besides, you'll be seeing more'n you ever wanted."

Reluctantly the little boy shimmied through the opening in the canvas and disappeared from view. Within minutes he poked his head out.

"You're going to have to slow down, Grandpop. Sara Jean said she can't take much more of this jostling."

The old man frowned beneath bushy white eyebrows. He tore his gaze from the team to glower at his grandson. "Can't stop in the middle of this godforsaken wilderness, boy. Tell her we're going to keep going till we reach someplace that'll offer shelter from the storm."

The boy's head disappeared inside and the old man turned his attention to his older granddaughter.

"What's that in the distance, Lizzy? A town? These old eyes can't see that far."

Lizzy gave her grandfather a gentle smile. If the truth were known, he could hardly see ten feet in front of him. But he refused to admit it. Since leaving Georgia, they had hit every rock and rut along the trail. She had the blisters on her backside to prove it.

She peered through the swirling snow kicked up by the team. "It's mountains, Grandpop. We're heading toward mountains."

The old man muttered an oath under his breath before adding, "I guess it would be too much to hope that someone would be living way out here. A man would have to be some kind of fool to make his home in this barren wasteland."

Like us, Lizzy thought. Some kind of fools. Leaving behind everything they'd ever held dear, and hoping to make a new start in this… What had Grandpop called it? This barren wasteland.

The wagon rattled on, up hills, down dry gulches, with the horses straining in the harness. The snow was thicker now, stinging cheeks, blinding eyes. The wind howled, swirling it into drifts.

From the back of the wagon came the sound of Sara Jean's low moans. It was enough to cause the hairs on the back of Lizzy's neck to rise. Every so often the old man would bite down on the stem of an empty pipe when the sound went on too long. The girl beside him spoke not a word. But the knuckles of her hands were white as she gripped the edge of the hard seat.

"Careful Grandpop. You're heading—" Before the words were out of her mouth, the wheels tipped precariously and there was the terrible, wrenching sound of splintering wood as the wagon slid down a ravine and landed on its side. In the confusion the team reared up and ripped loose the wagon tongue, dragging it through the snow until it became lodged in a pile of brush. There they stood, blowing and snorting in a frenzy of terror.

Lizzy had been thrown free and found herself face-down in a mound of snow. As she sat up she heard the cries of the others. Picking her way through the drifts, she reached the wagon.

"Sara Jean. James. Grandpop." She frantically searched through the torn canvas and scattered household goods.

"I'm here." Lizzy saw James shake off a piece of canvas.

"Are you hurt?"

"No. But Sara Jean's awfully quiet."

Lizzy crawled over a shattered rocking chair and bits and pieces of broken china to find her sister lying on a pile of clothing.

"Sara Jean. Can you move?"

The younger girl opened her eyes and sat up. "Sweet Lord almighty, I thought I'd die when we went crashing over that hill."

Lizzy watched as the girl touched a hand to her stomach. "I'm fine, Lizzy. At least, nothing hurts more than it did before. Where's Grandpop?"

Lizzy scrambled up and peered through the blinding snow. Cupping her hands to her mouth she shouted, "Grandpop. Can you hear me?"

"Over here."

Lizzy found him sitting in the snow. From the dazed look on his face she knew he'd been badly shaken.

"Can you stand, Grandpop?"

"Forget about me. Find the horses."

"I will. As soon as I see to you." With her hand at his elbow she eased him to his feet. "Lean on me, Grandpop. I'll get you to the wagon."

With slow, plodding steps they slogged through the snow until they reached the wagon. James and Sara Jean were already collecting the household items that littered the bank.

"You sit here, Grandpop," Lizzy said, easing him down on a pile of comforters. "I'll fetch the horses."

By the time she'd managed to free the team from the harness that had tangled around brush and boulders, her fingers were stiff and frozen. Leading the frightened animals to the overturned wagon, she surveyed the damage.

One wheel had sheared off in the fall. The side of the wagon had caved in, the wood shattered beyond repair. But no one seemed to have sustained injuries except Grandpop. He was still sitting where she'd left him, looking dazed and confused.

"Are we going to right the wagon?" James asked as she approached.

"Can't. The wheel's broken. Maybe the axle, too. Besides, the three of us wouldn't be able to budge it."

"What about Grandpop?"

Lizzy glanced at the old man and shook her head. "Grandpop needs to save his strength right now."

"What are we going to do?"

Lizzy struggled to keep her fear hidden from the others. "First we're going to build a shelter."

"But we can't just stay here in this blizzard," Sara Jean wailed. "Lizzy, we'll all freeze to death."

Lizzy drew her arm around the younger girl and carefully kept the panic from her tone. "Now stop fussing. We have plenty of clothes, and Ma's old comforters to keep us warm. And there's enough of last night's stew to hold us for another day or more. I spotted a couple of big boulders over here that ought to offer shelter from the snow."

Leading the way, Lizzy dragged a piece of torn canvas to a niche between two towering boulders. The ground was snug and dry.

"Sara Jean, bring Ma's comforters. James, fetch more canvas."

Working quickly, they made a crude shelter and built a fire. While Sara Jean heated the stew, Lizzy helped Grandpop to a spot near the fire. Then she and James made frequent trips to the wagon, returning with enough splintered wood and wet logs to keep the fire going through the night.

As Sara Jean ladled their food, Grandpop turned his glazed eyes to Lizzy and said, "No telling how long it might snow. We can't stay here, girl, or we'll be food for the wolves in no time. Someone has to go for help."

Lizzy swallowed. There was only one person capable of that. But what he was suggesting was foolhardy.

"I don't know where to go, Grandpop."

"Just take one of the horses and give him his head. If there's a barn, he'll head right to it."

"And if there isn't?" Sara Jean asked.

Lizzy's gaze was drawn to the blizzard that obscured everything beyond the firelight. What sort of dangers lay out there in the darkness? How much cold could she endure before she would give up and close her eyes? How many hours before a body froze to death?

She glanced around at the people who were depending on her to do what was needed, and managed to push aside her fears.

Setting down her half-empty bowl, she plodded to the wagon. When she returned, she had a pile of clothes slung over her arm.

Sara Jean watched as Lizzy removed her petticoats.

"What are you doing?"

Lizzy forced a smile. "Haven't you heard, Sara Jean? This is what all the proper ladies wear to travel through blizzards these days."

She pulled on a pair of Grandpop's britches and tied them up with a length of rope. Over her chemise she pulled on a coarse homespun shirt, then sat down and laced up her high shoes.

When she picked up a shawl, Grandpop lifted a hand to stop her. "Here, Lizzy. Take my sheepskin jacket."

"No. You need that to stay warm."

"I have your ma's quilts. Don't argue. Take it."

Lizzy slipped into the warm jacket, turning up the collar. It smelled of sweat and tobacco and horses. Like Grandpop. It was oddly comforting.

"You'll need this to keep the snow out of your eyes." Grandpop removed his big, wide-brimmed hat and placed it on Lizzy's head.

As she started toward the horses Sara Jean grabbed her hand. "Don't go, Lizzy." Her eyes were wide with fear. "If you go out there, you'll never come back. I just know it."

"Now, girl, you stop...."

"It's all right, Grandpop." Lizzy dropped an arm around her sister's shoulders. "Don't you worry about me, Sara Jean. I'm coming back." She pressed a kiss to her cheek and drew away.

"Lizzy, wait." James rushed forward and thrust something into his sister's hands.

"What's this?"

"The mittens you made for me last winter. You'll need them."

"Why, thank you, James."

She put them on, then drew him close and hugged him fiercely.

Seeing the tears in his eyes, she tousled his hair and whispered, "Take care of your sister and Grandpop until I get back. And say your prayers before you fall asleep."

"I will, Lizzy."

Since there was no saddle, she pulled herself onto the horse's back and dug her hands into his mane. This was the way she had learned to ride across the vast lands of the Willows. Though Ma had complained that it was unbecoming to a lady of breeding, Lizzy had always loved pulling herself onto the bare back of a horse and racing across the meadows to find Pa.

She took a last lingering look at her family, then nudged the horse out into the blinding snow.

From the safety of the fire, this had seemed like merely a foolish idea. But from where Lizzy was now sitting, the whole scheme was crazy. The countryside was blanketed in white. For as far as the eye could see, there was no trace of civilization.

She felt a moment of panic. How would she ever know if the horse was making progress or merely walking in circles? She fought back the fear that threatened to paralyze her and reminded herself that life was no more dangerous in this wilderness than it had been in fiery Georgia during the darkest days of the war. Then, the enemy had been man. Now, it was nature.

Taking a knife from her pocket, she carved a notch on the trunk of a tree, then urged the horse forward. At least she'd know if she passed this way again.

The snow had begun drifting, smoothing out the hollows and dips in the land. Had it not been for the raw cold that bit clear to her bones, Lizzy might have enjoyed the pristine beauty of the stark landscape.

The mountains, which earlier had seemed so far away, now loomed directly ahead of her. As the temperature continued to drop, trees groaned beneath the weight of the snow. The crack of branches splitting away from trunks could be heard over the howling of the wind.

Her horse, spooked by the sound, reared, then began racing headlong into the blinding snow. Lizzy bent her head low and was grateful for Grandpop's hat. But even with that protection, snow trickled down the back of her neck.

The horse stumbled, and for a breathless moment Lizzy thought they were going to take a spill like the one that had overturned their wagon. But the horse found its footing and began moving doggedly forward.

With her chin resting inside the upturned collar of her jacket, she gave the horse his head. As the snow continued to pile up and the temperature continued to drop, the horse slowed to a walk, and Lizzy could no longer feel her hands or feet.

She closed her eyes against the blinding snow. It felt so good to keep her lids shut. The slow, plodding movement of the horse lulled her. Her head bobbed. Her breathing slowed. She thought about sliding into the softness of the snow, just for a few moments. Just until the storm passed. It would be warm under the snow. And soft. So soft.

Her head jerked up at the sound of something. Something louder than the wind. She heard it again. It was the unmistakable howling of a pack of dogs. If there were dogs, she reasoned, there would be people around to feed them.

Though the snow had drifted to the horse's belly, Lizzy dug in her heels and urged him forward. He took several tentative steps, and the howling and barking grew louder.

The horse lifted its head, nostrils flaring. Then it began rearing. It took all Lizzy's skill to keep from being thrown. With soothing words and firm control, she doggedly held on.

Looking up, she saw in the distance the outline of a man standing with his legs apart, moving toward her.

"Oh, thank God. Thank God," she cried.

But even as the words were escaping her frozen lips, she saw the man lift a rifle to his shoulder and take aim.

"Don't shoot," she shouted, struggling to be heard above the howling of the wind. "I'm alone and unarmed."

She lifted her arm and waved, hoping desperately to make him understand that she meant no harm. But still he aimed the rifle. And as her horse struggled forward, then sank to its knees directly in the path of the man, she saw him squeeze the trigger.

The sound of the rifle fire echoed and reechoed across the hills, rolling like thunder. For long moments Lizzy could hear the impact of it rumbling inside her chest as her horse seemed to stumble, before jerking convulsively. And then she was falling into the deep, soft snow.

The gunfire continued, on and on, until, as abruptly as it started, it was over.

The silence was incredible.

She waited for the pain of dying. Instead there was only a strange numbness. Then she felt strong hands lifting her, and realized it must be Ma and Pa, come to take her to the other side.

For a moment she clung to their hands and felt the heavenly warmth of them. How sweet would be the reward. Then a troubling thought intruded and she began to fight the hands that were guiding her.

"I can't come with you, Pa. Not yet. There's Grandpop and Sara Jean and little James. They're depending on me. I promised them I'd be back with help."

When the hands continued to hold her she began a frantic struggle. "Don't you see? It wouldn't truly be heaven if I didn't see to them first."

"Take it easy."

His voice was as rich and resonant as she'd always known it would be. And His touch as gentle. But somehow, she had never expected God's voice to sound like a Yankee's.

Something warm was being wrapped around her. A white gown? Wings?

"You'll see to Grandpop and Sara Jean and little James?"

"I'll see to them. As soon as I finish with you."

She relaxed. As long as she had His word, it was as good as done.

Dying wasn't so bad, she thought, as she sighed and gave herself up to the spirits. At least she wasn't alone anymore. Or quite as cold.

Chapter Two

Cody stared at the strange-looking creature in the snow. The clothes were crude. Oversize britches, a man's shirt, a hat pulled down all the way to the forehead. But there was no mistaking the soft womanly curves beneath the clothes.

He removed the hat and was astonished by a spill of waist-length hair the color of leaves in autumn. Her face was exquisite, with a small, upturned nose, high cheekbones and a perfectly sculpted mouth.

When he started to lift her, she protested in a gentle Southern drawl that reminded him of warm honey. It did something to his insides that was not at all unpleasant.

The minute she heard his voice she seemed to relax. Her struggles ceased. It was a good thing she gave in. She was no match for his strength. He'd already decided that, if necessary, he'd knock her out before he'd waste any more time in this storm. She didn't have much time left before she'd be frozen.

He examined her horse. It was too badly wounded to survive. What a shame to sacrifice good horseflesh. It had obviously been a farm animal, trained to the plow. Another blast of gunfire echoed and reechoed through the hills as he ended the horse's suffering.

Minutes later, cradling the girl against his chest, he pulled himself into the saddle and urged his horse up a steep ravine. Within a short time they had taken refuge from the storm in a snug log structure.

Unrolling some fur hides from behind his saddle, Cody wrapped the girl in one, then bent to the task of getting a fire started.

Lizzy's teeth chattered uncontrollably. Nearby a fire crackled. She wanted to crawl closer, to feel the heat of the flames against her flesh. But something was restraining her.

Hands. Strong hands.

She inhaled the fumes of something potent an instant before a bottle was pressed to her lips and she was forced to drink liquid fire. She coughed and sputtered, then felt the warmth trickle through her veins. A moment later the bottle was pressed to her mouth again and she swallowed more of the fiery brew.

Choking, she mustered her strength and pushed the hands aside.

"Now you're looking better."

That voice again. She opened her eyes, expecting to see her first glimpse of eternity and a host of heavenly creatures there to welcome her. Instead there was only a man. He was tall, with broad shoulders and muscled arms straining the rolled sleeves of a faded shirt. The britches he wore were made of fur, as were the coverings on his feet. He stood over her with his feet planted far apart. As if ready to do battle, Lizzy thought. One hand rested on a pistol in a holster slung low on his hips. In the other hand he cradled a bottle of whiskey. The upper half of his face was shaded by a wide-brimmed hat. The lower half was clearly visible. A heavy dark beard covered his cheeks and chin. She couldn't tell much about his lips, except to note that he was frowning.

The dog at his feet was staring into the raging storm, his lips drawn back to bare his fangs.

For a brief moment she was overcome with disappointment. "But you're not God."

His frown was replaced by a quick, charming grin. "I've been called a lot of things, ma'am, but I've never been mistaken for the Almighty."

"But I thought . . . Ma and Pa had come to get me. I heard the voice of God." She struggled to remember. Then she suddenly recoiled. "You're the man who shot me."

Beneath the heavy fur robe she began to feel for the bullet wound. He couldn't have missed at such close range. But miraculously, there was no wound, no pain.

"I wasn't shooting at you. It was the wolves that were snapping at your heels."

"Wolves?" She felt faint. "You mean that barking and howling?"

"So that's what made them so bold. You must have been half out of your mind from the cold not to fight or evade them. They were closing in for the kill. They'd already crippled your horse."

"My horse?"

"I'm sorry. I had to put him down. He was too badly wounded."

Lizzy swallowed. Now they would be left with only one horse to pull the wagon. Grandpop would be furious.

"How many wolves were there?"

He shrugged. "Maybe eight or ten. I managed to get most of them, but a couple are still out there. That's why old Beau is snarling. He hates wolves."

An involuntary shiver passed through her. She glanced around. "Where are we?"

"A lean-to I have up in the hills. Comes in handy if I find myself too far away from home. You needed a fire fast or you weren't going to make it."

She felt the painful tingling in her hands and feet, a signal that she was slowly returning to normal. "Where do you live?"

"Up the mountain." He pulled a stick from the fire and offered it to her. On the end of it was a sizzling piece of meat.

As she ate she slowly felt restored. He handed her a cup of steaming coffee laced generously with whiskey.

"Now why don't you tell me what brought you out in this storm. I'm guessing, from what you were trying to say, that there are others."

She nodded. "My grandfather, my sister and my little brother."

"Any of them hurt?"

"I don't think so. Just shaken up. Our wagon tipped over and lost a wheel. We made a shelter and got a fire going. There was plenty of food and warm blankets. But now I'm worried about the wolves.''

"As long as there's a fire, they'll keep their distance. Besides, as soon as we left, I'm certain they feasted on horseflesh. Does your grandfather have a rifle?''

She nodded.

"Good." He wrapped himself in a fur robe and lay down beside her.

"What are you doing?''

"I'm going to sleep.''

"Aren't we going after my family?''

"We're not going anywhere until this storm passes. Now get some rest. You're going to need it.''

Lizzy watched as he drew his hat down over his face. Minutes later she could hear the slow, steady breathing that indicated he was sound asleep.

She felt an overwhelming gratitude that this stranger had rescued her. But the gratitude was already giving way to some other emotions. She was annoyed that he could calmly sleep while her family was trapped in this raging blizzard. She knew she'd never be able to rest until she was assured that they were safe.

On the far side of the shelter, she noticed a chestnut stallion dozing, safe from the storm and the predators. It was the most magnificent animal she'd ever seen. Somehow it seemed to suit the man.

She thought about the horses Pa had bred at the Willows. They were some of the finest horseflesh in the South. By the time the war ended, they'd been left with only two broken-down plow horses. All the others had been stolen or run off by bands of marauding soldiers. Lizzy turned her thoughts away from that terrible time.

At the entrance to the shelter the dog lay, his head on his paws, his ears lifted to the sounds of the night. There was something about this man and his dog that gave her a feeling of security.

She turned her attention to the man beside her. His hat completely covered his face. Such a dark, mysterious face. She suddenly had an overpowering urge to see him. Mustering all her courage, she propped herself on her elbow and touched a finger to the hat, lifting it until it slipped aside. For a moment she held her breath, fearing that he would rise up and rage against her boldness. When he continued to lie very still, his eyes closed, his breathing slow and even, she became even bolder.

Leaning over him, she studied the fierce, bearded face. Up close she could see long spiky lashes, casting shadows across the hollows of his cheeks. The hair on his chin, like the hair on his head, was thick and dark and curly. His lips, nestled in all that hair, were perfectly formed, with the lower lip full. His lips were slightly parted, and while she watched, she thought they curved into the merest hint of a smile.

Alarmed, she started to draw back. Instantly a hand with a grip like iron closed around her wrist, holding her still.

"Just what was it you were looking for?" His voice, low and sleep roughened, frightened her.

"I..." She couldn't let him see her fear. Lifting her chin she said, "I have a right to see the man who intends to sleep beside me."

"Do you now?" He chuckled, low and deep in his throat, and drew her fractionally closer. "And do you like what you see?"

She tried to draw back but his grasp was too firm. He held her by the wrist, forcing her to press her hands on his chest. A most uncomfortable position, because she could feel the steady, even hammering of his heart.

"What I see is a man who looks like a hairy beast."

Her eyes widened as he drew her even closer, until her lips were hovering mere inches above his.

He laughed. His breath was warm against her cheek, and she looked down. That was her first mistake. His eyes glinted with laughter. She felt herself being drawn into them. She had to struggle against those laughing eyes, those hands that held her, or she would be caught.

As she began to push frantically, she realized her second mistake. The more she fought, the firmer his grasp became. The laughter suddenly fled from his eyes. They became as dark and mysterious as the night sky.

A thread of fear curled along Lizzy's spine. If this man was dangerous when he was laughing and teasing, he was far more dangerous when this look came into his eyes. She saw the way his gaze was drawn to her mouth. Her throat went dry.

If he dared to kiss her, what would she do? She had never been kissed by a man. The very thought terrified her.

"Did anyone ever tell you you have the most incredible lips?"

She swallowed and tried to speak, but no words came out.

"I'm going to have to taste those lips."

"No." She stiffened in his arms.

"My mother used to say there was an ornery streak in me that always made me do what I was told not to." He drew her down across his chest until their heartbeats were joined in a single throbbing rhythm. "Don't ever tell me no. Those who've tried have found out that I don't know the meaning of the word."

His hand cupped the back of her head, guiding it down until her mouth brushed his. Her lips trembled, and he could feel the tiny tremors that raced through her.

Instantly he felt the jolt and cursed himself for being so foolhardy. How could he have known that her lips would be sweeter than any wine? How could he have guessed that his teasing would cause such a reaction? He felt as if he'd just taken a blow to his middle.

The girl pushed against him, breaking contact. He watched her eyes, seeing the cloud of confusion as she struggled to scramble away.

"Now, if you have no more curiosity about me, ma'am . . ." He was surprised at how difficult it was to speak. His throat felt constricted. "You'd better roll yourself into that fur and grab some sleep."

Sleep. Lizzy knew that sleep would never come now. Her cheeks were hot. In fact, her whole body was on fire.

She watched as he calmly rolled aside. Within minutes she could hear his breathing, slow and easy. It infuriated her that he could so calmly dismiss their kiss, while she was still too agitated to even lie still.

In his sleep Cody turned toward her and flung out an arm. To avoid being touched by this bold stranger, she rolled away, drawing the fur wrap up to her chin.

Reluctantly, lulled by the warmth and a strange curling sensation in the pit of her stomach, she finally joined him in sleep.

Cody poured a cup of coffee from a blackened pot and watched the sleeping girl over the rim of his cup.

He wondered now if the kiss they'd shared had been only a dream. He'd been sound asleep one moment, cradling her against his chest the next. He touched a finger to his lips and slowly shook his head. He hadn't imagined it. He could still taste her.

She was either a fool or a hero, going out in that blizzard to search for help. She'd sounded kind of odd, calling him God. A grin split his lips. By now she was probably calling him the devil.

Maybe she was addled. Or maybe the cold had made her crazy. It had that effect on some people. That's why this place was so sparsely populated. He'd settled here for that very reason. There'd be no one to bother him here. There weren't many people who'd choose to live in such isolation, pitting their skill against the elements. But to Cody, it was the haven he needed after the hell he'd been through.

He frowned, thinking about the herd of wild mustangs he'd spotted in a canyon not far from here. They'd be trapped by the blizzard, making it easy to catch them. He'd intended to start after them at daybreak. Now he'd have to alter his plans. But only for a day, he thought, draining his cup. He'd find the girl's family, help them repair the wagon and send them on their way. By tomorrow he'd be on the trail of the horses. And he'd have his solitude.

He tossed a chunk of meat to Beau, who lay guarding the entrance to the lean-to. The dog caught it in his powerful jaws and lay contentedly chewing until the meat was devoured. When Cody placed a fresh rack of meat over the fire, the dog's ears lifted and his tail began thumping.

Lizzy awoke to the aroma of coffee and the sizzle and snap of meat over a fire. It took her only a moment to remember where she was. In a lean-to, somewhere in the hills with a stranger who had a deep resonant voice and the look of a wild mountain man.

He had kissed her. Boldly, with no thought of her feelings. Just thinking about it brought the heat to her cheeks. She gathered her courage. Somehow she would have to face him. And she would have to pretend that the kiss they had shared last night was forgotten.

She listened to the silence. The wind had ceased its fierce howling. That meant the storm had passed.

Pushing aside the heavy pelts, she sat up.

The man kneeling beside the fire glanced over at her. "How are you feeling?"

"Fine." She crawled from the nest of fur and spotted her shoes near the fire. "I don't think I thanked you properly last night. You saved my life. For that, I'm most grateful." She walked closer. "My name is Lizz—Elizabeth Spooner."

"Cody Martin."

He extended his hand and noticed the way she hung back at first before placing her hand in his. He glanced down and immediately understood why. Her palms were so badly callused that they were cracked and bleeding.

"The trail can be rough," he said, turning her hands over to examine them.

Seeing the way her cheeks flamed he turned away and busied himself with the fire, giving her a chance to compose herself.

Lizzy picked up her shoes and hastily put them on and tied them.

Cody handed her a cup of coffee and broke off a piece of meat. "Better fortify yourself with as much food as you can manage. We won't be stopping again once we leave this place."

As Lizzy ate she asked, "How did you happen to find me?"

"Heard the howling of the wolves. Figured they'd cornered a deer." He grinned. "Thought I'd save the deer for myself. I can always use the meat. Besides, Beau and I enjoy a good fight now and then." He tossed a piece of meat to his dog. "When I saw them snapping at your heels, I knew I wouldn't get a second chance. Every bullet had to count."

Lizzy shivered and swallowed the strong, hot coffee. The thought of what had nearly happened left her weak.

"If you don't mind, I'd like to find my family now." She stood and began pulling on Grandpop's sheepskin jacket.

"Now that the storm's passed, the air will have a bite to it." Cody glanced at her flimsy shoes and her ragged britches. "You'd better wrap this around you. The cold can't penetrate it."

Lizzy accepted the wrap made of stitched coyote skins. "Did you do this?"

He nodded and busied himself tamping out the fire and rolling the hides they'd used for sleeping. When the shelter was in order he saddled his horse and pulled on a heavy fur parka.

He helped her into the saddle, then pulled himself up behind her. Immediately the dog set up a friendly yelping, eager to be on the trail once more.

As they left the lean-to they were blinded by a world of white. Now, Cody realized, the trick would be to find that family of hers. A storm like this had a way of changing the landscape. Unless she'd marked her trail, they might never come upon that overturned wagon and its occupants until the spring thaw.

Lizzy stared at the dazzling landscape and thought about what would have happened to her if Cody hadn't come along. Even without the wolves, she and her horse would have been doomed.

Cody turned the chestnut, forging a trail through the unbroken crust of snow.

"You were coming from this direction." With his head bent, his voice was right beside her ear, sending tiny shivers along her spine.

"I marked the trees with my knife. That is," she added, "I think I did. After a while, I was so cold I couldn't seem to think."

"That's what happens to everybody out here at first."

"You mean you get used to all this snow after a while?"

"A body can get used to almost anything."

"Were you born here?"

"No."

The tone of that single word alerted Lizzy that he didn't want to talk about himself.

"Up ahead, by those trees, is where I came upon you and the wolves."

As they drew close, Lizzy scanned the area for any sign of bloodshed. What was left of the wolves, even her horse, were now only soft white mounds of new snow.

"We'll backtrack from here." Cody guided his mount down a steep path, then began searching for trees with fresh markings on their trunks.

Wrapped in a warm fur, astride the most magnificent horse she had ever seen and cushioned against Cody's chest, it was difficult for Lizzy to imagine that scant hours ago she'd been fighting for her life. It seemed strange, trusting her safety to this man. And yet, for some reason she couldn't quite fathom, she did.

"Here's a mark. Is it yours?" He pointed to the fresh cut on the bark of a tree.

"I think so." Pulling out her knife, she made a cut below it. The two marks were identical.

"Good. Now we've got a trail to follow."

He urged his horse forward.

It was midday, and Lizzy had been in the saddle for hours. Whenever they encountered drifts too deep, or an incline too steep, Cody would dismount and lead the horse. Each time, he used a soft, easy way of talking to the animal that soothed it. Each time, Lizzy found herself believing that this fierce-looking man would get them through.

Lizzy drew the fur wrap tightly around her, grateful for its warmth. Cody had been right. The air had more than a bite to it; it cut like a knife.

Ahead of them Beau set up a yammering that filled the air. Cody urged his horse into a run.

At the top of a ridge they looked down on a sight that had them transfixed.

The wagon and its contents had been completely covered by snow. All that could be seen was the top of one wheel, poking through the layers of white frosting. A short distance away the towering rocks were so covered with snow, they were nearly indistinguishable from their surroundings.

Beau stood in a clearing just beyond the wagon, barking at Grandpop, who was facing him.

As Lizzy and Cody watched, Grandpop lifted the rifle to his shoulder and took aim at the dog.

Cupping her hands to her mouth, Lizzy shouted, but from this distance, her voice was carried away before it could reach the clearing.

Cody slid to the ground and lifted his gun from the holster. Lizzy watched in horrified fascination as he took aim.

''No. Cody, that's my grandpop.''

But even as she yelled, his finger closed around the trigger and he fired. The sound rolled and thundered across the hills.

Chapter Three

For a moment Lizzy couldn't see for the tears that sprang to her eyes. But as she blinked the tears away, she saw that Grandpop was unharmed. Slowly she let go of the breath she'd been holding.

"I wasn't going to shoot him," Cody said gruffly. "I just wanted to get the old man's attention."

She saw that his ploy had worked. The gunshot distracted Grandpop momentarily, causing him to look up at the ridge where they were standing.

A moment later Sara Jean and James came rushing out of hiding. They waved and cheered as Lizzy and Cody mounted and rode toward them.

"So you made it," Grandpop said when their horse drew near. For a moment his voice roughened and he cleared his throat. "Girl, when I saw how bad this storm was last night, I figured you for a goner."

"I would have been if it weren't for Mr. Martin." Lizzy slid from the saddle and hugged her sister and brother. "He found me in the hills."

"Half-frozen and being attacked by wolves." There was an accusing tone to Cody's voice as he studied the man who'd sent an innocent out into the wilderness.

Sara Jean's eyes widened. The idea of being rescued by a handsome stranger sounded so romantic, she was almost willing to risk cold and wolves herself. Almost. At any rate, she felt a twinge of jealousy that it had been Lizzy who had brought this stranger to their midst.

"We're much obliged." Grandpop eyed the man with mistrust. "I'm Amos Spooner, and these are my other grandchildren, Sara Jean and James."

"Cody Martin." He extended his hand in greeting.

The stranger's voice was low and deep. A brusque Northern voice. And not at all friendly. At the sound of it Grandpop tightened his grip on the rifle and reluctantly offered his hand.

"Your granddaughter said you have a broken wagon wheel and possibly a broken axle." If Cody noticed the snub he chose to ignore it. "Where's the rest of the wagon train?"

"We're traveling alone." At Cody's surprised look Amos shrugged and cleared his throat again. It was a habit he wasn't even aware of. The more agitated he became, the more often he cleared his throat. "Just packed up what little we had and left. Didn't take time to plan."

Cody's mouth formed a grim, tight line. "The West is littered with the bodies of men who didn't take time to plan."

Lizzy glanced at her grandfather and saw his stricken look. Leaping to his defense, she said, "With our parents gone, Grandpop feels responsible for all of us."

"Let's take a look at that wagon," Cody said abruptly. "I'm sure you want to get back on the trail before the next storm hits." Besides, now that he'd seen this ragged band, he wanted to be rid of them as soon as possible. He had no liking for unexpected company. No matter how urgent their needs.

Draping an arm around Lizzy's shoulders for support, the old man led the way toward the mound of snow that covered the wagon. He walked with a strange, stiff-legged gait.

Seeing the way Cody watched him, Amos felt he owed an explanation. "Yankees left me a little memento. Pieces of musket ball in my knee."

Cody said nothing. But he felt the accusing stares of the others as they strode toward the wagon.

James trailed along behind. "Is that your dog?" he asked timidly.

Cody turned and nodded. "His name's Beau."

As the boy made a move toward him, Amos warned, "Don't go trying to pet him, boy. He looks more like a wolf than a dog."

"Grandpop thought Beau was a wolf. He was going to shoot him, weren't you, Grandpop?"

"Fool critter came at me with his fangs bared. What else could I think?"

As the boy started forward, the dog growled a warning deep in its throat. But at a single word from

Cody he stopped, lowered his head and merely sniffed as the boy touched his head.

"Hello, Beau," the boy crooned, stroking his fur. "Good old Beau." He looked up. "We had a dog once, didn't we, Grandpop?"

"We had a lot of things once, boy. No sense crying over spilt milk. Here's the broken wheel." Amos brushed away snow. "Haven't checked the axle yet. Probably cracked, too."

"Let's have a look."

Lizzy and her sister stood aside. Ignoring the snow, Cody crawled around the wreckage. When he was finished his frown had deepened into a scowl. "Looks like your wagon suffered some serious damage, Mr. Spooner. I think it'll take a couple of days to make the repairs." So much for his plans to find those mustangs today.

"Repairs? Except for a hammer, I don't have any tools."

Cody stared at the old man. "No tools? How far have you come?"

"We're from Georgia." Lizzy spoke the words proudly.

Cody's eyes narrowed on the man who had set himself up as their leader. It was hard to believe anyone would uproot an entire family and attempt a journey like this without some thought to the things they'd need along the way.

"I guess you have no choice, then." He spoke without emotion. "I have a place in the mountains. We'll have to drag your belongings up there until the wagon can be repaired.''

"How long?" Amos eyed him suspiciously.

Cody shrugged. "A couple of days. A week maybe."

Amos swallowed. A week under the same roof as a Yankee. "Guess it can't be helped. All right, Lizzy, Sara Jean. Let's start bundling everything."

Cody set to work removing the remaining wheels and broken pieces from the wagon. Then he attached the flat cart to the plow horse in much the same way the Indians affixed a travois. Onto this they lashed their household goods and bundles of clothing.

When the cart was loaded Cody turned to Amos. "You and the younger girl will ride my horse. The rest of us will have to walk."

Though the old man's pride was wounded, he knew better than to argue. He wouldn't get more than a few feet in this snow before he'd collapse. As for Sara Jean, she wouldn't fare much better in her condition.

Cody studied Lizzy's flimsy high-topped shoes and her little brother's worn boots. "First we'd better see to the two of you."

From the back of his saddle he unrolled several fur pelts. Rabbit hides were wrapped around their feet and secured with leather strips. James was given a parka of elegant fox pelts stitched together.

Cody showed Lizzy how to wrap her fur pelts around her to form a hooded cape. "Keep your hands tucked inside," he said sternly.

He draped fur throws over Amos and Sara Jean that would keep them snug and warm on the long ride.

At first, when the strangers were helped onto the stallion's back, the animal balked. But when Cody took the reins and led his mount, along with their plow horse, the stallion followed meekly.

Lizzy caught hold of her brother's hand and led him through the deep drifts, wondering how they would even make it to the base of the mountain that loomed ahead of them, let alone climb it.

"Can we stop soon?" Sara Jean wailed. "My back's so stiff, I swear I don't think I can sit another minute."

Cody glanced at Lizzy and James, plodding silently in the wake of the horses. Though they had to be nearly asleep on their feet, they continued on without a word.

"Maybe you'd like to change places with your sister for a while."

Sara Jean sulked. She should have known she'd get little sympathy from a savage. She'd been watching Cody Martin since they set off. Never once had he stumbled, or slowed his pace, or turned to see if they were all right. He just marched into the bitter wind, plowing on through the heavy drifts, leading the horses. He wasn't a man, she thought angrily; he was a beast of burden. She didn't care for his crude manners or his surly attitude or his curt tone. He would never be mistaken for a Southern gentleman.

Lizzy, too, had watched Cody. And admired his strength. Though the arms holding the reins must be tired, he never dropped them to his sides. And though the wind cut like the blade of a razor, he never bent, but merely faced it head-on.

Each time she thought she couldn't take another step, she had only to look at the man leading their tired party, and she found new strength within herself to take just one more step, and then another.

"Lizzy. I'm so tired." James sank to his knees.

"You have to keep going, James. Just a little farther."

"I can't."

She saw the exhaustion on his face, and her heart went out to him. He'd been through so much in the past months. How could she ask any more of him?

"Come on, I'll carry you." She knelt and helped him onto her back. He wrapped his chubby little arms around her neck and she struggled to her feet.

Taking a deep breath, she stumbled forward, determined to keep up with the others.

Cody didn't like the color of the sky. There was more snow coming. He didn't know how much longer the two on foot could keep up this pace. But he had to keep pushing if they were going to reach safety before the next storm hit.

Beau growled and Cody stopped to see what had caught the dog's attention. He glanced behind him and bit back a savage oath. The girl was stumbling through the drifts with the little boy on her back. How long did she think she could keep that up?

As he was watching, he saw her fall forward, then get to her feet, still balancing the boy on her back. With a sigh of resignation Cody dropped the reins and closed the distance between them. Without a word he took the boy from her and swung him onto his shoulders.

Lizzy watched as he strode forward and caught up the reins, then continued plodding at the same steady pace. She had no choice but to force herself to move ahead.

Several times she stumbled and fell. Each time, Beau stopped and growled. Each time, she pushed herself up and continued on. And each time, satisfied that she had her footing, Cody turned away and resumed a brisk pace.

A short time later, when Beau gave a warning growl, Cody turned. He couldn't see Lizzy's figure trailing behind the horses. Dropping the reins, he went back and found her lying, facedown, in a snowbank.

"Lizzy. Get up, Lizzy," James shouted from his perch on the man's shoulders.

She didn't move.

Bending, Cody caught her by the arms and lifted her to her feet. She struggled to stand, but her legs weren't capable of supporting her weight.

"Come on," Cody muttered, draping an arm around her shoulders. "Lean on me. We don't have far to go now."

She wrapped her arms around his waist and leaned into him, forcing herself to put one foot in front of the other.

"That's right," he encouraged. "Just a little farther and we'll be warm and dry. And you can sleep."

"Sleep." It was that word that kept her going. She wanted desperately to lie down and close her eyes. She was weary. So weary.

Cody handed the reins of the horses to the little boy on his shoulders. "You lead them, James. And see you do a good job."

"I will." The boy eagerly accepted the responsibility and turned to glance at the two figures hunched beneath a mound of fur. "I'll watch out for Sara Jean and Grandpop, too."

Lizzy gamely plodded along beside the towering figure who kept her upright whenever her legs threatened to fail her.

Cody marveled at the girl's inner strength. Despite her frail appearance, he could sense her iron will. She barely reached his chin. But he had a feeling she would finish anything she started, or die trying.

It had been a long time since he'd felt a woman's arms around his waist or carried a child on his shoulders. He'd convinced himself that he could live without such things. And maybe he could. But he suddenly realized how much he'd missed them. Maybe that was something that never stopped.

"How much farther?" Amos called.

"Just up ahead there." Cody pointed and they all strained to see through the curtain of snow that had begun falling.

In the distance, nestled between two mountain peaks, was a flat meadow frosted with snow. In the gathering dusk, the outline of two buildings could barely be distinguished from the trees that formed a protective half circle on either side of them.

It was almost like a fortress, Lizzy thought as they drew nearer. The mountains behind formed an impenetrable barrier. The trees on either side stood like sentinels. The only approach was along a sheer ascent leading to the meadow, which could easily be viewed from the front door.

Cody led them to a small log house with a wide porch across the front.

"I'm afraid my house isn't much more than a shack," he said apologetically. "I always thought I'd find time to make it bigger." He shrugged. "But it's big enough for me."

He released his grasp on Lizzy and she felt the chill where only moments before she had been warmed by the touch of him.

He bent down and deposited James on the ground, then helped Sara Jean and Amos from the horse. "Go ahead in. I'll just take the horses to the barn and see to them. I'll have a fire going in a few minutes to warm you."

He untied the latch and shoved open the door before heading toward the barn.

Sara Jean helped Grandpop inside, with James trailing them. Sara Jean quickly settled herself into the rocker and tucked the fur robe over her lap. Grandpop and James flung themselves down on the floor, too weary to move.

Lizzy was the last to enter. She stared around the single room, noting the rocker pulled up in front of the fireplace and the table and chairs made of rough timber. A bench stood just inside the door, and beside it a pair of unfinished boots. There was a loft built just below the log rafters, and though she couldn't see what was up there, she knew that was where Cody slept.

The house reflected the man. Solid, sturdy, neat.

"How did this man happen to come upon you, Lizzy?" Grandpop asked sternly.

"I was lost, and a pack of wolves were attacking me." Lizzy closed the door but kept her voice low, in case Cody should come in behind her. "And suddenly he was there, with his horse and dog and rifle. It was like a miracle."

"What's a miracle, Lizzy?" James asked.

"Pa always said it was the hand of God touching us."

"How do we know when God touches us?"

"When there's just no other explanation for what's happened," Lizzy said. "Ma used to say, if we saw the Christmas star and wished for something purely unselfish, we'd see a miracle."

"Have you ever seen a miracle, Grandpop?"

"No," the old man said abruptly. "And I don't suppose I ever will."

"Then how do you explain what happened out there?" Lizzy demanded.

"You just got lucky, girl. That's all. And stop filling your little brother's head with nonsense. We're just humble folk. We have no right to ask for miracles."

Cody nudged the door open and entered carrying an armload of logs. His dog walked beside him. A blast of frigid air and snow swirled in behind them.

Lizzy forced the door shut and tied the latch.

"There's a lantern on that shelf," Cody said.

Lizzy handed it to him and he held a match to the wick, then to the tinder in the fireplace. Soon the room was full of light and heat. Cody placed a blackened pot over the fire, and their mouths watered as the rich aroma of coffee filled the air.

"I keep my food down here." He seemed to be speaking to no one in particular. "Care to give me a hand?" Cody moved aside a rag rug, revealing a small door in the floor. Holding the lantern aloft, he led the way to a root cellar beneath the house.

Lizzy was the only one with the strength to follow. Her eyes widened at the shelves loaded with potatoes, carrots, apples, dried meats. "I don't believe our cellars at the Willows were better stocked than this."

"The Willows?"

Lizzy felt her cheeks grow hot when he turned to study her.

She stared at the hard-packed dirt floor. "Our home in Georgia."

It wasn't what she said, but what she didn't, that told him all he needed to know. The entire country was aware of the torching of Atlanta and the plundering of the plantations surrounding it. He didn't press the issue.

"I guess, coming from that part of the country, this snow must seem overwhelming."

She shrugged, grateful to talk about anything except the war. "At least I've seen snow once or twice, when I went with Pa to Washington. Poor James had never seen it before."

"More than likely he's seen enough for a lifetime. Here." Cody handed her some potatoes and carrots.

"Did you grow these yourself?"

"Most of them. Some I took in trade for pelts or horses." He sorted through the smoked meats and selected a chunk of venison. "What did your father do in Washington?"

"He went to plead for more time." Her voice trembled. "But it was already too late. While he was meeting with the president, the Confederacy became official and Uncle Alex accepted the vice presidency."

Cody turned to study her in the light of the lantern. "Uncle Alex?"

She shrugged uncomfortably and looked away. "Alexander Stephens, of Georgia. He was a good friend of my father's, and we all called him Uncle Alex."

"I see." He saw a whole lot more. "Your father knew President Lincoln?"

"Not very well. But Pa respected him, and thought they might be able to avoid..." She shrugged again. Her voice lowered. "On the train ride home, Pa said that such matters were out of men's hands now, and in the hands of God. But he was still praying that neither side would resort to war."

Unanswered prayers, Cody thought. He had a firsthand knowledge of those. In grim silence he lifted the lantern from a peg and turned toward the stairs. Lizzy followed.

Grandpop was asleep on the bench by the door. Sara Jean was still settled in the rocker. Her breathing was slow and easy. James had curled up on a rug in front of the fire beside Cody's big dog. The little boy gamely lifted his head and smiled at Lizzy. Then he couldn't fight the need to sleep. His eyes slowly closed. He snuggled himself into the dog's soft fur.

Lizzy understood their weariness. While she cut up the vegetables and meat and placed them in a pot over the fire, she brushed damp tendrils from her forehead. How good it was to have finally escaped the frigid air. Here in Cody's cabin it was snug and warm. It was the first time, Lizzy realized, that she'd been truly warm since they left home.

"Did you grow cotton on your place in Georgia?" Cody picked up a rifle and began to oil and clean it.

"Some. That was Grandpop's love. The soil." Lizzy glanced lovingly at her grandfather, whose mouth was slightly open, emitting an occasional snore. "But Pa didn't share Grandpop's love for the soil. He wanted to breed horses."

Cody's interest was instantly piqued.

"What kind of horses did he breed?"

"Thoroughbreds. Some of the finest racehorses in the South," Lizzy said with pride. The light in her eyes suddenly faded. "But the war ended Pa's dream. The army needed all the horseflesh we could provide. General Lee himself signed the orders. Though it broke Pa's heart, he couldn't possibly refuse. He said it was his duty as a Southern gentleman.''

She tossed a handful of carrots into the pot of water and wiped her hands on her britches.

Cody watched as she stirred the pot, then rolled out a batch of biscuits and placed them over some hot coals. Lifting a hand, she brushed the damp hair from her face and leaned back on her heels, staring into the flames. In the firelight her eyes gleamed amber. Her skin was as smooth and pale as alabaster.

Unable to battle the overpowering weariness, her lids slowly flickered, then closed. Her breathing slowed. Her head nodded.

She felt herself being lifted in strong arms and carried to the softest bed she'd ever known. She was enveloped in something incredibly comfortable and warm. And for one brief moment she felt the scratch of a rough hand across her cheek. Then sleep claimed her.

Chapter Four

The fragrance of freshly baked biscuits filled the air. Voices washed over Lizzy. Happy voices. Contented voices. Grandpop, Sara Jean. The muted giggles of a child. James.

Lizzy sat up, momentarily confused. She must be home. The Willows. It was suppertime.

The voices paused as a door opened. Frigid air wafted in, causing a sudden chill, not only in the room, but in the occupants of the room.

Not the Willows, Lizzy realized. A cabin in the mountains.

"My biscuits..."

Lizzy glanced from Cody, standing in the doorway, to her family, seated around the crude table. The biscuit in her grandfather's hand was perfectly baked, with no trace of having been burned.

"Oh, Lizzy, we woke you," Sara Jean said. "Cody told us to go ahead and eat and let you sleep."

Lizzy shoved the hair from her eyes and got to her feet, uncomfortably aware that the man in the doorway was studying her. Without asking, she knew he was the one who had carried her to the pile of pelts and gently covered her. She felt the blood rush to her face as she recalled the brush of his rough hand against her cheek.

"Sorry. I guess the heat of the fire did me in. I didn't mean to fall asleep before my chores were done."

"Nothing to be sorry about," Cody muttered, standing his rifle alongside the door. "You walked nearly ten miles today. And in those drifts it probably felt like a hundred." He glanced toward Amos. "I examined your wagon more carefully. I don't think that axle can be repaired. It's broken in several places. But I have a log we can hew that's just about the right length to replace it. It'll hold you until you find a blacksmith."

"More delays," the old man said with a trace of irritability. He shoved away from the table, and Sara Jean and James followed suit.

Lizzy glanced at Cody. It occurred to her that it was his house that had been invaded by strangers. And his life that had been disrupted. Yet, whatever his feelings were, he kept them carefully hidden behind a polite mask.

"Have you eaten?" she asked.

"No. I wanted to check that wagon first."

"I'll fix you something now."

As he removed his fur parka, Lizzy tried not to stare at the broad shoulders that strained the faded shirt. She ladled steaming stew into a bowl and placed several biscuits on a plate, while he rolled his sleeves and washed his hands in a basin of water.

As he sat down she said, "I guess I should thank you for saving the biscuits before they burned."

"It's been a long time since I smelled cooking as good as that, ma'am. I'm not fool enough to see it go to waste." He looked up as she placed his meal in front of him. "You aren't eating?"

"I... Yes, of course." Flustered at the nearness of this man, she filled a plate for herself and took the seat across from him.

He watched as she bowed her head and whispered a silent prayer before tucking into her food.

"How long do you reckon it will take us to get under way?" Amos tamped ash from his pipe into the fire.

"Depends. You can get started hewing the log tomorrow. The wheel's cracked but it can be mended. There's a side of the wagon that's smashed and will have to be completely rebuilt. And there's the torn canvas that will have to be mended." Cody watched as the old man filled his pipe and pulled a flaming stick from the fire to light it. "A little longer than I first thought. A week. Maybe more. I can lend a hand. But not until I chase up a herd of mustangs first. I can't afford to let them get away."

"Wild mustangs?" James's eyes widened with interest.

Cody nodded.

"Are you bringing them here?"

"If I catch up with them."

"Why?"

"That's how I earn my living. I break mustangs to the saddle and sell them to the army."

A sudden awkward stillness settled over the occupants of the room.

It was James who said, "Yankee soldiers come here?"

"The last time I looked, the war was over." Cody spoke quietly, deliberately. "There's just the United States Army now, son. Think you can remember that?"

"Yes, sir." James knew he'd been gently chastised. Something in the way Cody had spoken stirred his memories of Pa. Memories that had begun to fade.

The boy glanced at his grandfather, who was staring silently into the flames of the fire.

Cody pushed away from the table and turned to Lizzy, who kept her eyes downcast. "Thank you, ma'am. The food tasted as good as it smelled. It's been a long time since I've tasted anything that good."

Lizzy lifted her gaze. Her cheeks reddened when she felt his piercing stare.

Needing to be busy, she picked up their plates and filled the basin with hot water from the kettle. While she washed the dishes she felt a warm glow. She didn't know why this man's words should please her so, but they did.

"Sara Jean," Amos called. "Lend a hand to your sister. Can't you see she has need of some help?"

"I'm so tired, Grandpop. I just don't think I can move."

"You don't think Lizzy's just as tired? I won't have her doing everything herself."

"It's all right, Grandpop." Lizzy picked up a small linen square and admired the handiwork. Someone had gone to a great deal of trouble stitching delicate rosebuds along the edge. It seemed so out of place in this rough cabin. "I can manage fine without Sara Jean's help. Let her rest."

Her younger sister sank gratefully back into the rocking chair and closed her eyes.

Minutes later they all looked up at the sound of horses, approaching hard and fast.

"Snuff out that lantern," Cody called sharply as he picked up the rifle and opened the door a crack to peer out into the darkness.

Lizzy did as she was told, then hurried across the room to steady Grandpop, who had lifted his rifle to his shoulder.

"James," she whispered, "take Sara Jean and hide under those pelts."

The two knew better than to argue at a time like this. Within seconds only their eyes could be seen peering out from the pile of furs in the corner of the room.

It occurred to Cody that these people knew a whole lot about dealing with unexpected company. He himself knew firsthand about the bands of former soldiers from both sides who roamed the battered country brutalizing innocents.

His finger tightened on the trigger of the rifle.

"Who's there?"

"We're looking for horses. Heard you had some."

"Who said?"

"Fellow in town said you had mustangs."

Realizing the fireplace illuminated the room and its occupants, Cody stepped outside. Like a silent shadow, Beau slipped out to stand beside him.

Cody counted six men on horseback. In the darkness all he could see were the silhouettes of wide-brimmed hats, long leather dusters and six rifles, all trained on him.

"You aiming to buy?" His voice lowered. "Or steal?"

"We got money," came a voice in the darkness. "But we need fresh horses right away."

"Sorry. Can't oblige you. But if you come back tomorrow night, I'll have all you want."

A savage curse broke the stillness. "We need 'em now."

Men on the run. Cody had seen enough of them to recognize the desperation in the tone. "Sorry. Like I said—"

"Maybe we didn't make ourselves plain enough," came the angry voice. "We can't wait until you get a new supply. We'll take any horses you got in that barn."

With Beau at his heels Cody stepped off the porch and walked toward the horsemen, keeping his rifle aimed at the one who was doing the talking. Cody assumed he was their leader.

In a shaft of moonlight they could see his eyes, narrowed in concentration. His voice was deadly calm. "I'm afraid I can't let you do that."

At the sound of his voice, one head came up sharply.

"Cody? My God, is that you? Cody?" At the boy's strangled tones, Cody strained to see through the darkness.

"My name's Cody Martin. Who are you?"

"It's me. Ned."

At his words Cody stiffened, and for a moment he nearly forgot the danger as he let the rifle drop to his side.

One horse separated itself from the others. A boy, as tall and slender as a sapling, slid from the saddle and started forward. Beau growled a challenge, but at a word from Cody sniffed the stranger and let him pass.

Cody's words stopped the youth in midstride. "Have you traveled far with this bunch, Ned?"

"No, I..." The boy swallowed and tried again. "They found me in a blizzard last night, carrying my saddle. I'd had to shoot my horse when he went lame. They said if I could handle a gun they'd let me tag along with them."

"Looks like you hitched yourself to a real winner this time, Ned. If you ask me, they're not about to ride out of here until they've helped themselves to everything that's mine."

"That's not so. Tell him, Whit. Tell him you just want to buy some fresh mounts."

Cody saw the gleam of white teeth as the leader smiled. "Sorry, kid. It didn't take this stranger long to figure us out. Now step back. 'Cause if you stay in the line of fire, we're going to have to believe you've taken sides with him against us."

"You can't shoot him."

The man laughed. "Did you really believe we were going to pay him for his horses?"

"But you said..."

"You're wasting your time. Now mount up and pull back, or you'll get the same thing he's going to get."

Inside the cabin Lizzy felt Grandpop begin to crumple to the floor. The effects of the journey, combined with the sudden danger, left him too weak to remain standing on his injured leg any longer.

"Here, Grandpop. You sit here on the floor behind this table." She dropped the table on its side like a shield to protect him from gunfire. Then, taking the rifle from his hands, she crept toward the opened door.

"This is your last chance, boy," the leader called.

"You don't understand." Ned's voice was a high-pitched note of pleading. "This man isn't just another stranger. The last time I saw him was two years ago and thousands of miles from here. Cody Martin is my brother."

For a moment it seemed as if the entire world went silent. Except for the snow that fell, there wasn't a sound to break the stillness that greeted the boy's words.

Lizzy's mouth dropped open in surprise. In the moonlight she studied the two profiles. Both men held their heads at a proud angle. Both had broad foreheads, finely sculpted, aristocratic noses. But where Cody's face was covered with dark hair, Ned's was clean-shaven. Though both men were taller than average, Ned was thin, almost frail, while Cody's arms and shoulders were corded with muscles.

The leader swore again, loudly, savagely. "You're a fool, boy. Now we're going to have to kill the both of you. And two men against five don't stand a chance."

Lizzy never even stopped to calculate the odds. Cody had saved her life. She owed him as much. Besides, it was what Pa would have done.

Stepping outside quickly, she took up a position on the other side of Cody and aimed her rifle at the horsemen. Wearing ragged britches and a faded shirt, with her hair hidden beneath Grandpop's hat, she looked like just another shabby traveler.

"Now it's three against five," she said in her soft, Southern drawl.

Though Cody was stunned by her boldness, he heard the mutterings among the men on horseback and quickly took advantage of their surprise.

"Looks like the odds keep getting better, gentlemen. Now would you like to ride out of here peacefully, or would you like to face three rifles?" He gave a low, menacing chuckle. "We might not get all of you, but one thing is certain. At least three of you won't be leaving the way you came."

There was a long, expectant hush as the others waited for their leader's command. At last he lowered his rifle. "You win. This time. But the horse Ned was riding is ours. We want him back."

At a gesture from Cody, Ned unsaddled his horse and handed the reins to the leader.

The man called Whit had a voice as cold and cutting as the night air. "You'd better look over your shoulder the next time you ride these hills, mister. And you, too, boy. We don't take kindly to those who cross us."

"And I don't take kindly to those who'd steal from me," Cody called. "Now get off my land. Before I lose my patience. And my temper."

The three continued to stand side by side on the porch, rifles aimed, until the six horses blended into the darkness.

Slowly Lizzy let go of the breath she'd been holding. She turned toward Cody and the boy called Ned, expecting to witness a warm reunion. Instead, Cody lowered his rifle and turned on her in a rage.

"Don't you ever put yourself in harm's way like that again. That damned fool act could have gotten you killed."

Stung by his attack, she reacted with similar anger. Her words were spoken in a low, throaty whisper. "It worked, didn't it? They left without firing a shot."

His eyes blazed. "And what if they'd called your bluff and opened fire?"

"It wasn't a bluff. I know how to shoot a rifle. Pa taught me to shoot better'n most men."

He caught her roughly by the arm and dragged her close. His breath stung her temple as he warned, "Don't ever do a thing like that again. The last thing I want is for you to get yourself killed for me."

She pushed away from him. "Don't you worry your head about that, Cody Martin. I have no intention of dying for the likes of you."

Enraged, he turned his full wrath on his brother. His tone was controlled and as cold as steel. "You'd better come inside and warm yourself before you go."

Go? Lizzy was mystified. Hadn't the lad claimed to be Cody's own brother, separated for the past two years? Hadn't he just journeyed halfway across the country to find him?

"Only for a few minutes," Ned said calmly, after a moment's hesitation. His tone was equally controlled. And equally frosty. "If you have a horse I can buy, I'll be on my way."

"I'm fresh out of horses." Cody held the door and waited until Lizzy entered the cabin. "But I expect to have a fresh herd tomorrow."

"Tomorrow." Ned followed Cody inside. "I'd planned on being in the town of Commencement by morning."

"You'll have a long walk." Cody secured the door and stood his rifle alongside it.

"How far is it from here?"

"About thirty miles. Even on a fresh mount it's a hard day's ride."

"What's Commencement?" Sara Jean asked.

Ned glanced toward the soft Southern voice and his eyes widened at the sight of a pretty face surrounded by a veil of pale blond hair. Whereas the girl on the porch had been dressed in tattered men's clothing, this young woman looked like a proper lady, dressed in a pale gown that matched the blue of her eyes.

"Evening, ma am." He whipped his hat from his head and blushed clear to his toes.

"Ned, this is Sara Jean Spooner."

Sara Jean dimpled.

"She and her family got caught in the blizzard and damaged their wagon. This is her grandfather, Amos, and her little brother, James. And this is her older sister, Elizabeth."

Peals of laughter issued from James's throat.

"What's so funny?" Lizzy asked.

"Cody called you Elizabeth."

Lizzy wished the floor would open up and swallow her. It was bad enough that Cody had hollered at her for doing what she thought was right, but now he would know that she'd put on airs when she'd first introduced herself to him.

If Cody noticed her humiliation, he said nothing.

"You still haven't told me what Commencement is." Sara Jean was determined to draw Ned's attention to her.

"It's the only town in these parts," Cody explained.

Ned avoided his brother's eyes. "I'm supposed to meet a man there who has a job for me, ma'am."

"Maybe we could settle there, Grandpop," Sara Jean said excitedly.

"It's not much of a place yet. A few dozen families or so." Cody lifted a bottle of whiskey from a shelf and poured three glasses. He offered one to Ned and one to Amos before lifting the last to his lips. "What kind of work are you being offered?"

Ned studied the toe of his worn boot. "They need someone to ride shotgun on the stage."

Cody's eyes narrowed, but he kept the anger from his tone. "That's a long way from your original calling."

"And this is a long way from yours." Ned drained his glass and set it down hard on the table. "Would I be imposing if I asked to sleep in your barn tonight?"

"Might as well stay in here where it's warm." Cody glanced toward the loft. "I guess there's room for the two ladies up there. The rest of us can sleep on the floor around the fireplace."

He rested a ladder against the loft, then picked up a lantern and headed toward the door. "I'll check on the horses before I turn in."

He pulled open the door, sending sparks dancing up the chimney.

When the door closed behind him, Ned crossed the room and poured himself another drink.

Lizzy kissed Grandpop's cheek, then drew James close. "Don't forget your prayers."

"I won't."

She dropped a kiss on the top of his head and climbed to the loft. Reluctantly Sara Jean followed her.

Cody's sleeping loft was larger than Lizzy had imagined. Every inch of space was covered with fur pelts. The bed was several thicknesses of fur, with two down pillows covered by delicately embroidered linens. It was obvious, from the fine stitches, that the same hand that had embroidered the linen towel had embroidered these pillow covers.

As Lizzy and Sara Jean rolled themselves into the comfort of fur, they could hear the men's voices just below them.

Amos cleared his throat in agitation. "Did I hear you say you were Cody's brother?"

"Yes, sir." Ned removed his wide-brimmed hat and duster and carefully hung them on a peg by the door.

"You two don't seem to hit it off too well." Amos watched as the young man carefully washed his hands and face, then began removing his boots.

"I haven't seen Cody, nor spoken to him, since the winter of '64."

That date struck a nerve with Lizzy. That was the year her father had gone off to war. It was the last time she'd seen Pa alive.

"And this is how you greet each other after all these years?" Even Amos Spooner, as crotchety as he was, couldn't imagine a more strained reunion than the one he'd just witnessed.

"I didn't come here looking for my big brother. And it's plain he wasn't hoping to see me, either."

From his tone, it was obvious that Ned had no intention of making any more conversation. He wrapped himself in a blanket and used his saddle for a pillow. Within minutes he was fast asleep.

Amos smoked his pipe in silence for long minutes. Then, placing a fur on the floor, he invited his grandson to join him.

Up above, in the loft, Lizzy lay wide awake, unable to sleep.

There was nothing Sara Jean or James could ever do that would change the way she felt about them. No matter what, she knew she would always love them. Something terrible must have happened to drive such a wedge between those two brothers.

She listened to the sound of the door opening and heard the sparks leap in the fireplace as the wind danced through the room. Crawling to the edge of the loft, she watched as Cody latched the door and hung his coat and hat on a peg.

She saw him stare across the room toward the place where his brother slept. She could feel his sadness as surely as if it were her own.

What had happened between Cody and his brother? she wondered. And what would it take to remove this barrier between them?

She thought of the prayers she'd whispered each night since she was a little girl. She would say them tonight for Cody and his brother. And for Sara Jean, and James, and Grandpop. But though her intentions were honorable, exhaustion overtook her. Before the first words of the prayer flitted through her mind, she was sound asleep.

Chapter Five

Lizzy lay snuggled in the warm fur and listened to the stillness of the early morning. A horse whinnied in the barn. The wind whistled through the bare branches of the trees. High above, a bird cried. Below, Grandpop snored softly.

Beside her Sara Jean slept as peacefully as the babe she carried within. Lizzy studied her sister and felt a welling of love. How tragic to have been married and widowed within the span of months.

Sara Jean rarely spoke of the boy who had won her heart, or of the future that must seem bleak without him. Lizzy wondered if her sister was afraid at the thought of childbirth. If only Ma had lived. She would have brought Sara Jean a wealth of knowledge and experience. She would have been such a comfort. Lizzy could only pray that when the time came, her sister's natural instincts would take over.

Lizzy tucked the fur around her sister's shoulders and crept down the ladder. Moving stealthily past the sleeping figures on the floor, she pulled on her shoes and, wrapping a shawl around her shoulders, picked up a pitcher and basin and headed toward the privacy of the barn.

Once inside she breathed in the sharp scents of hay and dung and rich, moist earth. It was in the barn at the Willows that Lizzy had always felt the most comfortable. From the time she was a child she'd mucked stalls and scattered hay. And it was at Pa's side, during a foaling, that she had first been allowed to stay up all night.

As the horses nickered, she rummaged through the bundles of clothing and household goods left on the wagon until she located one of her few remaining dresses. Smoothing the wrinkles from the cloth, she laid the garment in the hay while she shed the oversize britches and shirt.

The water in the pitcher was cold as she poured it into the basin and dipped the corner of a clean cloth into it. With her precious supply of soap she lathered the cloth and began to wash herself.

Cody had come out in the early morning to see to the horses. When the door to the barn suddenly opened, he lifted his head and reached automatically for his rifle.

From his position in the stall, he could see the slender figure move forward in a swirl of snowflakes. Then the barn door was latched shut and he watched as Lizzy breathed deeply. A smile touched her lips and she sighed as she walked toward the remains of her family's wagon and began rummaging through her belongings.

From the light in her eyes it was obvious that she liked his barn, and for some strange reason that made him happy.

By the time Cody realized what she was up to, it was too late to let her know that he was there. As she began stripping her rough clothing away, he knew that he would have to remain silent. To reveal his presence now would be to invite her wrath.

He grinned at the thought of that fiery little creature's temper. If she knew he was here, enjoying the vision of her naked flesh, she'd tear him apart.

He leaned a hip against the stall and watched as she stripped away the last of her tattered garments. He ought to feel guilty for invading her privacy. But the truth was, he was enjoying himself too much to suffer guilt.

She was so perfect, she took his breath away. He felt a wild rush of heat as his gaze moved from the slope of her shoulders to her tiny waist. He drank in a quick glimpse of her breasts as she washed herself, then slipped into her petticoats.

She lifted a delicate ivory chemise over her head, then began to lace the ribbons that held it across her breasts. He felt another rush of heat as her fingers tied the ribbons, and he thought of his own rough fingers brushing her silken flesh. The mere thought set him on fire.

She turned her back on him and picked up the dress that lay in the hay. She slipped on the dress and smoothed it down over her waist and hips. Then, pulling a brush and comb from her pocket, she sat cross-legged in the hay and tossed her head, sending her waist-length hair spilling forward over one breast.

Cody had an almost overpowering desire to take the brush from her hands and smooth the silken strands himself. The little tune she was humming played through his mind, reminding him of one his mother had once crooned.

Beside him the mare stomped and snorted, causing Lizzy to glance toward the stall. For a moment she merely stared at the shadowy figure. Then, as realization dawned, she scrambled to her feet and stood facing the man who had dared to violate her privacy.

"How could you? How dare you?" She advanced on him, her eyes flashing fire, her hands tightened into fists at her sides. "You are nothing more than a vile, low-born..."

She lifted her fists and began pounding on his chest. "Grandpop warned me that Yankees were no better than dogs. You stood there, watching me undress, watching me bathe myself, and you have no remorse, no shame."

She struck him again and again, and he did nothing to block the blows. "You are mean. Cruel. Horrible."

Tears sprang to her eyes and she felt ashamed that he should see her crying. But as she tried to turn away, he caught her by the wrists and held her.

"Don't cry, Lizzy."

"I am not crying." But at the denial, her tears flowed even harder and she felt them stream, hot and wet, along her cheeks.

Cody knew there was no explanation he could offer that would be acceptable to her in her present mood. Besides, if the truth were known, he wasn't sorry for what he'd witnessed. And given the chance, he'd do it again.

She tried to yank her hands free but he continued to hold her firmly by the wrists.

"You're laughing at me," she cried. "Oh, how can you be so cruel?"

"I'd never laugh at you." His tone hardened. "I'm sorry that I startled you. But I'm not sorry for what I saw." His voice lowered. "What I saw just now was a very beautiful woman who was taking great pains to make herself even more beautiful, if that is possible."

Her tears faded. Her eyes widened at his words. But though his tone was deadly serious, a part of her still didn't want to listen.

"It's so easy for you, isn't it? The words just flow like honey from your lips. You probably know all the right things to say to make a woman forget to be afraid of you."

"Are you afraid of me, Lizzy?"

She straightened her spine and looked him in the eye. "I'm not afraid of any Yankee."

He started to smile, then caught himself. She reminded him of a kitten tossed into a rain barrel. She was so incredibly small, and brave, and angry.

He drew her closer and plunged one hand into the tangle of hair at her temple. Soft. Her hair was as soft as a snowdrift. He twisted a strand around his finger and drew her face close.

"Maybe you ought to start being afraid of me." His gaze focused on her mouth and she saw his eyes narrow.

Suddenly she was afraid. But not of him. She was afraid of the way her heart had begun tripping over itself. Her throat went dry as he lowered his head to her. She ran a tongue over her lips, and he watched the movement.

His hand stayed in her hair, but his fingers gently massaged her scalp as he drew her fractionally closer.

She stiffened. "You must not do this...."

Her protest was swallowed by the brush of his lips over hers. For a moment all thought scattered.

He lifted his head, and his dark eyes stared down into hers. He thought about fighting the urge, then gave up the battle. From the moment he'd touched her, he'd known that all was lost.

He drew her close, then framed her face with his big, work-worn hands.

Lizzy closed her eyes, ashamed that, for all her shock and outrage, she yearned for the feel of his lips on hers again.

"Open your eyes." His tone was low, almost gruff.

Lizzy's lids snapped open.

He stared into pale amber eyes and saw himself reflected there. And then whatever last thread of sanity he'd managed to salvage was lost.

He crushed her mouth with his. His arms came around her, drawing her into the warm circle of his embrace.

Heat. It was so intense, he'd never known anything like it. His blood heated until it flowed like liquid fire through his veins, roaring in his temples.

She tasted clean and fresh and new. The fragrance of bayberry soap clung to her hair and skin.

He felt the trembling of her lips beneath his and knew that she'd never before been kissed like this. But though the urge to leave her unsullied was great, the need to taste her was even greater.

Lizzy felt little splinters of ice snaking through her veins, chilling her. Then a moment later the ice became sparks, heating her flesh, her blood.

She had never dreamed a man's lips could bring such pleasure, a man's hands could unlock such feelings. Feelings she'd never known before.

A tiny fist seemed to tighten deep inside her, then slowly open, sending strange curling sensations pulsing through her. As Cody's mouth moved over hers and his tongue lazily traced her lips, she clung to him until, growing bolder, she opened her mouth to allow him to explore the intimate recesses.

Cody took the kiss deeper and felt a tiny shudder pass through her. He knew he was taking her too far, too fast. But he needed one more taste, one more touch.

He'd known passion before. And desire. But never before had he known such hunger. A hunger so deep, so great, he was certain nothing would ever fill this void.

He knew he had to end this before he took them over the edge. But still he lingered, savoring the taste of her, the fresh, clean scent of her that filled his mind.

Struggling to the surface, he called upon every ounce of willpower, and finally lifted his head.

His voice, when he finally managed it, was rougher than he'd intended. "Go back to the house. Now. This minute."

Her eyes were wide. Her lips were still swollen from his kisses.

Without a word she crossed the barn and picked up the basin, tossing the water into a trough. Wrapping her shawl around her, she grabbed up her brush and comb and hurried away.

Cody stood where he was until the door to the barn was closed behind her. Then he let out a long, slow breath and picked up a pitchfork. His hands, he noted, were trembling.

With a muttered oath he tossed the pitchfork into a mound of hay and stormed away.

The door to the cabin opened with a swirl of snow-flakes. Lizzy kept her attention rigidly focused on the food she was preparing for breakfast. But she knew the exact moment when Cody removed his jacket and turned toward her. She felt her cheeks flame and blamed it on the heat of the fire.

"How far is that herd of mustangs?" Ned asked as Cody took a seat at the table.

"Couple of hours, if they haven't moved on."

"If you don't mind, I'd like to go with you."

As Lizzy served their plates, she saw Cody's head come up sharply.

"What would you ride?"

Ned shrugged. "I saw a mare in the stall out in the barn. I thought maybe I could ride her."

Cody quickly shook his head. "The mare's getting ready to foal soon. The only horse left is the Spooners' plow horse."

Ned glanced at Amos. "Would you mind?"

"He's slow," the old man said, "but dependable."

Ned glanced at his brother. "Can I go with you?"

"Suit yourself." Though his words were curt, Lizzy thought she detected a hint of pleasure in his tone.

As Ned and Cody began to eat, they noticed that the Spooner family had gone very still. Glancing up, they paused, then set down their forks and bowed their heads as the others were doing.

"For this food we thank Thee," Amos intoned.

"Amen," the others said in unison.

Cody had a flash of memory of his own father, a stern army general, who was also a loving father and a man of deep faith.

He glanced across the table at Ned, who had gone very still. Suddenly Ned wolfed down his food and bolted from the table. "I'll get my saddle and bring the horse around to the door."

When he was gone Amos said conversationally, "Is the mare wild?"

"She's skittish. I found her with a herd of mustangs up in the hills. But from her lines and coloring, I'd say she has more Thoroughbred in her than mustang." For the first time that Lizzy could remember, Cody allowed his emotions to show in his voice. "She's the most perfect mare I've ever seen. She mated with my stallion. If her foal is as perfect as she is, I'll have a whole new line of breeding stock. There's no limit to what I can sell them for."

"Can I see her?" James asked.

"You can look, son. But don't go near her. Like I said, she's skittish."

James nodded solemnly.

As they finished eating, Ned hurried in, shaking snow from his hat and duster. "Looks like another storm coming in."

"That's nothing new in these parts." Cody slipped on his coat and pulled his hat low on his head. Turning to Amos, he said, "We should be back before dark. But if we're not, don't worry. I have several shelters in the hills." His gaze moved to where Lizzy stood beside the table. His tone grew stern as he directed his words to her grandfather. "If anyone should come here, lock the door and blow out the lantern. Whatever you do, don't go outside to face them."

He saw the way Lizzy lifted her chin and faced him with a scowl. Softening his tone, he added, "If you have to, take shelter in the cellar under the cabin."

Amos nodded.

"Come on, Beau."

The dog's tail thumped, but he remained where he was beside the fire. James had his chubby arms locked around Beau's neck. His face was buried in the dog's fur.

"James," Grandpop said sternly. "How many times do I have to tell you, the dog isn't a pet?"

"Yes, sir." James stood and the dog scrambled to his feet and raced to the door, eager to join his master on a new adventure.

When Cody pulled the door open, the dog raced outside where two horses stood saddled and ready.

"All my tools are in the barn," Cody called, pulling himself into the saddle. "Help yourself to what you need."

Amos nodded. "I'm much obliged."

For a moment Cody looked beyond the old man to where Lizzy stood, and their gazes met and held. She felt the heat stain her cheeks as he touched a hand to the brim of his hat. Then he wheeled his mount.

The horses' hooves beat a tattoo as they crossed the frozen meadow and disappeared down a ravine.

Lizzy plunged the dishes into a basin of hot water and took comfort in the hours of hard work that lay ahead.

Chapter Six

"Hold that log steady, Lizzy."

"I'm trying, Grandpop."

"Trying's not good enough. You got to lean into it, girl, else I'll never get it hewed smooth enough to replace that axle."

As her grandfather planed the wood, Lizzy's hands were scraped raw from her struggles with the rough bark.

"Where are James and Sara Jean?" the old man growled. "They could lend a hand."

"I sent them back to the house, Grandpop. Sara Jean's back was aching, and I saw James shivering in the cold."

Lizzy was shivering, too. But she knew that the harder she worked, the warmer she would get. She forced herself to ignore the cold in order to give her grandfather the help he needed.

Amos worked the plane over and over the log, filling the barn with the sweet fragrance of wood shavings. The two of them bent to their task, oblivious to the wind that howled outside the barn door.

They both looked up as the sound of horses' hooves drummed like the roar of a train, drowning out even the sound of the storm.

Throwing open the barn door, they peered through the swirling snowflakes and watched as Cody and Ned drove a herd of horses into the corral. Whenever a horse tried to break away, Beau nipped at its heels and sent it back to the herd. When all the horses were inside the enclosure, Cody closed the gate and secured it.

The horses milled around in confusion, many of them rearing and bucking in their eagerness to escape. But as the men tossed feed over the rails, the horses settled down and began to eat.

"Come on, girl. We've wasted enough time." Amos led the way back to the log, and while he began to plane it, Lizzy held it securely.

Cody and Ned led their horses into the barn. When they entered its warmth, they shook the snow from their wide-brimmed hats. The horses eagerly trotted to a trough. Beau dropped down into the hay and lay panting. Exhausted, Ned dropped down beside the dog and closed his eyes.

"I see you found your herd," Amos said without looking up.

"The storm had them trapped in a box canyon." Cody walked closer to watch as the old man worked over the log. When he caught sight of Lizzy's hands, his smile turned into a frown.

Embarrassed, Lizzy looked away, refusing to meet his eyes.

Cody kept his tone casual. "Why don't I plane for a while, Amos, and you can hold the log."

The old man looked up with pleasure. "You aren't too tired from the trail?"

"I think I have an hour or two left."

From his position in the hay, Ned's mouth dropped open in surprise. Cody had done the work of three men this day. He couldn't figure out how his brother was still standing.

"You go on inside, Lizzy, and get supper started," Amos said sharply.

Cody looked around. "Where's Sara Jean and James?"

"Resting."

"Can't they help?"

Seeing his frown of disapproval, Lizzy quickly added, "The journey's been hard on Sara Jean in her condition. I don't know how she does it."

At the mention of her sister, Ned was on his feet. "I'll walk with you, if you don't mind, Miss Spooner." He hurried to the door and gallantly held it open for her.

Cody watched as his brother followed Lizzy from the barn. Then he attacked the log with a vengeance.

"It took us at least two good hours of chopping before that old tree broke free. Then we had to use both horses just to drag it far enough to clear the opening to the canyon. It's a good thing your horse was trained to the plow, Miss Spooner. Otherwise we'd be there still."

Over supper Ned was regaling them with tales of the day spent with his brother. He was clearly still excited about their adventure. And though he tried to be polite to everyone, it was obvious that he directed most of his conversation toward Sara Jean.

The young woman was equally enthralled. "How many horses did you find?"

"Thirty. And from the looks of them, they were lucky we came along. With that fallen tree blocking their exit, they would have starved to death within a few more days. If the wolves didn't get them first," he added dramatically.

Cody leaned back, sipping strong, hot coffee. He hadn't said a word since the meal began.

"Such excitement." Sara Jean propped her elbows on the table and rested her chin on her hands, studying the young man across the table. "I envy you. It must be wonderful to be free to go where you choose." She glanced at her grandfather and saw his disapproving frown. "What I mean is, when you're a woman expecting a baby..." She blushed. "All I did today was crochet a little more of the blanket I'm making."

"Sara Jean does beautiful handwork," Lizzy put in. "Ma used to say she was even better than Grandma, who was considered the best in Georgia."

"I'd like to see your work," Ned said.

"Really?" Sara Jean's eyes sparkled as she pushed away from the table.

She crossed the room to the rocker and picked up the square of fabric. "I unraveled one of Ma's good sweaters for the yarn. It was supposed to be Lizzy's, but she said I needed it more than she did."

Amos started to grumble something about Lizzy being a sucker for her sister's sad stories, but Lizzy managed to cough loudly enough to drown out most of what he was saying.

Sara Jean and Ned bent their heads together while she showed him the intricate stitches she'd used to form the pattern.

Still grumbling, Amos pushed away from the table and went in search of his pipe and tobacco.

James yawned loudly and Lizzy said, "You put in a long day, James. Roll yourself up by the fire. And don't forget to say your prayers."

"Will you come and hear them later?"

"Of course I will. As soon as I've finished."

He wrapped his chubby arms around her neck and hugged her, then made his way to the fire.

Cody drained his cup and watched as Lizzy began to clear the table. He saw her wince as she lifted the plates. Instantly he was on his feet, taking the dishes from her hands.

"I'll take care of these."

"No." She stubbornly clung to them. "I heard what Ned said. From the sounds of it, you did more than most men today."

"Ned likes to exaggerate."

She shook her head. "You've done enough, Cody. We invaded your home, ate your food and stole your privacy."

"And now you're going to take orders from me."
With a smile he firmly took the dishes from her hands
and placed them in the basin of hot water. "I'll wash,
you dry." Before she could protest, he began to wash
the dishes.

"I can't let you do this, Cody. It isn't right."

"Woman, before you came along, I not only had to
wash my own dishes, but I had to come in from the trail
and make my own supper, too. So you see, you didn't
just invade my privacy, you brought along some tal-
ents, as well. As long as I'm enjoying your good cooking, I don't mind doing a few chores in return."

As Lizzy picked up a square of linen, she said, "I've
been admiring the handwork on these towels. Where
did you get them?"

The minute the words were out of her mouth, she
saw the way his smile faded. Whatever fragile cama-
raderie had begun to develop between them was suddenly shattered.

She tried several times to start a conversation, but it
was plain that Cody's mind was elsewhere.

As they finished the dishes in silence, James called,
"Lizzy, will you come and hear my prayers now?"

Lizzy was torn between trying to smooth things over
with Cody and her obligation to her little brother.
Turning away, she knelt beside James, who was already wrapped in a fur throw. From the corner of her
eye she saw Cody pull on his coat. The door closed behind him. A short time later, when she kissed James
and tucked him in, she realized that the others had all
retired for the night. Sara Jean could be heard shuf-

fling around in the loft. Beside the fire, Ned and Grandpop were already snoring softly.

She should be tired, too. Her muscles ached from the day's work. But instead of feeling weary, she experienced a strange restlessness.

She poured coffee from the blackened pot that hung over the fire and walked to the small window that looked over the snow-covered expanse of land.

Out on the porch, Cody rolled a cigarette and held a match to the tip. He drew smoke into his lungs, then lifted his head to study the path of a falling star.

Lizzy watched it, too, and squeezed her eyes tightly shut while she made a wish.

Minutes later she finished her coffee and carefully washed the cup before putting it away. When she turned, Cody was just entering the cabin.

He hung up his jacket and crossed directly to her. In a gruff whisper he said, "Hold out your hands."

"What? I don't..."

"Woman, why do you always argue with me?" He lifted one hand for his inspection and began applying a salve. When he finished one hand he caught the other and did the same.

Because the others were sleeping, he kept his voice low. "This is something I use on my horses whenever they've been injured. I've never seen hands quite as raw as yours, but I'm hoping it will help."

Within minutes the burning pain began to fade. She stared down at her hands, then up at him.

His eyes narrowed as he caught her hands in his. "Have I made it worse?"

She shook her head. "No. They're beginning to feel better already."

"Good." He continued holding her hands. "Tomorrow Ned and I will get busy on that log. You shouldn't be doing rough work like that."

"I don't mind."

"I know you don't. But I do. I've watched you work like a mule." His voice lowered intimately. "You deserve better, Elizabeth."

She felt her cheeks grow hot. Though it was painful, it was time for some honesty.

"My name isn't really Elizabeth. I mean, I was christened by that name. But I've always been called Lizzy. I guess I was just putting on airs, pretending something that wasn't really me." She swallowed. "I didn't want you to think you'd wasted your time rescuing someone who wasn't worthy of the effort. For a little while I just didn't want to be plain old Lizzy Spooner."

His voice warmed. "Believe me, you could never be plain." He lifted her hands to his lips and pressed a kiss to her knuckles, then turned them over and opened them, pressing a kiss to each palm. It was the sweetest gesture she'd ever known, and for a moment Lizzy felt tears spring to her eyes as he drew her arms around his waist and gathered her close.

Against her temple he murmured lazily, "And I will never regret rescuing you, Lizzy Spooner."

The touch of his lips against her temple sent threads of pleasure skittering along her spine.

If his words were lazy, his mouth wasn't. He moved it across her eyebrow, along the curve of her cheek to the corner of her lips. And though she longed for his mouth on hers, he changed direction and explored her ear, her jaw, her neck, until she moaned and arched her head for his further inspection. He ran hot, moist kisses along her throat until she gasped and clutched at him.

His mouth covered hers with hot, hungry kisses. His hands pressed against her back, drawing her firmly against him. The scrape of his teeth had her gasping, and when his tongue moved seductively over hers, she moaned.

Her hands clutched at the front of his shirt, then curled around his neck as she returned his kisses. She suddenly strained against him with an urgency that matched his own.

The change in her had him reeling. He'd known passion, had even had his senses clouded by a woman a time or two. But never like this. The moment she responded to his kisses, he felt a need so hot, so compelling, it seemed to burn through his mind, sear his very soul.

Suddenly, all he knew was Lizzy. All he could feel was her warm, moist skin beneath his fingers. All he could taste was the honeyed sweetness of her lips.

Never before had Lizzy known such needs. Needs sharper than any hunger. Stronger than anything she'd ever experienced. It was like the undertow she'd once encountered in the river near her home. She'd been pulled down, down, until her lungs felt like exploding.

Until her head throbbed and her limbs became weightless. And then, when she'd thought she couldn't survive another moment, she broke the surface of the water and filled her lungs with air, clearing her mind. In no time she found herself swimming safely to shore.

Cody's lips moved over hers, slowly, seductively, causing her to sigh and move in his arms. If she was about to get caught up in another undertow, she was ready. Her head was already spinning. She could no longer hold a coherent thought. She was drowning in the heady taste of him.

"Lizzy." Slowly, carefully, Cody pushed her a little away.

Her eyes were heavy lidded, her lips swollen. Just looking at her brought another swift rush of desire. What had he been thinking of? With her family sleeping just a few feet away.

"I have to go out to the corral now."

"The corral?" Her head was still spinning. Nothing seemed to be making any sense.

"To check on the mustangs."

"Yes. Of course." She ran a tongue over her lips and prayed her legs would hold her.

"Can you see by the light of the fire?"

"See?"

"To climb to the loft."

She nodded, but continued to stare at him. He lifted the lantern from its peg and studied the way her eyes glowed. Amber, like a cat's. Even now, though he forced himself to act as though nothing had happened, he wanted her with a desperation that made him tremble.

"I'm going to take the lantern outside with me."

She nodded, and watched as he pulled on his jacket and opened the door.

He paused in the doorway. His voice was little more than a whisper. The tone was flat. But his words had more impact than if they'd been shouted.

"The towels were made by my wife, Mary. She died two years ago."

The door closed behind him.

Her eyes brimming, Lizzy continued to stand and stare.

Touching a finger to her lips, she shivered and turned toward the ladder.

Long after she had wrapped herself in fur and lay in the darkness, listening to the soft, steady breathing of her sister, Lizzy could still taste him on her lips. And she could hear his voice, struggling to show no emotion. But the pain had been there. From across the room she had recognized the pain. And had been moved to tears by it.

She knew that sleep would elude her this night.

Chapter Seven

Lizzy awoke with a start and realized that Sara Jean was already downstairs. She could hear her sister's laughter, and the deeper sound of Ned's voice joining in.

With everyone awake, Lizzy knew there wouldn't be time for a private moment to wash and brush her hair. Slipping into her dress and shoes, she climbed down the ladder and hurried to prepare breakfast.

She placed salt pork in a skillet over the fire and set a pan of biscuits to bake, then filled the blackened coffeepot with water from the kettle. Soon the little cabin was redolent with the aroma of good food.

Cody came in from the barn, where he had already begun his morning chores. Immediately Lizzy felt her cheeks grow hot and busied herself at the table. It wouldn't do to allow herself to think about what she and Cody had shared last night. In the light of day he must surely regret his impulsive behavior.

"Looks like it snowed some more." James peered out the window. "I can't even see our footprints from last night."

"Do you like the snow?" Cody hung up his coat and rolled his sleeves before plunging his hands into a basin of water.

"Yes, sir. We never got snow back home. But Pa told me about a time when he was a boy and it snowed at the Willows. It ruined all the crops, isn't that right, Grandpop?"

"Come and eat, James," Amos called irritably. "And quit pestering Cody with your talk."

"I don't mind the boy talking to me. In fact, I enjoy it."

Lizzy saw the relief on her brother's face as he took the seat beside Cody. The little boy watched as Cody bowed his head with the others while Amos intoned a prayer of thanks. When Cody lifted a steaming cup of coffee to his lips, James imitated him with the mug of warm milk Lizzy gave him.

"Could I help you with the mustangs?"

Cody set his cup down. "What could you do?"

James set his own mug down and thought. "I could muck out the stalls."

"I can't put them in the barn. My mare is too close to foaling. They'll have to stay in the corral for now."

"Won't they get cold?"

"Wild mustangs grow a protective coat of hair. They're used to the cold. That's what saves them from all these storms out in the mountains."

"That's good." It was obvious that the boy had worried about the horses in the pen. He thought a long minute. "I could feed them for you."

"They're too wild, son. They might get excited and trample you."

"I'm good with horses. Next to Lizzy, Pa said I was the best."

"That so?" Cody glanced across the table to where Lizzy sat, eyes downcast. "Just how good is your sister?"

The little boy puffed with pride. "Pa used to say the horse wasn't born that Lizzy couldn't ride."

"Maybe I'm wasting my time fighting those mustangs. Maybe I ought to let your sister break them to saddle."

"Lizzy could do it. I know she could."

Lizzy glanced up, intending to chide her brother for having such false pride. But before she could, her gaze was caught and held by Cody's.

There was an unusual warmth to his tone. "Well, James, I don't think I can let even an expert like Lizzy break those mustangs." He held her gaze a moment longer before turning back to the little boy. "But I would take it as a favor if you two would feed and water them today while I help Amos with that axle."

"You hear that, Lizzy? We're going to take care of wild mustangs." James pushed excitedly from the table and began to search for his worn boots.

"One thing," Cody said sternly. "Neither of you can go inside the corral. You fork the hay and grain over the rail. And you fill the troughs from outside the fence. Understood?"

James nodded solemnly.

Cody turned to Ned. "If you can spare another day, we could use your help with that axle."

Ned watched as Sara Jean spread blackberry preserves over a warm biscuit and lifted it to her lips. He could feel the delicate bite of those teeth all the way across the table. His insides turned to mush.

He cleared his throat. "I guess I can spare one more day. Commencement will still be there tomorrow."

"Good. I'll be out in the barn when you're ready to get started."

Cody pushed away from the table, then turned back. "That was a fine breakfast, Lizzy. Thank you."

It was the first time he'd spoken directly to her this morning. She felt the heat rush to her cheeks. "You're welcome."

"How are your hands?"

She saw the others look at her and she swallowed in embarrassment. "Much better, thank you."

He studied her a moment, seeing the way she kept her hands beneath the table. As he turned away, he called over his shoulder, "Amos, I'll see you in the barn."

He drew on his coat and was gone in a swirl of snowflakes, with Beau at his heels.

"Come on, James," Amos called as he began to pull on his shoes. "You can gather up the wood shavings from the barn. They'll make fine kindling for the fireplace."

As they dressed for the outdoors, Lizzy began gathering up the dishes. She noted Ned and Sara Jean smiling shyly at each other across the table.

"Where do you plan to settle?" Ned asked.

Sara Jean moved her shoulders in a shrug. "Grandpop doesn't know. He just said we'd keep going until we reached California and found a place that suited us. Isn't that right, Grandpop?"

The old man grunted a response.

"But how will I ever know where to look for you if you don't know where you're headed?"

Sara Jean stared at her plate. The thought of never seeing Ned again was too distressing. "If you're at Commencement, I could always send a letter there telling you where we've put down roots."

Ned shook his head. "I don't know how long I'll be staying there. Cody doesn't have much good to say about the town."

Sara Jean's voice sounded as petulant as a child's. "If you ask me, Cody doesn't have much good to say about anything."

Lizzy clattered dishes in the basin. "That's a fine way to talk about a man who's given us shelter. Besides, he's Ned's brother."

"I don't take offense," Ned said quickly. "Cody's always been prickly. He's a hard man to understand. And after Mary..." He stopped, realizing he was speaking out of turn.

Amos and James stopped what they were doing and glanced up expectantly.

"It's all right, Ned." Lizzy began to wash the dishes, and Sara Jean picked up a towel to dry them. "Cody told me that his wife died two years ago."

Sara Jean turned to her in surprise and Lizzy knew she was bursting with questions.

"What else did he tell you?" Ned studied Sara Jean's glossy yellow curls as she lifted a cup to dry.

Lizzy shrugged. "That's all. Nothing more."

"How did she die?" Sara Jean asked.

"I guess you could say she was a casualty of war." Ned's tone grew harsh. "After Cody left, she and the baby were on their own way out there on that isolated farm."

"Baby?" Lizzy felt the plate slip from her soapy hands and drop to her feet, where it shattered.

"Yes'm." Ned stooped and began picking up shards of china, with Sara Jean on her knees beside him.

For long minutes there was only silence as they cleaned up the mess. Then Sara Jean let out a cry as she pricked her finger, and Ned dropped everything to rush to her aid.

"Let me wrap that for you." He pulled a clean handkerchief from his pocket.

Lizzy finished the dishes alone while Ned and Sara Jean moved toward the window, where he could probe for the splinter that pierced her flesh.

When the dishes were done, Lizzy swept the floor clean, then reached for a shawl. It seemed to her that Grandpop and James were taking an inordinately long time to dress. But then, there had been little time for gossip these past months. And the man who had taken them in seemed so mysterious. It was only natural they would want to stay and hear as much as they could about him.

As she started toward the door, she heard Sara Jean say, "Did your brother have a son or a daughter?"

"A son." Ned seemed more concerned with Sara Jean's finger than his brother's loss.

"How old is he?" Lizzy asked.

"Who?" Ned lifted his head.

She found herself gritting her teeth. "Cody's son."

"He was almost five when he died along with Mary."

Almost the age of James. Lizzy felt her heart go out to the stern man who had suffered such a loss.

"How did they die?" Sara Jean continued boldly.

At her sister's question, Lizzy held her breath. Though she had no right to such information, the curiosity was eating at her.

"Don't know for sure." Ned carefully wrapped the clean linen handkerchief around Sara Jean's finger. "Some say they were bludgeoned by a crazy man. Others said it was a roving band of deserters from General Lee's army at Hagerstown, not far from the Pennsylvania border where Cody had his farm."

Sara Jean snatched her finger away from Ned's grasp. "Don't you dare say such a thing about our fine Southern soldiers."

"I wasn't accusing them, ma'am." Ned's face turned beet red. "I was just repeating what some said."

Sara Jean glanced at her grandfather, whose boots were forgotten as he stared into the flames of the fire.

"Southern soldiers wouldn't harm a woman and babe, would they, Grandpop?"

"I guess," the old man mused aloud, "there was good and evil on both sides. The war did terrible things to people." He glanced toward Ned. "But that doesn't excuse your brother from neglecting his duty. Where was he while his wife and baby were being brutalized?"

Ned flushed. "He was off fighting the war, sir."

Amos pinned him with a fierce look. "Which side did he fight on?"

After an awkward silence Ned said softly, "The North."

"And what about you?" Amos bellowed. "Were you off fighting in the war, too?"

"Yes, sir." Ned studied the toe of his boot. "When the war started, and my grandmother realized that Cody would be serving with the Federals, she packed up and returned to her childhood home in Louisiana, with me in tow. A short time later I joined up to fight under General Braxton Bragg for the Confederate Army of Tennessee."

North against South. Brother against brother.

A terrible silence descended upon the cabin. Amos turned away and snatched up his sheepskin jacket. Even James, as young as he was, seemed to understand the horror of what had been said. He ducked his head and struggled with the leather thongs on his boots. Sara Jean stared at the clean linen wrapped around her finger. Beside her, Ned hung his head and stared at a spot on the floor.

Lizzy gathered her shawl around her and pulled open the door. Now she understood why the two brothers hadn't spoken to each other in over two years. And why their reunion had been so strained. At least her own family had been united against a common enemy. What would they have done if Ma and Pa had chosen different sides?

When a blast of frigid air knifed into her flesh, she was almost grateful. At least now she had an excuse for the tears that stung her eyes.

"Grandpop, supper's . . ." The rest of Lizzy's words died on her lips.

While Amos and Ned strained against the ropes and pulleys lifting the wagon, Cody fitted the smooth, round log into place. He had removed his shirt, and despite the cold of the barn, his skin was slick with sweat.

Lizzy stared at the ripple of muscle across his back and shoulders as he bent to his task. She gave an involuntary shiver. She had seen plenty of men without their shirts before. Workers in the fields. Farmhands in the barns. Never had she been so affected by the sight of a man's body.

"That ought to hold it." Cody straightened and ran the back of his hand across his dripping forehead. "At least until you can get that broken axle to a black-smith."

"Is there one in Commencement?" Amos asked.

"There was the last time I looked." Cody reached for his shirt and pulled it on. "But the town keeps changing. There may not be a smith now."

Amos glanced toward his granddaughter. "Hear that, girl? I'll head on over to town tomorrow with

Ned. If there's a smith, we ought to be on our way within a couple of days.''

"That's fine, Grandpop." Lizzy had to dig to muster some enthusiasm. "Supper's ready."

"Did you feed the horses?" Cody asked.

She paused at the door to the barn and glanced back in time to see him tucking his shirt into the waistband of his pants. Fixing her gaze on a spot over his shoulder, she nodded. "They've been taken care of."

"Thank you."

She turned and ran all the way to the cabin.

Inside, the fragrance of freshly baked bread mingled with the sweet scent of wood shavings on the fire. The men took turns washing in the basin before sitting down at the table.

"Something smells wonderful," Ned commented as he speared a slice of venison and passed the platter to Amos.

"Lizzy baked corn bread. It's Grandpop's favorite." Sara Jean was seated beside Ned. Each time she passed him a plate or bowl, their fingers brushed, causing heat to stain her cheeks.

Ned bit into the corn bread and gave a sigh of pleasure. "It's just become my favorite, too, Miss Spooner."

Lizzy smiled. "Then I'll have to wrap you some to take along when you leave for Commencement, Ned."

"Thank you, ma'am. I'd be obliged."

"So you'll be leaving in the morning." Cody sipped strong coffee and stared across the table at his brother.

"I only hope the job's still waiting for me."

"If it isn't, you'll need something to hold you over until another job can be found." Cody drained his cup. "After supper I'd like you to pick out fifteen mustangs."

"Why?"

Cody shrugged. "You earned the right to half the herd. You did as much work as I did bringing them in. They should fetch a good price in Commencement. That'll give you a stake."

For a moment Ned seemed thunderstruck. "I don't know what to say."

"Don't say anything. Just see that you pick out some good horseflesh."

Ned pushed away from the table and pulled on his duster and hat. "Guess I'll go have a look at them right now."

Sara Jean tossed a shawl over her shoulders. "Mind if I come along?"

"No, ma'am." Ned's eyes registered his surprise. "I'd be pleased."

He held the door open and she hurried past him, ignoring the frown on her grandfather's face.

Seeing Grandpop's fury, the rest of the family finished their meal in uncomfortable silence.

Within minutes Amos lowered his fork and shoved back his chair. "Think I'll take my smoke outside and maybe amble down to the corral myself."

Lizzy knew that her grandfather would have rather smoked his pipe in front of the fire. But the idea of Sara Jean alone in the dark with a young man had him feeling protective.

When the door closed behind Amos, Lizzy began gathering up the dishes. As she washed them in the basin of hot water, she could hear James, seated in front of the fire, talking in low tones to Cody, who sat on the bench, mending some harness.

"My pa was a big man. Bigger'n Grandpop. Even bigger'n you, I guess. My pa could do anything. Like you. He worked all day in the fields and then spent half the night in the barn with his horses."

Cody ran the leather through his work-worn fingers. "You remember a lot about him, do you?"

"Yes, sir." James locked his arms around Beau's neck and buried his face in the thick ruff. "Well, some I remember. And some Lizzy told me." His voice grew wistful. "Lizzy says I look like Pa. But sometimes I can't even remember what he looked like anymore."

He glanced up, and Cody could read the fear in his eyes.

"Do you think someday I'll forget what Pa looked like?"

"Maybe. But your heart will never forget."

Lizzy swallowed the lump that had suddenly formed in her throat. With her back to them she continued to dry the dishes.

"Grandpop said we used to have some fine pictures of Ma and Pa. But they were all burned with the Willows."

"I'm sorry to hear that. But you won't need pictures to carry the people you love with you."

"Do you still remember what your baby looked like?"

Lizzy whirled. In that instant she caught the look of surprise in Cody's eyes before his gaze narrowed. Though he spoke to James, his words, Lizzy knew, were directed at her.

"I see my brother's been talking about me."

"He said—"

"James." Lizzy's voice was strained. "Get ready for bed now. I'll hear your prayers when I've finished the dishes."

"But..."

"Right now."

"Yes'm." The little boy began struggling out of his boots and britches. "Ned didn't mean any harm by it. He just said..."

One glance at Lizzy's face and he fell silent. When he was rolled into a fur robe, with Beau curled up beside him, he called, "I'm ready, Lizzy."

She could feel Cody's gaze burning into her back as she knelt beside her little brother and listened to his halting words.

"Bless Grandpop and Sara Jean, and Lizzy. And Ma and Pa in heaven. And bless Ned and Cody and Beau." His eyes opened wide. "Is it all right to ask God to bless a dog?"

"I don't see why not. Isn't Beau one of His creatures?"

Reassured, the little boy said, "And bless me, too, and help me to grow up to be as big and strong as Pa."

"That was a fine prayer, James." Lizzy bent and brushed a kiss across his forehead. "Now you get some sleep."

"'Night, Lizzy. 'Night, Cody," he called.

"Good night, James."

Lizzy straightened and glanced toward the door, hoping the others would soon return.

"Let me see those hands."

At Cody's deep voice she turned to find him standing behind her, holding a small vial of ointment.

"They're fine." She lifted them for his inspection.

"Good." He caught her hands in his and turned them palm up. "Now let's see that they keep healing." He smeared the ointment on her right hand, then lifted the left and did the same.

Each time his fingers pressed over hers she felt a wave of heat that weakened her knees and left her trembling.

"In a week or two they'll be as good as new."

At his words Lizzy felt a pain around her heart. In a week or two they'd be back on the trail. And there would be no time to worry about her hands. It would be her heart that would be chafed and bleeding.

"I'm sorry," she whispered, glancing toward the sleeping figure of her little brother.

"Sorry for what?"

Cody was so close. His breath feathered the hair at her temple.

"For James saying what he did to you."

"You can't control what a little boy says and does."

"But we all listened to the gossip about you."

"That's just human nature. We all want to hear about someone else's misfortunes. Maybe because it makes our own so much more bearable."

"That still doesn't make it right. We shouldn't have pried."

He placed his fingertips over her lips to silence her. Instantly she felt the jolt. Glancing up, she saw that he felt it, too.

His eyes seemed to darken. She could see herself reflected in his pupils. Slowly, he traced the outline of her mouth with his finger. Her lips parted invitingly and she heard his slight intake of breath as he leaned closer and lowered his head.

The kiss was the merest brushing of lips, yet the feelings poured through them, leaving them both trembling with need.

They heard the sound of booted feet across the porch, and the trill of Sara Jean's laughter.

Stepping apart, they looked up as the door was flung open and the others trooped inside, stomping snow from their boots as they did.

Sara Jean glanced at Cody and her sister, wearing similar frowns. "You two should get away from your chores for a while and appreciate the beautiful night. The stars look close enough to touch. Why, I declare, even the air doesn't seem as cold tonight. It would do you both a world of good to breathe in that air and walk through the snow."

"That's a fine idea. I guess I'll check on my mare." Cody pulled on his coat and stepped out into the night.

Lizzy climbed the ladder and fled to the loft, fearing that the color in her cheeks would reveal her confusion.

Chapter Eight

"Lizzy." Sara Jean's voice was a frantic whisper. "Are you awake?"

"Uh-huh." Lizzy rolled over to face her sister. She'd been tossing and turning for more than an hour, but sleep still evaded her. The thought of Cody's hands and lips tormented her, driving her to distraction. How could she possibly sleep when all she could think of was that silent, wounded man?

"Lizzy, please don't think I'm wicked."

"Wicked? Sara Jean, where did you get such nonsense?"

Her younger sister placed a hand on her swollen stomach. "Here I am, expecting one man's baby, and allowing myself to think about another."

"But that isn't wicked. Ben's been dead all these long months, Sara Jean. It's only natural to think about someone who's alive and young and strong. Besides, it's plain to see how Ned feels about you."

"Is it? Do you think he cares about me, Lizzy?"

"Of course he does."

"Listen to what that does to my heart." Sara Jean caught her sister's hand and brought it to her breast. "Doesn't that mean I must be wicked? How can he make my heart pound like this when I don't even think about Ben like that?"

"You were married for only a few days before Ben went off to war. Why, the two of you didn't even have time to get acquainted, let alone miss each other."

"Oh, Lizzy." Sara Jean hugged her close. "I'm so glad you're not mad at me. I know Grandpop thinks I'm wicked. Why, he practically accused me of being a loose woman for going out to the corral with Ned."

"Grandpop just feels responsible for you. For all of us. Put yourself in his place, Sara Jean. He's lost his only son, his land, his heritage, everything he ever worked for. He feels like a stranger in a strange place. And now, on top of everything else, he has to start all over raising another brood. I'll bet," Lizzy mused, "if you could look inside his soul, you'd find out that he's just as scared as the rest of us."

"Grandpop? Scared?" Sara Jean gave a mirthless laugh. "The only thing Grandpop is is mean and mad at the world. And right now he thinks his youngest granddaughter is an evil, wicked woman."

Lizzy took her sister's hand and squeezed it. "In Grandpop's day, a man didn't even speak to a woman unless he had her pa's approval first. To him, going off with a man in the dark is an invitation to Satan. He doesn't mean to judge us harshly. It's just his way."

"Oh, Lizzy. What am I going to do?" Sara Jean suddenly wailed. "Ned's going away in the morning.

And I'm never going to see him again. I don't think I can bear to lose another man who makes me feel like this."

"Shh." Lizzy drew her sister close and brushed away her fine, blond hair, damp with tears. "It seems to me that you've forgotten how to pray."

"Oh, Lizzy, this is too important for silly, childish prattle."

"Silly." Lizzy knelt up and stared at her sister. Even in the dim light cast by the fire it was plain that her eyes were flashing with righteous anger. "Sara Jean, the silly things you can handle by yourself. But when it comes to the important ones, you'd better put them in the hands of someone you can trust. Now if you really want Ned to feel the same way you do, you'd better start praying."

"Oh, Lizzy. You're as mean as Grandpop." Sniffing back tears, Sara Jean rolled away and drew the fur robe over her head.

For long minutes Lizzy knelt very still, listening to the sound of silent weeping. Her own heart was as heavy as a stone.

There was a time, she realized, before the war, when she'd believed in miracles. But after watching the Willows burn to the ground, with everything she cherished in it, she had begun to lose heart. Seeing the land she loved destroyed, learning that Pa was dead, had been the darkest hours. And burying Ma along the trail, far from the ones she loved, had been the heaviest burden of all.

She thought about the little boy who lay sleeping by the fire, trusting that everything she taught him was the truth. And the sister who had just turned her back on those childhood lessons after pouring out her heart's secrets.

Closing her eyes in desperation, Lizzy began to whisper the prayers she'd learned at her parents' knees.

"Breakfast is ready."

Ned glanced up from the rope he'd been examining. "This one looks sturdy enough to hold better than a dozen frisky mustangs."

He handed it to Cody as they took their places at the table. Cody ran the strands through his fingers, then returned it to his brother with a nod. "That ought to work."

Sara Jean climbed down the ladder. Glancing up, Lizzy tried to hide her surprise.

Sara Jean was wearing her best Sunday dress, which had once belonged to their mother. It was pale blue, and Pa had always said that it made Ma's eyes seem as blue as the bluebells that grew wild in the meadows. By letting out a few seams, and adding a shawl, Sara Jean's condition was hardly noticeable.

She had brushed her hair until it glistened like spun gold and fell in soft curls around her pretty face.

Seeing her, Ned scraped back his chair and nearly tripped over his feet in his haste to assist her down the final rungs of the ladder.

"Sara Jean, you look so—" his cheeks turned bright pink and his Adam's apple bobbed furiously "—pretty."

"Thank you, Ned." She swept to the table like a grand lady and waited until he held her chair. "I thought, since this was to be your last meal with us, that I'd make it as festive as possible."

Lizzy smiled as she placed a platter of venison on the table. Leave it to Sara Jean to make a lasting impression on the poor boy. One that he'd never be able to forget.

"Now that we're all here," Grandpop said with a scowl at his youngest granddaughter, "we'll say grace."

They bowed their heads.

"For this food we thank You, Lord. Stay our feet along a safe trail to Commencement."

With a murmured amen they began to pass the food.

"I've been thinking, Grandpop." Sara Jean chose her words carefully. She'd given this much consideration while she dressed. "We all know that sometimes you have trouble with your eyes." When he opened his mouth to protest, she added quickly, "At least when the light begins to fade. Now on the journey to Commencement, you'll have Ned along to guide you. But on the journey back, you'll have no one. That could be very dangerous."

Lizzy's head came up. For once, her sister made sense. "Sara Jean's right, Grandpop. I don't know what we were thinking of. You ought to have someone with you."

Amos studied his younger granddaughter, sitting as close to Ned Martin as she dared. He knew what she was up to. "And you think that someone ought to be you, Sara Jean?"

"James is too young for such a long journey. And Lizzy takes much better care of him than I do, so she really ought to stay here with him. And I thought maybe we'll find a doctor in Commencement."

"Oh, yes, Grandpop," Lizzy said with enthusiasm. "It would be wonderful if Sara Jean could find a doctor to deliver her baby." That way, Lizzy wouldn't have to face the awesome task by herself.

"Seems to me you've done an awful lot of thinking on this, Sara Jean." Grandpop's eyebrows drew together as he regarded her over the rim of his cup.

"I have. And I've been praying on it, too, Grandpop."

"That so?" He glanced at Ned, who had forgotten all about the food in front of him. If his eyes got any bigger, Amos thought, they'd fall clear out of his head. "Well, I'll think on it awhile now, if you don't mind."

Sara Jean ducked her head and picked at a biscuit. Ned's knees brushed hers under the table and she felt a rush of heat that had nothing to do with the fire that crackled in the fireplace. She wanted to look at Ned, but she was afraid Grandpop would see her, so she kept her gaze averted.

When the meal was finished, the men pushed back their chairs.

"Time to get started," Amos announced. Out of the corner of his eye he saw Sara Jean watching him. With exaggerated movements he stretched, then reached for his sheepskin jacket and pulled it on.

"I guess," Amos announced to no one in particular, "while I'm hitching the wagon, you may as well pack up a few things and come along for the ride, girl."

Sara Jean's mouth dropped open. "You mean it, Grandpop?"

"Well," he admitted, "I do have trouble seeing when the light fades. And a town the size of Commencement might have a doctor. Though Lord knows how we'll be able to pay him."

"I'll be ready, Grandpop." She flew to the ladder and began to climb to the loft. "By the time you get the wagon hitched, I'll be waiting."

The three men made their way to the barn.

"You think this wood will hold until we get to Commencement?" The horse's breath plumed as Amos hitched up the wagon.

"It's solid." Cody checked underneath, then crawled out and wiped his hands along his pants. "As long as you don't carry a heavy load, or go over any embankments, you ought to make it to town."

Amos chuckled. "Maybe it's a good thing Sara Jean's going along. Staring at all this snow can blind a fellow."

Cody turned away. It was obvious that the old man couldn't see very well. But it wasn't Cody's place to point it out.

He watched his brother lasso the mustangs he'd chosen to take along. "Tie them all on a lead to the back of the wagon," Cody shouted. "If you keep them close together, they won't bolt."

The door to the cabin opened and Sara Jean made her way to the wagon, followed by Lizzy and James.

Ned helped Sara Jean up to the seat of the wagon.

"I packed venison for the journey," Lizzy said, handing up a package wrapped in several thicknesses of linen. "And extra corn bread for Ned."

"Thank you, ma'am." He tipped his hat.

"You'll need this," Cody said, handing Amos a fur robe.

"Much obliged." The old man draped it over Sara Jean's lap, then cleared his throat in agitation. "James, you mind your sister, now."

"Yes, sir."

"Lizzy..." He shrugged. "No need giving you orders. I know I can trust you to do what's right. We'll be back in a couple of days."

Lizzy swallowed, wishing there were some way she could say the words she felt in her heart. What if she never saw Sara Jean and Grandpop again? There were so many dangers along the trail. She loved them so much. But the words just wouldn't come. Instead, she merely called, "Goodbye, Grandpop. Sara Jean."

"'Bye, Lizzy. Goodbye, James," their sister called from the wagon.

"I'll need a hand with this mare," Ned shouted to his brother.

As Cody held the reins, Ned tossed a blanket over the one horse that would stand still long enough to be saddled. Though the mare allowed him to mount, she was still half-wild, and pranced nervously as he settled his weight in the saddle.

"You're going to have your hands full," Cody warned.

"Looks like." Ned met his brother's eyes for the first time and struggled for something to say. "I'm—glad I had this chance to see you."

Cody said nothing as he handed the reins to Ned.

"You take care, now," Ned called.

"You, too." Cody stepped aside as the mare danced.

Amos cracked the whip and the horse began plodding through the snow. The mustangs, tied to the wagon, followed along behind, blowing and snorting nervously. Beside the wagon Ned struggled to keep his mare under control.

Lizzy dropped her arm around her little brother's shoulders and drew him close as the wagon wheels drew lines through the new snow across the flat meadow. Beside them Cody stood, ramrod straight, his eyes unblinking as his brother rode out of his life as casually as he'd ridden in.

When the party dipped out of sight below a ridge, Cody turned and headed for the barn. But not before Lizzy saw the look of pain that clouded his eyes.

"Do you think Grandpop is in Commencement yet?" James glanced at Cody, who sat at the head of the table.

"I don't know, son. With only one horse pulling that wagon through the snow, thirty miles will seem like a mighty long trek."

"I never thought." Lizzy clapped a hand to her mouth. "What will they do if they have to stop for the night?"

"What did you do all the way from Georgia?"

"That was different," James piped up. "Lizzy was along to take care of everything."

Cody glanced up to see the flush that touched Lizzy's cheeks. The boy wasn't making an idle joke. It was obvious who kept things running smoothly in the Spooner family.

"They have Ned." He drained his cup. "He'll see to their safety."

It had come as a shock to Cody, seeing that stranger with the face of his brother. It pained him to think of the years they'd missed. And now, after all that had happened, they could never again be what they were before.

Lizzy wrapped a towel around the blackened pot and poured coffee into his empty cup. Though he absently thanked her, she could see by the look in his eyes that he had slipped away to another place, another time.

James pushed away from the table and pressed his nose to the window. "It's snowing again. Do you think Grandpop could get lost like before?"

Cody pulled himself from his reverie and crossed the room to stand behind the little boy. "It's just a little snow, James. It doesn't look like it'll grow into anything more."

"But what if it does? What if they slip over the mountain? What if the wolves . . . ?"

Cody surprised them both by picking him up. Crossing to the rocker, he sat down and planted the boy on his lap. Beau, drowsing by the fire, trotted over and pressed his nose to the little boy's hand.

"But Grandpop's eyes . . ."

"He has Ned and Sara Jean."

"And what if Sara Jean should have her baby?"

"It's too soon. But if she did, she'd have Ned and your grandfather there to take care of her."

"But Ned has all those mustangs. They might run away."

"They might. If they did, I guess Ned would just have to chase after them. The worst thing that could happen is that they'd find themselves free again."

"But . . ."

"You're still worried, aren't you?"

The little boy nodded. In a frightened voice he said, "I'm afraid Grandpop and Sara Jean will end up like Pa and Ma."

Cody thought about his own carefree childhood, and found himself cursing the circumstances that had robbed so many children of such a blessing.

"Sometimes, James," he said softly, "you just have to trust that everything will be all right."

"Do you?"

Cody nodded. "Of course I do. You'll see. They'll be back in a couple of days."

Within minutes the little boy climbed down from his lap and began petting Beau. Soon the boy and dog were engaged in a game of fetch the stick. Except that James seemed to fetch it more often than Beau. Before long the big dog was sprawled out in front of the fire, with James asleep against his neck.

As Lizzy finished the dishes, she turned to see Cody wrapping James in a fur robe. For a moment her heart stopped as she thought about the way her father had looked, so big and strong and handsome, carrying his infant son to bed. She had the strangest urge to weep.

Cody watched as she untied her apron and smoothed her skirts. Her hair had pulled loose from its neat knot, and damp little tendrils kissed her cheeks. By the light of the fire her eyes seemed more green than amber. There was the faintest blush of color to her cheeks that hadn't been there earlier.

"There's coffee," she said. "And a last sliver of corn bread."

"It isn't coffee I want."

As she started past him, he dropped his hands to her shoulders.

She stopped in midstride, as if frozen.

Maybe it was the overflow of tender feelings toward the little boy, though he doubted it. More probably it was the fact that they felt like a family. A man, a woman, a child.

It couldn't be because she stirred feelings in him, he told himself sternly. Feelings that had been buried so deeply he'd believed they were dead. Now those same feelings were struggling to be free. And he was torn between need and honor.

"For the longest time I've wanted to do this." Reaching up, he removed the pins from her hair and watched as it tumbled down past her waist. His eyes narrowed as he plunged his hands into the tangles.

"You mustn't do this, Cody."

"Shh."

He stared into her wide eyes and slowly combed his fingers through the waves, reveling in their silken texture.

"How could I have forgotten what a woman feels like?" He moved his big hands across the slope of her shoulders, down her sides, then up her back, sending shivers of pure delight along her spine.

"And the taste of a woman." He expertly parted her lips with his tongue and drank long and deep from her mouth.

Her muffled objection was forgotten. Even while she lifted her hands to push him away, her limbs betrayed her. Her arms encircled him, pulling him close, while her mouth moved under his, eager, avid.

The cabin was quiet. So quiet she could hear the roar of her heartbeat as it pounded in her temples. The room had become hot. So hot she thought her flesh must surely be on fire.

He kissed her with a hunger that matched her own. With teeth and tongue and lips, seducing, possessing. She clung to him, eager to taste, to feel. To give.

Somewhere on a distant hill a wolf called to the moon, and Beau stirred in his sleep. But neither of them heard.

When Cody moved his hands along her spine, she felt his touch over every inch of her body. Her breasts tingled with unexpected need. Her thighs pressed to his, filling her veins with liquid fire.

He tore his mouth from hers and pressed it to the soft, sensitive hollow of her throat. When she moaned softly and moved in his arms, he became inflamed, pressing hot, moist kisses along her neck to her shoulder.

He struggled to hold on to some sense of sanity. But the need for her had him slipping over the edge. He wanted to feel her, warm and moist and willing. He wanted to be free to touch and taste and explore until they were both sated.

Desire clawed at him, driving him closer to the edge. He had to have her. Or go mad.

"I want you, Lizzy." He spoke the words against her mouth. "Say that you want me, too."

"No. I ... No."

She tried to remember what Grandpop had said before he left. Something about trusting her to always do the right thing. But the words were lost in the buzzing in her mind. She couldn't think. Couldn't even hold a single coherent thought. All she could do was cling to him and soar, higher and higher, while his hands and lips drove her mad.

What had happened to him? All that cool control had suddenly been torn free, and he'd become some sort of madman. God in heaven, what had he been thinking of?

Framing her face with his hands, he rested his forehead against hers for a moment, struggling for breath. Very deliberately he placed his hands on her shoulders and took a step back, needing a moment to clear his head.

When he looked at her, his eyes were dark. And cold as ice.

"I'm going to check on the mare before I turn in."

She watched as he pulled on his jacket and strode out into the night.

For long minutes she remained standing, as still as a statue, staring at the closed door. Then, climbing the ladder to the loft, she undressed and covered herself with the fur wrap.

More than an hour passed before Cody returned. Lizzy heard his boots drop, then listened to the wind howling against the walls of the cabin.

It shamed her to admit that, had it not been for Cody's strength of will, she would be downstairs right now, lying in his arms.

Chapter Nine

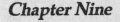

Lizzy was awake before dawn. It had been the longest night of her life. All night she had tossed and turned, reliving every touch, every kiss, every word. And always, in her mind, she had tormented herself with thoughts of what it would have been like to take their lovemaking to its inevitable conclusion. Then she tortured herself with guilt over such wicked thoughts.

She knew it would be awkward to face Cody. But it would be worse if she had to climb down that ladder knowing he was already up and watching her. So as soon as the first light of dawn streaked the sky, she dressed and hurried downstairs to start breakfast.

The first thing she noticed was that Cody's blanket was empty.

When he returned from the barn, she would have to pretend she wasn't aware of him.

As she added more logs to the fire, James stirred, then sat up.

"Is it morning already?"

"Just barely. If you'd like to sleep a little longer, you go ahead."

He glanced at the empty blanket. "Where's Cody?"

"Probably out in the barn."

James jumped up and began dressing. "Maybe he'll let me help with the horses."

The door opened. Cody stamped snow from his boots and took off his coat. Snowflakes glistened in his dark hair as he crossed the room.

"I'll be gone for a couple of days," he announced without warning. "Think you and the boy will be all right alone?"

When Lizzy turned anxious eyes to him, he looked away. Though he would give her a reason why he was leaving, it would be a lie. He was leaving not only because of what had happened last night, but also because of what had almost happened. He couldn't afford to be around her another night. He didn't have that much willpower.

"Where are you going?" James asked.

"I spotted hoofprints in the snow. A lot of them. Looks like a good-size herd of mustangs. Thought I'd trail them."

"Can't Lizzy and I go with you?"

"I'll need someone to stay here and take care of the horses. Think you can handle that?"

"I guess so."

For the first time Cody met Lizzy's troubled gaze. "Can you manage alone?"

"Of course." She turned away, feeling his gaze burning her back. "You'd better eat. I'll pack up what's left for your saddlebags."

"There's no need. Keep it for you and James. There'll be plenty of game along the trail. But I will eat some of that venison, as long as it's hot."

When he sat down to eat, James and Lizzy bowed their heads. Realizing they were expecting him to lead the prayer, he cleared his throat and said awkwardly, "For this food, we thank You."

While he ate, he found himself grateful for all the little boy's questions. It kept him from thinking about the woman who had suddenly complicated his life.

"What if the mare starts to foal?"

"She won't. She still has a couple of weeks."

"What if Grandpop returns and wants to get back on the trail?"

Cody glanced at Lizzy, then away. The thought had occurred to him. "I guess you'll have to do what your grandfather wants."

"But we wouldn't get to say goodbye."

"We'll say it now. And if there's anything you've forgotten to say, you can leave me a note."

"I can't write yet."

"I'm sure your sister can write it for you."

"It's not the same."

"I know, James." He pushed back his chair and stood, towering over the little boy. "You be sure to help your sister with the horses."

"I will."

"And remember. Don't go inside the corral."

"I'll remember."

Taking a rifle from a shelf, he handed it to Lizzy. There was a speck of flour on her nose and he had an almost overpowering urge to bend down and kiss it off.

"This rifle has been oiled and cleaned and filled with ammunition." He dropped a small sack of bullets into her hand. "Do you know how to load it?"

"Yes."

"Good." She smelled of soap and water. The same bayberry soap he'd seen her use in the barn. "Keep this rifle with you. When you go to the barn, it goes with you. When you're here in the cabin, you have it by the door."

She nodded.

He was laying too much responsibility on her. But he didn't see any choice now. She'd become a fever in his blood. If he could just avoid her for a couple of days, she and her family would be gone. And she would be safe from him.

"I'll be back in two or three days."

She swallowed and found that no words would come. She looked down, blinking furiously, hoping he wouldn't see the tears that threatened.

He pulled on his coat and called to Beau. In a flash the dog was bounding through the opened door, yelping in anticipation of the hunt.

Cody closed the door firmly behind him. As Lizzy and James watched through the window, he pulled himself into the saddle and set off across the wide expanse of snow-covered meadow. Within minutes horse and rider disappeared from view.

Lizzy stood a moment, feeling the terrible curtain of loneliness slipping over her, dragging her spirits down.

When Pa had gone off to war, she had found only one cure for the sickness that had crept over her spirit. Work. Hard work.

Pulling on a shawl, she called, "Come on, James. Let's get to our chores."

As she stepped outside, she welcomed the bitter cold. By the time she reached the barn her fingers were nearly frozen to the barrel of the rifle. But at least she was feeling something. Something besides emptiness.

The day passed in a blur of work. Lizzy decided to make a special supper, so in the early afternoon she cut up chunks of venison and carrots and potatoes and placed them in a pot over the fire. Knowing how much James loved her biscuits, she prepared a batch.

She and James fed and watered the mustangs, always careful to stay outside the corral. With half their number gone to Commencement, the horses had room to run and leap and nip at one another. Fascinated by their antics, Lizzy and James leaned against the rails.

"If I was bigger," James said, "and these were mine, I'd keep that one for myself." He pointed to a black stallion with white stockings.

"He is a beauty." Lizzy joined in the game. "I think, if they were mine, I'd keep that one." She singled out a smoky gray mare that shied away from all human contact.

"Why?"

"She's afraid. So she hides it by keeping her distance. But I'd win her over. In no time, I'd have her eating out of my hand."

Lizzy glanced at the darkening sky and picked up the bucket. "Come on, James. We'd better feed the mare and get back to the cabin. It'll be dark soon. Besides, I'm eager to eat that stew I put over the fire."

"Me, too. And the biscuits. I can smell them clear out here."

She laughed and led the way to the barn. Inside, it was warmed by the hay and the dung and the heat from the mare as she moved restlessly in her stall.

Lizzy mucked the stall and spread fresh straw while James carried a bucket of water and filled the trough with oats.

They both looked up at the sound of horses' hooves, riding in hard and fast.

"Do you think it's Grandpop and Sara Jean?"

"I don't hear a wagon." Lizzy picked up the rifle and headed toward the door of the barn.

The little boy's eyes lit. "Then it must be Cody, back with more mustangs."

"Maybe. But until I'm sure, you get under that straw and stay there." She checked to see that the boy had done as she ordered. Then, throwing the brace, she opened the door a crack and stole a peek. What she saw turned her blood to ice.

There were five horsemen circling the corral. And though she couldn't see their faces, she knew immediately that they were the same five who had threatened to steal Cody's horses.

* * *

Cody followed the hoofprints up a steep incline. There was no doubt that they were mustangs. None of the horses were shod.

Leaving Lizzy and James alone in his cabin still nagged at the edges of his mind. But he'd been given no choice. After last night, he knew what would happen if he stayed. An innocent like Lizzy deserved better.

As he stared out at the vast expanse of white, he was reminded of another time, another place. It had been winter when he'd left Mary and little Rob and went off to do what he'd been trained at West Point to do. And while he'd been away, trying to hold the country together, his whole reason for living had been torn apart.

He wondered again, as he had so often since that time, why his life had been spared when so many other people had died. With his wife and son brutally murdered, he'd lost the will to live. It was only here, in this pristine wilderness, that he'd begun to heal. But he wondered if he would ever again find peace of mind, peace of soul.

Deep in thought, it took him a minute to realize that the hoofprints that crisscrossed in the snow were not the ones he'd been following. These horses were shod.

As he climbed from the saddle and studied them more carefully, he felt his heart begin to race.

There were five of them. One had a distinctive circular groove in its right front hoof. He'd seen that same print in the snow in front of his cabin the morning after Ned had arrived. It belonged to the horse ridden by the one called Whit.

From the wide spaces between the prints, he determined that these horses were traveling at a gallop. And
headed toward his cabin.

God in heaven. Lizzy and James were there alone.

Pulling himself into the saddle, he called to Beau and
set out at a gallop. His jaw clenched in anger. It
couldn't be happening again. He wouldn't let it.

Lizzy slammed the door and threw the board that
braced it.

"Who's there?" James called from his hiding place.

"Those men who came by the other night."

"They'll steal Cody's horses."

"Be quiet, James, and let me think."

Maybe, if she was lucky, they would just take the
mustangs and leave. Even as she prayed it would be so,
she knew better. Seeing the horseflesh in the corral,
these men would want to see if something better was
kept in the barn.

Her heart was pounding so hard she could feel her
blood hammering in her temples. If they found the
door locked from the inside, they would know that
someone was in here. Someone who didn't want to be
found.

She looked around for another way out. There was
none. No door. No window.

She heard the rattling of the door and knew that
someone was trying to pry it open.

"James," she called, picking up the rifle, "cover
yourself with straw. No matter what, don't show

yourself unless I say so. Do you hear me? No matter what, you mustn't let them know you're here.''

She could taste the fear that clogged her throat. She would have to make a decision. If the men broke into the barn, they would surely take the mare. And they would kill anyone who stood in their way. Or worse, she realized with a new rush of fear. She knew what men like this would do to a helpless woman. She forced the thought aside. If James could hold his silence, at least he would survive.

She heard muffled voices from beyond the door.

''It's locked. Someone's in there, I tell you.''

''Cody Martin,'' came a deep voice Lizzy recognized as belonging to Whit, the leader. ''Come out now with your hands up. If we have to go in and get you, we're coming in with guns blazing.''

Lizzy swallowed and aimed the rifle at the closed door. ''Remember, James,'' she called softly. ''No matter what happens, they mustn't find you. Even if I cry out, you must not reveal yourself.''

After a few moments of silence she heard muffled comments, followed by a low rumble of laughter. She listened to the crunch of snow as several booted feet walked the perimeter of the barn.

They were searching for another entrance, she guessed. When the sound of footsteps grew louder, she knew that they had returned.

''So, Martin,'' the leader shouted. ''You have only one way out. Unless you come out by the count of five, we're going to burn you out.''

Lizzy's throat went dry. For a moment she felt paralyzed as she realized the enormity of their threat. A minute later she smelled the acrid stench of smoke as the fire began to lick along the dry timbers.

Now it was not just her life that hung in the balance. There was no way to protect James from that fire. And when she brought him out, they would kill him, as well.

"Lizzy. What'll we do?" Her brother crawled from his place of concealment, his eyes enormous with fear.

"If we go out there, they'll kill us," she said firmly.

"If we don't, we'll burn."

The mare danced nervously in her stall, nostrils flaring, eyes terror-filled as the straw along one wall went up in flame.

Lizzy thought about how bravely her father had gone off to war, knowing that he might never return. It gave him comfort, he'd said, to know that if he died, at least his loved ones would be safe. She drew herself up straighter. She could do no less. If she had to die, at least she would see that James was safe.

There might still be a way.

"Come on, James."

She strode into the mare's stall, with James tugging on her skirts.

"Cody said she was skittish. He said we couldn't come in here."

"Easy," Lizzy crooned, catching the terrified animal's head. "James, hand me that bit and bridle. And move very slowly. We wouldn't want to spook her."

The little boy did as he was told. Lizzy eased the bit between the mare's teeth and slid the bridle over her head. "Now, James, we're going to slip you on her back. She's too fat to saddle, so you're going to have to ride her bareback."

"Ride?"

"Now you listen, James. What I'm going to tell you is very important." Holding the reins, Lizzy eased him onto the back of the horse. "Do you remember the trail we took here, across the flat meadow, then through the hills?"

He nodded, his eyes wide and unblinking.

"You're going to take the same trail out of here. You don't stop, no matter what you see or hear. You just give the mare her head and keep riding until you either find Cody or you get to Commencement."

"But what about you?"

"I have to stay here, James. And see that nobody stops you."

"But I don't under—"

"There's no time." Lizzy turned as the wall beside them went up in flames. Leading the mare, she headed her into the wall of flame. "You're going to race right through that back wall, James. And you're never going to look back."

"I can't."

"Do it for Pa. Do it for me. Make me proud, James." She felt the tears course along her cheeks as she slapped the mare's rump as hard as she could.

The terrified animal raced into the wall of flame, with the little boy clinging to the reins. Moments later they broke free and sped across the field of white.

With smoke and flames blinding her, Lizzy leapt out of the way of a fiery timber. She could wait no longer. Any minute now, the entire roof would cave in. The barn had become an inferno.

Cody crested a hill and looked down on a scene of horror. Black, acrid smoke filled the air. Flames leapt high as his barn crumbled in on itself.

In the corral the horses milled around in fear and confusion. A man could be seen moving among them, securing them with ropes.

Three other men were moving stealthily around the burning rubble. All held rifles in their hands. Even as he watched, Cody spotted movement on the far side of the burning barn. He felt his heart stop.

God in heaven. Lizzy. Standing alone, rifle in hand, about to face certain death.

He'd hoped and prayed that she would be safe in the cabin. Now he knew her fate. And what was worse, he would be forced to be a witness to her death, and would be helpless to stop it.

He knew that from this distance he wouldn't reach her in time. But at least, he reasoned, those savages would pay.

He pulled himself into the saddle and lifted the rifle to his shoulder. As soon as he was within range, they would feel the sting of his fury.

* * *

"Will you look at this."

As the three men rounded the side of the burning barn, they stopped short at the sight of the woman in the soot-blackened gown, holding a rifle at her shoulder.

"You don't look like Cody Martin to me."

"Must be his whore," one of them said with a laugh. "Probably picked her up in Commencement."

"Where's your man?" another called.

"Stop right there." Lizzy's eyes narrowed as the men glanced at each other, then continued moving toward her.

"I'm not a very good shot." Her finger was slippery on the trigger, and she longed to rub it on her skirt. But she knew she couldn't afford even a moment's distraction. "So don't make me angry. There's no telling who might get shot by accident."

The three men glanced at each other for direction.

One of them grinned. "We don't want to see anybody shot. Just put down the rifle."

"You don't understand," she said evenly. "I'm not putting down this rifle until you ride out of here. Now get on your horses."

"All right."

The two glanced at the third in surprise. He merely smiled and said, "Go get our horses, boys."

She watched as, moments later, the two rounded the burning rubble on their horses, leading a third. She felt a wave of relief and glanced toward the corral, where a man could be seen leading a string of mustangs.

Too late, an alarm sounded in her mind. "Where is the fifth man?"

"Right here," came a voice behind her.

She whirled to see James struggling in the arms of a man on horseback. "Is this little ragamuffin yours?" he asked.

James was crying. She saw blood on the front of his clothes.

In the next instant she saw a flash of fur and heard the savage snarls of a wild creature as Beau leapt through the air, closing his jaws around the horseman's shoulder. She could hear the snap of bones as the animal's teeth sank into the man's flesh, and he let out a piercing scream.

James dropped to the snow at her feet.

Something in Lizzy's mind seemed to snap. She could focus on only one thing. James hadn't escaped. Unless she acted immediately, these men were going to harm her little brother.

Everything seemed to happen in slow motion. She saw the man on horseback reach for his gun. She fired, and was only dimly aware that he clutched his chest and dropped to the ground, with a snarling Beau on top of him.

She turned and fired again and again at the men racing toward her.

It seemed to Lizzy that even after her rifle was empty, the sound of gunfire continued. The roar of gunfire echoed through her mind as she bent and wrapped her arms around her little brother and cradled him to her chest.

"Oh, James. Hush now. Don't cry. No one's going to hurt you. No one's ever going to hurt you."

She crooned gentle words of love as she kissed away his tears and ran a hand across his bloodstained chest. Though there was blood on his clothing, she could find no wound. She lifted him, eager to get him inside where it was safe and warm.

She knew only one thing as she stepped around the bodies and carried James toward the cabin. These men would never hurt her little brother again.

Chapter Ten

Cody saw what was happening as he sped down the ravine behind the barn. His heart nearly stopped when he saw the horseman carrying James. Beau needed no command. He reacted instantly to the little boy's cries.

When the first gunshots rang out, Cody didn't have the luxury of sorting out who was shot. He dropped one of the men with his first shot, and before he could fire off another, he saw one of the gunmen drop. That meant that Lizzy must still be alive and fighting. For the moment.

He opened fire on another gunman, then was caught by crossfire from the man in the corral.

Pinned down, Cody managed to crawl to the cover of a rock. By the time he brought down the only gunman still facing Lizzy, he heard the thunder of hoofbeats and realized that the one in the corral had gotten away.

The sudden stillness frightened Cody more than the sound of gunshots echoing across the hills.

For a moment he was afraid to look. Afraid of what he'd see. When he pivoted toward the place where

Lizzy had been standing, he saw a tiny figure moving slowly across the snowy expanse toward the cabin. With a shout he began to run. When he drew closer, he could see that Lizzy was carrying her little brother.

In that moment, Cody could taste the fear, bitter and foul in his throat, as he struggled to speak.

"Lizzy, is James . . . ?" He couldn't say the word.

"They were going to kill him," she said softly. Too softly. "He's wounded. They made him bleed."

Cody felt his heart begin to beat again. He wasn't dead. Yet.

"How bad is it?"

"I don't know." She snatched him away when Cody reached for him.

Seeing the set of her jaw, Cody realized that she had to do this herself. He walked along beside her and opened the door. She went to the rug and laid James down, then began removing his jacket and shirt.

"What are you doing?" the little boy demanded.

"Be still, boy. Your sister said you were wounded."

"They didn't hurt me, Lizzy."

"But the blood . . ."

"That was the bad man's blood. I bit him."

Cody looked thunderstruck. When he could find his voice, he threw back his head and started laughing. "You bit him?"

"Uh-huh. And that's when he hit me. But I didn't cry until I saw that they were going to hurt Lizzy. Then I cried hard. I guess that makes me a baby, doesn't it?"

"No, son." Cody hugged the boy close to his heart. "Crying doesn't make you a baby. What you did was brave. And your sister..."

Cody noticed that Lizzy had walked to the fireplace and was stirring something in a pot.

"What are you doing?"

"The stew," she said softly. "I promised James a special dinner tonight. Stew and buttermilk biscuits."

Cody crossed the room and took the big wooden spoon from her hand. "Lizzy, what you did out there..." He noticed that she was shivering violently and drew her into the circle of his arms. "That was very brave."

"Not brave. I killed those men," she said softly. "Because they were going to hurt James. I had to kill them."

"Yes, you did. And you were very brave."

"No." She shook her head and pushed away from him. Drawing her arms around herself, she said, "I was afraid. I've never killed a man before."

"Sit over here," Cody said, leading her toward the rocking chair. "James, get your sister one of those furs. She's cold."

Cody pushed her gently down in the rocking chair and wrapped the fur around her.

"Supper," she said, starting to rise. "I promised..."

"I'll see to supper. You sit here."

He left her, rocking gently, to prepare a meal for the little boy.

While James ate, he filled Cody in on what had happened. "And Lizzy said I had to ride through the wall of fire and keep on riding until I found you or got to Commencement."

"That's just about the bravest thing I've ever heard of," Cody said. He was amazed at the grit shown by both James and Lizzy.

"What about your mare?" James fretted. "Will she run off and be wild again?"

"Beau will bring her back. He'll stand guard until I get a proper shelter."

The little boy glanced at his sister, rocking gently, her gaze fixed on the flames of the fire. "Will Lizzy be all right?"

"Yes. But she needs a little time to herself."

A short time later Cody wrapped the little boy in a fur robe and listened to his prayers. Then he made a cup of tea laced with whiskey and placed it in Lizzy's cold hands.

"Drink this," he said softly.

She looked surprised to see him. "Cody? I'm sorry about your horses."

"What about them?"

She tried to remember. "I think they were stolen."

"No, Lizzy. You stopped the thieves."

"I did?" She sipped the tea.

He knew the moment when she remembered. A chill shot through her.

"James." Her hand shook and some of the tea spilled on the floor.

She started to clean it up, but Cody placed a hand on her arm. "Leave it. James is fine. He's sleeping."

She gazed tenderly at the figure of the little boy on the rug in front of the fire. "I'm sorry about those men. But I couldn't let them harm James."

"Don't be sorry, Lizzy. It was their choice to bring death and destruction on themselves." He waited until she'd emptied the cup, then took it from her hands. "I had no right to leave you alone."

"It wasn't your fault."

"If anything had happened to you or your brother, I would never be able to forgive myself."

She touched a finger to his lips to stop his words. "We've intruded on your life, Cody. We've robbed you of your freedom to come and go as you please. And now, because of your kindness, you've lost your barn and your beautiful mare."

He smiled at the sound of Beau's barking. "Unless I miss my guess, the mare is right outside, with Beau standing watch. As far as the barn is concerned, it can be rebuilt. But you, Lizzy—" he touched a finger to her cheek "—there could never be another one as precious as you."

She felt tears well up in her eyes and lowered her head to hide her weakness.

"I'm tired, Cody. So tired."

She stood and began to walk to the ladder. But before she took two steps, all the blood seemed to drain from her. She turned as pale as the snow outside the window. Before she could drop to the floor Cody caught her and scooped her into his arms. Gathering her close to his chest, he carried her to a pile of furs and lowered her to them, wrapping her in them as he lay beside her.

Through the long night he held her. Whenever she awoke, or cried out, he soothed her with murmured words or the gentle brush of his lips across her cheek.

He'd been given a very special gift, he realized. Another chance. This time, he would keep all those in his charge safe.

Lizzy awoke to the aroma of freshly baked buttermilk biscuits. Coffee bubbled over the fire. Venison and potatoes sizzled in a skillet.

She sat up and glanced at the man who moved around the table, filling a plate for James.

When Cody saw her, he hurried over. "You stay here, Lizzy, and I'll bring you something to eat."

"I can walk to the table."

"You need your rest."

She smiled at the look of concern in his eyes. "Cody, I'm fine."

"But last night..."

"I was tired and confused. Today I feel strong enough to face up to what happened."

"It was my fault. I never should have left you alone."

She shook her head. "We are not your responsibility. You had every right to go after that herd of mustangs."

His voice deepened. "That wasn't really why I left."

She shook her head to stop him. She would hear no more. Besides, she was afraid of what he might say. Afraid and ashamed. What they had shared had been too filled with passion to speak about.

"Now, why don't we eat that good food you fixed."

He followed her to the table, marveling at the strength she displayed.

As they ate, Lizzy thought about the man who had tenderly held her each time she had awakened through the night. His quiet strength had brought her more comfort than he would ever know.

When they finished eating, Cody began to clear the table, but Lizzy stepped in.

"I know there's much to be done. You'll need to bury the dead and build a shelter for the mare. And there's the task of rebuilding the barn."

He touched a hand to her cheek. "Are you really feeling up to this?"

She placed her hand over his and met his concerned gaze. "I'm fine."

"You certainly are. You are one fine woman, Lizzy Spooner." He turned and walked to the door, pulling on his jacket as he did. "Come on, James. We have our work cut out for us."

"Yes, sir." Proud to be included in men's work, James hurried to keep up with him.

All day the air was filled with the sound of an ax biting through wood as Cody chopped down enough trees to build a lean-to. While Lizzy sawed off the branches, James stacked them neatly beside the cabin for firewood.

By building the lean-to against the back wall of the cabin, they needed to erect only three walls. Before darkness settled over the land, they spread straw and led the mare into her new shelter. It was snug and dry, and warmed by the stone fireplace of the cabin.

"I think she's going to like this," Cody commented as he filled a trough.

Fresh snow was falling when they made their way to the cabin door. Once inside, Cody added another log to the fire and lifted out a pot of stew that had been simmering in the coals.

"I think there are enough biscuits left over from this morning," he said as he began ladling the food onto plates.

When no one spoke, he glanced at the two figures lying in front of the fire. James was fast asleep with his arms around Beau's neck. The dog's eyes didn't even open when Cody tossed a chunk of meat near him.

He glanced toward the rocking chair, where Lizzy was seated. She was curled up like a kitten with her head resting on the arm of the chair.

A slow smile spread over his face as he crossed the room and tucked a fur around Lizzy's shoulders. He studied her face as she slept. There was a freshness, an innocence, that belied her inner strength.

Her breathing was slow and even. Her hair had fallen forward, covering one eye like a silken veil.

What an amazing woman she was. She had worked alongside him all day without stopping. Never once had she slowed her pace, or issued a word of complaint.

He wouldn't have believed that such a delicate-looking creature could accomplish so much.

He blew out the lantern, leaving only the flames of the fire to light the room. As he ate, he thought about all the lonely meals he'd eaten in this cabin. Tonight, though he sat alone at the table, the room seemed full of life.

It was full of love, he realized. The love of a brother and sister. And, though he had tried to deny it, the love of a man for a woman.

Indulging in a rare luxury, he shook out a small amount of his precious tobacco and rolled a cigarette. Leaning back, he filled his lungs with smoke. He didn't know how it had happened. Or when. But somehow, some way, this little woman had completely won his heart. The thought didn't fill him with any particular joy. It was, he told himself firmly, a fact of life. And a complication.

He smoked the cigarette until it was too short to hold. Tossing it into the fire, he tucked the robe tightly around the little boy's shoulders, then stood a moment watching Lizzy's slow, even breathing. Yes. A serious complication.

He climbed the ladder to the loft. It was the first time since the Spooner family had arrived that he was free to sleep in his own bed. As he wrapped himself in the fur robe, he knew he'd have no trouble sleeping this night, despite the thoughts that tormented him. He was surrounded by the fresh, clean scent of Lizzy that still clung to the folds of the fur.

"So Grandpop told the soldiers to step down off his porch with their muddy boots and go around to the back door."

Cody bit back the smile that threatened. As a measure of his respect, James had carefully refrained from calling them Yankee soldiers.

"Ever the Southern gentleman, I see. Did they do what he ordered?"

"Yes, sir. And at the back door they told him they were taking our pig, our horses and all the chickens that were left."

The laughter fled from Cody's eyes.

"What did your grandfather do then?"

"Nothing. But Lizzy flew out the door with the rifle and told them if they touched the plow horses, they'd be dead."

"Good for Lizzy. Did they leave the horses?"

James nodded. "You don't want to cross Lizzy when she's riled."

"I've learned as much." Cody emptied a bucket of water into the mare's trough, then looked up at the sound of horses. As he snatched up his rifle, he became aware of the creak of wagon wheels.

"It's Grandpop," James called, rushing from the lean-to.

They hurried around to the front of the cabin just as the horse drew to a halt. The cabin door opened and

Lizzy stepped out onto the porch, wiping her hands on a towel.

"What happened to the barn?" Amos called.

"A little trouble." Cody glanced at Lizzy, then back to Amos. "I'll tell you about it later. Was the blacksmith able to fix the axle?"

"See for yourself," Amos invited, stepping wearily down.

He helped Sara Jean to the ground and she pressed a hand to the stiffness at her back. It seemed to Lizzy that her sister had added several more inches to her girth in the few days she'd been gone. The babe inside her had grown.

Cody crawled under the wagon and carefully inspected the axle. He got to his feet, dusting his hands on his pants. "He did a good job."

"That he did." Amos tousled his grandson's hair and dropped an arm around Lizzy's shoulders. "I sure hope you have some supper left, girl. It's been a long ride."

"Come on inside, Grandpop. There's plenty."

"Where will I put my horse?" Amos asked.

"I'll take the wagon around to the back. There's a shelter big enough for him and the mare."

"She hasn't foaled yet?" Sara Jean asked.

"She's waiting for you." Lizzy grabbed her sister's hands and drew her close for a quick kiss on the cheek.

"Then she won't have long to wait." Sara Jean moved slowly toward the door, and Lizzy noticed that she winced as she walked.

"You mean the baby's coming? Did you find a doctor in Commencement?"

"Yes and no," Sara Jean answered quickly. "Grandpop finally located the doctor, in the saloon. Grandpop said his words were all slurred when he told him he wouldn't ride this far to deliver a baby if the mother were the Queen of Sheba. So it looks like it's going to be up to you, Lizzy."

Lizzy turned a worried look in Cody's direction. Facing five gunmen was nothing compared with the thought of helping her sister deliver a baby.

Amos followed Cody to the small shelter behind the cabin. When they were alone inside, he said, "Now maybe you'd better tell me what happened here."

Cody told him in as few words as possible. Amos listened in silence while he unhitched the horse from the wagon.

"You left them alone."

"Yes."

"A herd of mustangs, you say?"

Cody filled a trough with oats. The silence hung between them for long minutes.

"Lizzy stood up to the gunmen?"

"I've never seen a finer, braver woman. She was willing to risk her life for James."

"Lizzy was raised to live her faith. Greater love hath no man," Amos said solemnly, "than to lay down his life for another." His head came up. He regarded Cody in the dim light of the lean-to. "I'm grateful you returned in time."

"Not nearly as grateful as I am."

"Did you get all of them?"

Cody shared the secret he'd kept from Lizzy and James. "The leader got away."

"You saw him?"

"Only a shadowy figure in the corral. But I found his horse's hoofprints. I'd know them anywhere. Believe me," he added solemnly, "I'll never give him a chance to get close to your granddaughter again."

As they traced their steps in the snow to the cabin, Amos glanced at the hard, chiseled profile of the man beside him. There was a lot more to Cody Martin than he'd first imaginèd. The man was quiet, thoughtful, competent. And he was also, Amos thought with alarm, much more attracted to Lizzy than he let on.

Chapter Eleven

"We can go up on that ridge and cut timber," Amos said over breakfast. "James and I can haul the logs back in the wagon. Why, we can have that barn rebuilt in no time."

"It isn't your obligation," Cody said firmly.

"We accepted your hospitality when we needed it. Now you'll do the same." Amos softened his tone. "Besides, the women will need a few days to mend the canvas. And if Sara Jean has that baby, she'll be grateful for the extra time to build up her strength for the journey ahead."

Sara Jean got up from the table and walked to the rocker. Picking up the blanket, she began to add another row of fancy stitches. A strange sense of calm had descended on her. Let the men talk about cutting trees and building walls. It was nothing compared to the task that was before her. Though she feared the pain, she was resigned to it. In fact, if truth be told, she was eager to be through with this discomfort.

"I'll hitch the wagon." Cody pulled on his jacket. "Come on, James. You can lend a hand."

"Yes, sir."

Amos started out the door behind them, then turned. "While you're mending that canvas, Lizzy, you'd better start a pot of hearty stew. We'll be plenty hungry by noontime."

Lizzy nodded. He was gone in a whirl of snowflakes.

"How big was Commencement?" Lizzy and Sara Jean sat at opposite sides of the table, mending the seams in the tattered canvas.

"It wouldn't have been worth mentioning back in Georgia," Sara Jean said with a laugh. "But after all those miles of wilderness, it looked big enough to me. There's a stable at one end of town, and a saloon at the other. And in between there's a blacksmith, a mercantile and general store, and a sheriff's office and jail. There's talk of building a schoolhouse and a church, if they can find a preacher."

"Where did you and Grandpop sleep?"

"The blacksmith sent us to one of the houses on the edge of town. The widow Purdy runs a boardinghouse. Oh, Lizzy, she had real feather beds with rag rugs on the floors and frilly white curtains at the windows." Sara Jean's eyes danced. "She served eggs and fried potatoes for breakfast. Eggs. Can you imagine? And what she can do to a roast chicken." She rolled her eyes. "I haven't seen Grandpop eat like that since Grandma passed away."

For a minute Sara Jean's needle and thread were forgotten as she smiled. "After supper Mrs. Purdy made Grandpop prop his feet up on a footstool and she massaged horse liniment into his knee.''

"Horse liniment?''

Sara Jean's smile grew. "He said it was the best night's sleep he's had in years."

Lizzy shook her head, knowing how Grandpop had suffered nights with the pain in his knee.

"As soon as Mrs. Purdy laid eyes on Grandpop, it was plain she was sweet on him."

"Sara Jean." Lizzy was clearly shocked. "How can you say such a thing?''

"Furthermore, if you ask me," Sara Jean went on, "I think Grandpop was sweet on her, too. He didn't seem to mind in the least that the blacksmith took so long to fix the axle. It just gave him one more day to sample the widow Purdy's fine cooking. Not to mention having his knee massaged with liniment.''

Lizzy walked to the fire to stir the pot of stew. It was true that Grandpop had seemed milder tempered since his return from Commencement. It had been his idea to stay on here to help Cody rebuild the barn. A scant week ago, the thought of helping a Yankee with such an awesome task would have been unthinkable.

Before she could ponder all that her sister had told her, the men stomped into the cabin, shaking snow from their clothes.

Removing the canvas, Sara Jean hurriedly set the table while Lizzy ladled food onto their plates.

They bowed their heads while Grandpop said, "We thank Thee for this food, Lord. And for the fine timber Thou hast provided. With Thy help, the new barn should be up in no time.''

"Amen," the others intoned as they began to pass around heaping plates of stew.

"Sara Jean said that Ned's job with the stagecoach was still waiting for him," Lizzy commented.

Cody's fork paused in midair. His eyes narrowed slightly. "So he took it?"

"He said the pay was too good to pass up."

"Did he know how far the run would be?"

"Between Commencement and a place called Los Ranchos de Albuquerque."

"That's over a hundred miles. What're they carrying?"

"Gold," Amos said softly. "At least from what I heard."

Cody's voice lowered. "If you heard it, it stands to reason that everyone else did, too. That's why no one was willing to take the job except a greenhorn. Every gunslinger from here to Texas will be watching that stage."

Everyone grew very quiet. Lizzy saw Sara Jean drop her fork and lower her head.

To change the subject Lizzy asked, "What did Ned do with the mustangs?"

"Sold five of them the first day. He's boarding the rest at the stable, and hoping to break them to saddle when he comes in from his first run. That way he'll be able to sell them for even more than the first five."

Amos broke open a hot biscuit and cleared his throat in agitation. He understood Cody's concern for his brother. But there was nothing any of them could do now. He'd follow Lizzy's example and keep the conversation flowing.

"If you had a cow, Cody, Lizzy could churn you some fresh butter. Anna Purdy had the best butter I ever tasted. And big thick glasses of buttermilk every night after supper."

Lizzy glanced at Grandpop over the rim of her cup. "Sounds like you enjoyed your stay at Mrs. Purdy's."

"That I did, girl." He pushed away from the table and tamped tobacco into his pipe. Lizzy saw him idly rub at his knee before he sank down in the rocking chair and began to puff contentedly.

Across the table, Sara Jean had grown very quiet. As had Cody. When he'd drained his coffee, he pushed away from the table. "Guess I'll get back to chopping trees."

"Yep. There are still a few good hours of daylight. Come on, James," Amos called as he picked up his sheepskin jacket.

They all turned to glance at the little boy who had been quietly eating. His head now rested on the edge of the table. His eyes were closed.

"I think we'll let him spend an hour or two in front of the fire, Grandpop." Before Lizzy could reach him, Cody picked him up and carried him to the rug, where he deposited him.

"The boy worked as hard as a boy twice his age. He deserves his rest," he muttered as he dropped a fur over him.

Grandpop placed his pipe on the mantel and followed Cody out the door.

When they were gone, Lizzy cleared the table and draped the canvas over it. But when Sara Jean joined her to resume sewing, her earlier happy chatter was forgotten.

After long minutes of silence she lifted her head. "Do you think Cody is right? Could Ned's life be in danger?"

"You mustn't think about it, Sara Jean."

"But how can I stop thinking?" She tossed down her needle and thread and began to weep. "Before he left, he told me that this was going to be the start of a new life for him."

She turned and began to sob.

Lizzy pushed away from the table and hurried to her side. Gathering her sister into her arms, she murmured, "It's all going to work out now. You'll see. Grandpop has decided to stay here and help Cody with the barn. So when Ned returns, he'll find you here."

"You don't understand. It's all happening again. Ben asked me to wait, and he never came back from the war. And now, even though Ned hasn't said anything, I have this feeling about him. And . . ." Great, wrenching sobs tore from her throat. "I just know he's never coming back from this stagecoach run."

"You don't know any such thing." Lizzy pulled Ma's treasured lace handkerchief from her pocket and handed it to her sister. "Ned made it through the war, didn't he? You have to trust that he can make it through this, too."

"But, Lizzy, what'll I do if he doesn't?"

"You stop that now." Lizzy took the handkerchief from Sara Jean's hands and wiped away her tears. Kneeling, she grasped her hands and whispered, "You just have to put Ned in the Lord's hands. And you'll see. He'll come riding up to claim the prettiest girl in Atlanta, Georgia."

Sara Jean almost smiled. Instead she sniffed. "I don't live in Atlanta anymore. And look at me. I'm fat and ugly."

"You're beautiful. Pretty enough to turn Ned Martin's head. And wait until you see your baby. You'll know it was all worth it when you look at that sweet little face."

Sara Jean blew her nose and turned to her sewing. "At least I'll be able to lace my shoes again. And fit into that midnight blue dress of Ma's."

Lizzy smiled as she picked up her needle. The storm had passed. At least for the moment.

"Another day or two and we can start the walls," Amos said over supper.

"That's pretty ambitious." Cody bit into a tender biscuit and wondered how he'd managed to eat his own cooking for so long.

"I think tomorrow Lizzy and Sara Jean can pitch in. That way we'll get the work done in half the time."

Lizzy glanced at her grandfather. "I don't mind doing the work of a man. But not Sara Jean, Grandpop."

"And why not?"

"Because her pains have started."

Amos met Cody's look across the table. Both men started to scramble to their feet.

Lizzy laughed. "You can relax and finish your meal. She isn't going to have the baby this minute."

Suddenly Amos was all grandfatherly concern. "How are you, honey? Is it bad?"

"No, Grandpop. At least not yet. There's just a twinge of pain now and again. It hasn't fallen into any kind of a pattern yet. Lizzy says I'll know when it's time."

The men finished their meal in silence. But occasionally they shot furtive glances at the young woman whose slightest movement had them worried.

After supper Cody took a lantern and made his way to the lean-to to check the mare. He was surprised when, minutes later, Amos and James joined him.

"Why don't you stay inside by the fire?" he asked.

"Sara Jean let out a howl." The little boy's eyes were wide with fear. "And Lizzy said we might want to take a walk."

"Well, it's a fine night to watch the stars." Cody sat down in the straw and James joined him. Amos stood in the doorway, smoking his pipe.

"Will it hurt Sara Jean to have the baby?"

"Some," Cody said, hoping to ease the boy's fears. "But they say the pain is quickly forgotten when that small, perfect creature is placed in its mother's arms."

He thought about his own wife, ensconced in a fine big feather bed with satin hangings. There had been a doctor and a midwife in attendance, along with three or four women from town. His grandmother, the matriarch of the family, had come from Louisiana to stay with them, bringing her own cook, butler and maidservant.

All during her stay, the talk had been of secession and war, neither of which Cody had taken seriously. He never would have believed that two short years later he would be fighting against his own countrymen.

"I'm scared for Sara Jean. She isn't strong like Lizzy."

"She'll do fine." Cody dropped an arm around James and drew him close. Feeling the tremors that rocked the little boy's body, he said, "I think I'll go inside and fetch a few furs. We might end up sleeping here tonight. And while I'm there I'll see how Sara Jean is."

"Good idea," Amos said. "Better see how Lizzy's holding up, too. She looked a little pale when I left."

Cody made his way to the cabin and opened the door. He could see that Lizzy had made a pallet in front of the fire, on which Sara Jean was lying. Lizzy knelt beside her, bathing her forehead.

"I wish there was something more I could do for you."

"I guess this is something I have to do for myself."

Lizzy squeezed her sister's hand and fell silent. Cody crossed the room and helped himself to a handful of fur robes.

"It's funny," Sara Jean mused aloud. "I can't think of another single thing I ever had to do all by myself. Pa and Ma were always there to do everything for me.

It's got me pretty scared.'' She glanced at her sister. ''I'll bet you wouldn't be afraid if it was you.''

''Why wouldn't I be? Every woman's probably afraid the first time.''

''But you'd just grit your teeth and get through it, like you get through everything.''

''You're talking silly.''

''You know I'm not.'' Sara Jean waited while another pain held her in its grip. Then, breathing easier, she said, ''I've never known a time when you didn't just do whatever needed doing.''

Cody went very still. He hadn't meant to eavesdrop on their conversation. He'd assumed they knew he was there. But from the open way they were speaking, he realized that they thought they were alone. For a moment he mulled over the proper way to signal his presence. But even before he had a chance to act, Sara Jean's voice went on.

''When they brought Pa home in a box, you put Ma to bed, fixed supper for all the soldiers, then sat up all night to keep an eye on Grandpop while he drank the last of the spirits.'' She paused, biting down on a hard contraction. When it passed, she said softly, ''And when they burned our house down, I watched you beat at the flames even after the rest of us had collapsed. All we could do was sit and watch, while you were fighting a fire that had already consumed everything in its path.'' She was silent a moment before asking, ''What drives you, Lizzy?''

When Lizzy at last responded, her voice was hardly more than a whisper. ''I don't really know. I'm just no good at taking beatings, I guess. I just have to stand up and fight back, even though I know I'm going to lose.''

"I've always envied you, Lizzy."

At her sister's admission, Lizzy gave a little laugh. "Me? Sara Jean, you were the prettiest girl in our town. The boys just couldn't take their eyes off you. And look how Pa favored you. He'd have done anything you asked."

"That was because he thought I wasn't able to do it for myself. He thought I needed to be taken care of. But not you, Lizzy. Everybody always knew you could take care of yourself." Her voice lowered. "I guess that's why I wanted everything you had."

Lizzy laughed again, a soft, husky sound.

Cody stood in the shadows, trying not to think about the woman whose voice, whose husky laugh, did strange things to his insides.

"Now what did I ever have that you wanted, Sara Jean?"

"Everything. Your red hair. It's different, you know. Your eyes. And that pretty green velvet gown you wore to the dance the night before Pa went away to the war."

"Ma saved that gown for you."

Sara Jean tried to laugh, but a pain cut her off. Grasping her sister's hand, she said, "It never looked as good on me as it did on you."

"Shows how little you know. You looked beautiful. What else did you want?"

"Ben."

There was silence for long minutes.

Cody found himself frowning.

"That first time Ben called on us," Sara Jean said, "I saw the way he looked at you, Lizzy. I knew Ben was stuck on you. That's the only reason I set my cap for him. I wanted to see if I could take him away from my pretty older sister."

"That's enough, Sara Jean." Lizzy made a move to stand but her sister caught her hand and forced her to stay. "Don't, Lizzy. Don't run away from the truth."

Lizzy gave a long, drawn-out sigh. "All right. For whatever your reasons, you wanted Ben. And you got him. But he must have loved you, Sara Jean. He asked you to marry him. And you loved him, too, because you agreed."

"I—guess I loved him." She shrugged. "How can I know after only two days together?"

"If you love someone, you just know. You can't measure it by days or years."

Sara Jean looked away, unwilling to meet her sister's eyes. "I guess I figured in time we'd learn to love each other the way Ma and Pa did."

Lizzy fell silent. Ben had been just a boy who'd wanted someone to love him and keep his memory alive while he went off to fight the war. She hadn't been attracted to him, but she had really believed that Sara Jean loved him. No wonder the thought of having his baby had her sister so terrified.

"Will you do something for me, Lizzy?"

"You know I will."

"Will you take my baby and raise it like your own?"

"Sara Jean. What a terrible thing to ask. This baby's yours. Yours and Ben's. You can't just give it away like an old ball gown."

"I'm asking for the sake of the baby. Don't you see? I've never been able to do anything right. Look at me. Married for two days, and already a widow with a baby to take care of. What makes you think I can raise it?"

"Nobody knows how to raise a baby till they have one."

"You've never had a baby. And look how good you are to James. He's closer to you than he was to Ma."

"That's just because he knew Ma was too drained to take care of things." She patted her sister's hand. "Don't worry, Sara Jean. When this baby comes, you'll do just fine. You'll see."

Sara Jean began to moan as another pain surged. This time the pain didn't stop, but went on and on until Lizzy said softly, "The baby's coming, Sara Jean. Just bear down now. And in a few minutes you'll be able to greet your new baby."

Cody made his way from the cabin and carried an armload of furs to the lean-to. Once the two sisters had begun their conversation, there was no way he could have warned them of his presence without causing them embarrassment. And so he'd kept his silence.

And heard more than he'd intended.

Chapter Twelve

Amos and his grandson had long ago given up waiting for word about Sara Jean and had fallen asleep in the hay, wrapped in fur robes.

Cody leaned a hip against the doorway of the lean-to and rolled a cigarette. Holding a match to the tip, he drew smoke into his lungs.

He thought about Ned, riding shotgun on a stage loaded with gold. Fool kid had no business taking on such a dangerous job. He seemed determined to get himself killed. Still, he'd come through the war, Cody reminded himself. And he wasn't a kid anymore. Ned was a man, and he deserved the same respect due any other man. It was just hard to stop being an older brother.

What Cody wanted to do was saddle up and ride off after that stage and haul Ned back here where he could keep him safe. He frowned in the darkness. That's what had started all the trouble between them in the first place. Big brother, West Point trained, quick with a gun, had decided that little brother had no business going off to fight, especially since he'd chosen the opposite side in the battle. After that, everything had fallen apart. Grandma dead. Mary. Little Rob. And two brothers, who'd once been the closest of friends, couldn't forget all the pain, all the heartache, all the words spoken in anger. Or forgive.

He heard the cry, more like the bleat of a lamb than a human sound. He crushed the cigarette into the snow and began running toward the cabin.

When the door opened, two heads turned toward the sound. Lizzy was kneeling beside her sister. Her cheeks glistened with tears. Sara Jean wore a radiant smile. In her arms was a tiny bundle.

"Look, Cody. Come see my beautiful daughter."

Cody crossed the room and knelt down beside them. A part of his mind noted that the towel wrapped around the infant was one that had been embroidered by Mary. But that thought was quickly forgotten as he caught his first glimpse of a perfectly round head dusted by soft, dark fuzz. Sara Jean opened the towel to display a tiny round face with a turned-up nose and lips pursed like a rosebud. The baby's eyes were squeezed tightly shut as she gave a lusty cry.

"Sounds like she has a good set of lungs."

"Isn't she perfect?" Sara Jean pressed her lips to the infant's cheek and nuzzled her gently.

"Do you need anything?" Cody asked.

Sara Jean shook her head. "I'm just going to close my eyes and rest beside my baby." She laughed. "But you might want to see that Lizzy has some coffee. I think I wore her out."

As Lizzy started to get to her feet, Sara Jean caught her hand. "I'll never forget this, Lizzy. Having you here made it all seem so right." She swallowed. "I did it, didn't I? All by myself. Without Pa or Ma to do it for me."

"Yes, you did. You did just fine." Lizzy pressed a kiss to her sister's forehead, then got slowly to her feet.

"Come on," Cody said, taking her hand. "You look much more exhausted than the baby's mama."

"Oh, Cody." Lizzy sat weakly in the chair and accepted the steaming cup of coffee from his hands. "I was so afraid I'd do something wrong. But it was so beautiful." Tears started again and she wiped them away just as the cabin door was flung open.

Amos and James rushed inside, looking disoriented.

"Cody. Lizzy," Amos said gruffly. "Is something wrong?"

"Not a thing, Amos." Cody nodded his head toward the sleeping figures.

Instantly Sara Jean's lids opened and she smiled dreamily at her grandfather and little brother. "Come see what I did."

As the two knelt beside her, she unwrapped the bundle to display her new baby. Grandpop kept clearing his throat.

At his first glimpse, James was clearly enthralled. "Did you count its fingers and toes?"

"Her fingers and toes," Sara Jean corrected. "She's a little girl."

Lizzy crossed the room to join them. "See that smile?" She touched a finger to the baby's cheek. "Ma used to say that when a baby smiles, it's a sign that the angels kissed her."

Sara Jean laughed. "She's my little angel. And I've decided to name her Josephine Elizabeth, after Ma and Lizzy."

Lizzy felt her heart swell with pride and happiness.

"Josephine Elizabeth." James tried out the name.

"Mighty big words for such a little creature," Grandpop muttered. "How about . . ." He thought a minute. "Jobeth?"

Sara Jean's smile grew. She placed a hand inside her grandfather's callused palm. "Jobeth. I like that, Grandpop." Her lids closed from sheer exhaustion. "Say good-night to your great-granddaughter Jobeth."

Amos turned away and made a great show of cleaning his pipe and adding fresh tobacco. By the time he turned, he'd managed to compose himself. "Well, this calls for a celebration."

Cody nodded and lifted a bottle of whiskey from a shelf. Pouring three glasses, he handed one to Amos and one to Lizzy before lifting his own glass in the air.

"Here's to little Josephine Elizabeth, and her mother," Amos said proudly.

They touched glasses and drank.

"And here's to Ben." Cody's voice suddenly lowered with passion, and though he'd never met the man, he felt a kinship with him. "He gave his life for his country. But through his daughter, he lives on forever."

Lizzy felt tears burn her eyes and swallowed the whiskey in one gulp. It burned all the way down to her toes.

"I think you'd better get some sleep," Grandpop said, touching a hand to her shoulder.

As she walked to the ladder, he added, "Girl, you did fine tonight. Your Ma and Pa would be proud of you."

"Thanks, Grandpop."

Cody watched as she climbed the ladder to the loft. When the others had rolled themselves into furs, and the sound of their soft breathing filled the tiny cabin, he poured himself another glass of whiskey and walked to the window to stare at the night sky.

Thoughts of another baby filled his mind. And for the first time in two years, he didn't push the thoughts away. Instead he allowed himself to remember. And grieve. And begin to heal.

The days that followed flowed easily from one to the next. Cody and Amos fashioned a cradle from pine, and Lizzy stitched a quilt to line it.

Each morning the men went up to the hills and cut trees, then hauled them by wagon to the blackened space that had once been Cody's barn.

Lizzy and James spent the days cutting and smoothing the logs and piling the branches.

In the evening Cody worked on a sleigh he was making that would ease the burden of hauling logs.

"With a sleigh this big," Amos commented, "you could probably haul timber all the way to Commencement."

Cody grinned. "That's what I have in mind. With all the new settlers they're expecting, I could make enough money to build my herd, and even add to the barn and cabin."

"There's so much space here," Lizzy said. "Why, you could build an empire out here without crowding anyone."

"An empire." Cody's smile grew. "You do think big."

Lizzy lowered her head, embarrassed at having revealed her thoughts.

Sara Jean sat in the cozy warmth of the cabin and held her infant to her breast. From the fire came the fragrance of Lizzy's biscuits.

All that was needed to make her life complete, Sara Jean thought with a smile, was Ned rolling into the yard with a wagon to fetch her back to Commencement with him. Now that the baby was here, and her strength was slowly returning, she could begin to plan for the future. A future that had to include Ned Martin.

When she had laid the baby in the cradle, she glanced out at the sight of the logs piling up in the snow. At the rate they were going, they would be here another couple of weeks. The thought cheered her.

Within a week there were enough logs to begin forming the walls of the barn. Cody and Amos notched them into place, then sealed the logs with hot pitch. When the walls were complete, they built the roof. On the day they set the door into place and swung it closed, they sent up a cheer.

Cody led the mare and his stallion from their cramped quarters in the lean-to and brought them to their new stalls in the barn. Moving efficiently, he filled their troughs with food and water.

"I think she likes it here." Lizzy leaned over the rail and watched as the mare began to eat.

Cody glanced around. The others had gone back to the cabin.

"It will certainly be easier for her to foal here."

"How soon?"

He felt the mare's belly and crooned soothing words to her as she neatly sidestepped. "Another week. Maybe two."

"If you're looking for someone to give you a hand . . ." She smiled at his look of pleasure.

"You mean you didn't get enough of birthing yet?"

She shook her head. "Pa once let me watch a foaling. It was beautiful."

He nodded his agreement and moved to stand beside her. Together they watched as the mare moved around the stall, familiarizing herself with the new scents.

Cody breathed deeply. The structure smelled of new wood and sweet fresh hay and the sharp, pungent odor of newly turned earth.

It was quiet. Outside, the wind sighed and moaned as it swept across the meadow and fled up to the high country.

Inside, the light was filtered, casting them in a dim, golden glow. He turned, intending only to look at Lizzy. But the moment he looked, he had the overpowering need to touch.

He lifted a hand to her cheek and she moved against it, dropping her head so that her hair swirled forward.

"God in heaven, Lizzy. The things I feel..." He swallowed and opened his palm to caress her lips.

When she didn't move to stop him, he grew bolder, bringing both hands up to frame her face. That was all it took to have his heart pounding in his chest. One simple touch and he found himself wishing...

If only they had met at another time, another place. Before the world had gone mad and the country had become divided.

He ran his hands up her back, fingers burning a trail until they tangled in her hair.

When they were standing together like this, he could almost believe that he could make her his. That they were right for each other. That somehow, despite their different backgrounds, they could find a common ground.

Lizzy stood very still, wondering how long she could endure his touch before she would melt. Already her bones were turning to liquid. Her legs would soon collapse under her and she would be forced to cling to him like some helpless child.

Maybe, as Sara Jean had said, it was wicked to allow the thoughts that flitted through her mind. But she didn't care. She could no more control the thoughts than she could control the desire that flared at the first touch of his hands.

Now that she had tasted his kisses, she knew what it was to want, to need, with a desperation that bordered on insanity. At this moment she wanted, more than anything else, to taste his lips.

When he bent to her, she lifted on tiptoe to meet him.

"Lizzy, Lizzy," he breathed against her mouth. "The things I want..."

The rush of heat between them was instantaneous. The flow of passion swelled to a churning need.

She hadn't expected him to be gentle. When his hands were almost bruising in their eagerness to crush her, when his kisses were almost savage as his mouth moved over hers, she understood. Her own needs were equally primitive. And overwhelming.

So this was what it felt like to love. To want to give and give until, emptying herself, she would be filled with him.

She understood now how such needs could drive one to the very edge of reason and beyond. She wanted him. Loved him. It was that simple. She could no more fight the need than she could stop the wind that howled outside the door. Or stop the snow that blanketed the mountains.

She loved him. The thought seeped through her like a thin, tiny flame, wavering in the wind, inching closer and closer to her heart until it suddenly burst into a blaze of knowledge. She loved him. Though she didn't understand it, or take the time to question it, she had no more doubt.

Cody felt her slow, gradual surrender and gloried in it. In that moment his kiss gentled, his touch softened. Overcome with feelings of tenderness, he drew her close until he could feel her heartbeat inside his own chest.

His mouth moved over hers, feasting on her lips, drawing out all the wild, sweet taste of her. He took the kiss deeper, saying with his lips, his tongue, what he couldn't yet bring himself to put into words.

"Lizzy."

Her name was spoken against her mouth, like a whispered prayer.

Their breathing was strained, labored, as they poured out their feelings in touches, kisses and murmured phrases.

"There's so much..."

Cody's head came up sharply at the sound of someone approaching.

Desire fled. Now he was the fierce protector, willing to lay his life on the line before he would allow anything, anyone, to threaten her again.

"Stay here."

Lifting his rifle, Cody pulled open the door. Lizzy gave an involuntary shiver until she saw him replace the rifle and beckon to her.

"We'd better get to the cabin." He touched a hand to her face and stared down at her lips, still swollen from his kisses. He felt a moment's frustration, then swallowed it. "It's the doc from town."

He held the door for her, then secured it against the wind that had blown up from the north.

Together they walked the distance from the barn to the cabin. If anyone had taken the time to look, that person would have seen the proprietary way he caught her hand and led her.

When they entered the cabin, Lizzy was surprised to see not only a bewhiskered man holding a black bag, but a pretty, white-haired woman, as well.

"Doc Simms," Cody called in greeting. "We weren't expecting you."

"Didn't expect to come all this way myself. But Mrs. Purdy made a pest of herself until I agreed."

Lizzy inspected the woman carefully as she was introduced to Anna Purdy.

"So you're Lizzy. Amos bragged on you. And on you," she said to the little boy who hid behind his sister's skirts and peered out at her. "James, isn't it?"

"Yes'm."

She picked up the little boy and held him at eye level. "You're a handsome lad, almost as handsome as your grandpa."

The boy looked thunderstruck, and she chuckled, a deep, jolly sound that was so infectious it made everyone smile.

Anna set him down and bustled over to the new mother. "Has your milk come in yet?"

Too embarrassed to speak, Sara Jean could only nod. Such things were never discussed in mixed company.

"Good. How's the little one taking to you?"

"Fine." Sara Jean swallowed. "She's eating and sleeping about every four or five hours."

"That's good. Now you need to take good care of yourself." The widow unwrapped a bundle to reveal several plucked chickens, a container of eggs and a crockful of buttermilk. "I didn't know whether Cody Martin would have the proper food for a new mother. So I took it upon myself to provide what I could."

"That's very kind of you, Anna," Amos said. "Maybe you'd give Lizzy your recipe for roast chicken."

"I'll do better'n that. I'll fix it myself and show her how."

While she spoke she began bustling around the cabin, pouring water from the kettle, stuffing a chicken into a blackened pot. "Since we're not going to get to deliver a baby," she said to the doctor, "we may as well stay and take supper with these fine people."

The doctor arched a brow at Cody. "Now you see why I'm here. The woman could nag a stone into giving blood. Do you happen to have any whiskey?"

With a laugh Cody pulled the bottle from the shelf and poured a stiff drink for the doctor.

"Is that a new barn I spotted when we drove up?"

Cody nodded.

"Maybe I'd better unhitch my horse and lead him to shelter. No telling how long we might be here." As

Cody started toward the door, the doctor added, ''And maybe you'd bring that bottle. We wouldn't want to catch cold while we're out there.''

Still laughing, Cody led the way out the door.

Chapter Thirteen

"What Commencement needs is more people." Anna Purdy spooned vegetables onto James's plate. "When more people settle there, we'll have the farmers and shop owners and teachers we need to make it a thriving town. Of course," she added with a smile, "if everybody thought like Cody here, we'd all be living on our own little mountain, miles from anyone else."

Cody merely smiled and noticed that James ate every vegetable on his plate.

"I've tried everything I know to get Cody to come into Commencement. Lord knows there are enough eligible women there." Anna Purdy glanced at Sara Jean. "Women like you and me who lost their husbands in the war and have so much to offer a good man."

In an aside, the doctor muttered to Cody, "I bet it wasn't the war that killed her husband, it was the constant movement of her mouth. The woman never even comes up for air."

Anna Purdy speared both men with a look. "But except for an occasional stop for supplies, Cody Martin prefers to live out here like a monk."

"If you had a saloon on this mountain, I think a lot of the men in the town might be willing to join you." Doc Simms lifted his glass, much to the dismay of the widow. "Must be nice, having no one gabbing at you except your horse."

Lizzy watched Grandpop take seconds of the chicken and vegetables and wash it down with a tall glass of buttermilk.

When they thought they had eaten all they could, Anna surprised them with dessert. "I baked a fruit cobbler," she announced. "Lizzy, would you pour the coffee while I serve this?"

"None for me," Doc Simms said, lifting a glass of whiskey to his mouth.

The widow frowned at him, then turned her attention to the others.

At her first bite Sara Jean said almost reverently, "I can't remember the last time I had something so good."

"A year at least." Amos polished off every crumb, then leaned back, sipping hot coffee. "Anna, that was perfect."

The widow beamed as she glanced around the table at the smiling faces. "I just love cooking for people who know how to eat."

"Then you could cook for us every day." Sara Jean pushed away from the table and hurried to the cradle where the baby was just beginning to whimper.

"I'd like that. I miss cooking for my family. I guess that's why I decided to open my house to boarders. The trouble is, there aren't many people passing through Commencement." She glanced at Amos. "The truth is, you and your daughter were only the third boarders I've had this year."

"The town will grow, Anna." Amos patted her hand, and Lizzy noted that he kept his hand there a moment longer than necessary before lifting it to his coffee. "When the weather warms up, and the stage-coaches can get through from the east, you'll see more people heading this way."

"I wish you could see our town in spring and summer, Amos." Anna removed his plate and returned with more coffee. "When the snow melts, the land is so green and pretty. These mountains are covered with wildflowers. I swear, it's a little piece of heaven. The soil in the valley is so fertile." Seeing the light that came into the old man's eyes, she added, "Why, you could grow corn and beans and alfalfa."

"I know a lot about growing cotton." Amos looked thoughtful. "I suppose I could learn about growing other things."

"I don't see why not. If you're a man of the soil."

Lizzy listened to the widow's description of the valley and tried to imagine this land without the snow. Anna made it sound wonderful. And peaceful. After the horrors of war, peace was a precious commodity to all of them.

Cody waited patiently for the right moment to inject a question. He didn't want to cast a cloud on the widow Purdy's happy talk, but he was eager to hear news of his brother. When at last the widow stopped talking to sip her coffee, he asked as casually as possible, "Have you heard anything about the stagecoach?"

"Hasn't returned. Funny. It only takes a week for the round trip to Los Ranchos and back." Anna shrugged and turned to the doctor. "Have you heard anything?"

"Not a word. Of course," he added, lifting his glass to his lips, "there's been so much snow, the stage probably can't get through."

Everyone around the table grew uncomfortably quiet. Cody pushed away from the table and pulled on his coat. What he needed was fresh air and room to think.

When he opened the door, a bitter wind yanked the door from his grasp, slamming it against the wall.

He was surprised to note that the doctor's sleigh, standing just beyond the porch, was already piled high with snow.

"Looks like another snowstorm blowing in. I think it would be best if you folks stayed the night."

Anna seemed completely unconcerned. "Nobody's waiting for me at home anyway. And I brought plenty of food."

"Doc," Cody called, "want to give me a hand with your sleigh? We may as well take it to the barn."

He savored the thought of pushing the heavy vehicle through the drifts. He needed hard, physical work.

It would take his mind off his brother and the hundred or so reasons the stage hadn't returned.

"When you come back in, gentlemen," Anna called sharply, "be sure you remove your boots. I intend to scrub this floor. From the looks of it, it hasn't seen soap and water since it was built."

The doctor reached for his coat. As he stepped out onto the porch, he was heard to comment, "I hope you have a good store of whiskey, Cody. Looks like it might be a very long night."

Lizzy sat by the light of the fire, mending the last of the canvas.

Across the room old Doc Simms had nodded off in a chair. As the empty glass slipped from his fingers, Grandpop caught it before it hit the clean floor.

Sara Jean was in the rocker, holding her sleeping infant.

James was staring into the flames, his head resting between Beau's big paws.

After scouring the cabin, Anna Purdy had settled Amos on a chair, with his leg propped up on the kitchen table. She was rubbing liniment on his knee and chattering incessantly. Lizzy had never seen her grandfather looking happier.

Lizzy stopped her mending to watch Cody as he stitched together several beautiful wolf pelts. He hadn't stopped working since hearing the news of his brother's missing stagecoach. She understood his need to stay busy. It had always been her way of dealing with trouble, as well.

She wished there were something she could say or do to make the waiting easier for him. She longed to comfort him.

She glanced at his hands, moving over the lush fur. The thought of those work-worn fingers touching her, igniting sparks, sent a tremor along her spine.

He glanced up. In that moment, as their gazes met and held, she felt the edge of excitement slice through her. His dark eyes held secrets. Secrets she was driven to learn. Promises. Promises of pleasures untold, of endless delights, of passions fulfilled.

"Lizzy." At Anna Purdy's voice, the mood was shattered.

Lizzy's cheeks reddened. She had the feeling that Mrs. Purdy could see right into her mind and knew every thought she'd been thinking.

"You and James and I will sleep in the loft. Amos said that Sara Jean has fixed a bed in the corner, to be close to her baby. The men will sleep on the floor around the fireplace."

Lizzy saw the pleading in her little brother's eyes. "James will sleep down here with the men."

"But..."

"He's too big to sleep with us, Mrs. Purdy."

The woman glanced from the little boy to his sister, then nodded. "All right, then. Come along, Lizzy. Let's say good-night."

As Anna climbed the ladder to the loft, Lizzy set down her mending and knelt beside her brother. "I'll hear your prayers now, James."

A few minutes later, when she had made her way to the loft, Cody winked at the boy and muttered, "You dodged that bullet, James. Thanks to your sister."

"Yes, sir." James fell asleep with a smile on his face.

When the lantern was snuffed and the cabin was filled with the soft, muted sounds of sleep, Cody pulled on his coat and walked out to the porch. Rolling a cigarette, he filled his lungs and stared out at the snow that curtained the night.

Somewhere in this wilderness, if Ned was alive, he'd be looking at the same scene. Cody clenched his hand at his side. Ned was alive. Alive and well. He just had to be.

God, he thought, lifting his gaze heavenward, keep him safe.

The storm was still raging in the morning. When Cody tried to open the door, it was held by a wall of snow.

While Lizzy and Anna made breakfast, the men climbed out the window and shoveled the snow away from the cabin.

"Look," James shouted.

The men looked up from their work to watch a herd of several dozen mustangs race along the meadow and past the barn, their manes shaggy and their tails blowing in the wind. The horses in the corral began running in circles, eager to join their wild brothers.

James watched the graceful animals as they danced up a hill and disappeared into the high, wooded area.

"Look." Cody pointed and the little boy turned. "That's their leader."

One horse, as black as midnight, waited alone on a high peak, as if standing guard. He kept a watchful gaze on their party as the other horses filed past.

The wind ruffled his thick mane as he reared and stomped the ground before turning and following the others into the woods.

"They're so beautiful," James sighed.

Cody dropped a hand on his shoulder in understanding. "There's something special about a wild horse. Though I've caught and tamed hundreds, I never get over the beauty of them."

The little boy looked up at the man with shining eyes. In these few moments they had shared something very special.

Cody returned to his shovel while James joined Beau in a game of leaping into the drifts. Suddenly, while leaping into a particularly deep drift, the boy disappeared. Beau's frantic barking brought the men racing to the scene. But before they could reach him, the big dog plowed into the snow and emerged dragging the little boy by the back of his jacket.

Grandpop's first reaction was to hug the boy to his heart. But fear and anxiety got the better of him, making him react instead with fury.

"You can't go leaping into deep snowdrifts without figuring out beforehand how you're going to get out." He shook the boy, rattling his teeth. "It's the way with everything in life, boy. You always have to look first and figure things out. Now go on inside with the women where you'll be safe until you've learned that lesson.''

Choking back his tears, the boy headed for the cabin.

"Pretty rough on the kid, weren't you?" Doc asked.

Amos pulled a ragged scarf around his nose and mouth, muffling his words. "I'll, by God, be as rough as I please. It'd be a whole lot rougher putting his little body in a pine box in the ground.''

Cody turned away, feeling the jagged edge of a knife turning in his heart.

Each man hauled in an armload of split logs and set them beside the fireplace.

"This should keep us," Cody muttered, "in case the snow keeps falling.''

Sara Jean looked up from the baby in her arms. "Can a stagecoach get through snow this deep?''

"Only if it flies," Doc said, leaning close to the fire.

Lizzy saw the fear in her sister's eyes. But when she turned to glance at Cody, he was already striding out the door. They could hear the ring of the ax biting into frozen wood as he spent his frustration on another pile of logs.

The storm let up late that night. Lizzy awoke and listened to the silence that had settled over the land. Climbing quietly down the ladder, she padded to the window and stared at the snow-covered hills.

She had a sudden need to escape the four walls and the crush of sleeping bodies. She pulled on her boots and draped a fur around her shoulders, then stepped out onto the porch.

How vast the land. With a full moon casting its glow on the crest of new snow, it was like a dazzling fairy-land.

When a hand closed over her shoulder, she whirled and lifted her arms as if to defend herself. At the sight of Cody, she let out her breath in a long sigh of relief.

"I thought you were sleeping inside with the others."

"I wanted to check the mare. She's restless. But it isn't her time yet."

To keep from touching her again he busied himself rolling a cigarette. He held a match to the tip. In the flare of light, Lizzy saw his eyes, dark and hooded. He filled his lungs, then emitted a stream of smoke that instantly dissipated into the night air.

He turned to study the meadow, softened with a mantle of snow. "It's peaceful, isn't it?"

Lizzy felt an odd thickening in her throat.

"It's funny," he said, "hearing Anna Purdy rave about this place. Sometimes, when the storms rage or men take the law into their own hands, it's easy to see only the cruel side of nature or the danger of such isolation. But there's so much beauty here. Beauty and peace and solace."

"You came here to heal, didn't you?"

He nodded.

"I guess that's why we came, too. Only we didn't know it. We just knew we couldn't stay, and we felt like nothing would ever be home again."

"You'll find your home someday, Lizzy."

She wanted to tell him that she'd found it. Or thought she had. But she was too shy. She had no right to say such things. He had taken in a band of strangers and offered shelter. For all she knew, they had already overstayed their welcome. His cabin had been turned into a bunkhouse, with bodies everywhere. His precious store of food was quickly becoming depleted. The peace he was accustomed to was denied him, except during the silent hours of the night.

"I'd better go in now."

As she turned, he laid a hand on her arm. "Don't go." As soon as he said it, he seemed to think better of it. "No. On second thought, go ahead in. It's cold out here."

She turned to him. "What's wrong, Cody?"

"Nothing." Everything. He felt miserable, and didn't know why. No. That was a lie. It was because of her. Because every time he was near her like this, all he could think of was taking her like some sort of savage. And he knew that if he did, he would destroy something rare and precious.

What right did he have to take, with nothing to give in return? He had nothing to offer a woman like Lizzy. He had nothing to offer any woman. Except loneliness. And the pain and bitterness that festered in his soul.

"Go inside now, Lizzy."

She watched as he turned away and tossed the stub of his cigarette into the snow. He was unprepared for the touch of her hand on his arm. He turned to face her, his eyes suddenly narrowed in anger.

"What are you doing?"

"Touching you."

She lifted a hand to his face and traced the craggy contour of his cheek beneath the rough beard, the curve of his jaw, the outline of his lips.

He stood very still, fighting the feelings that ripped through him.

"I want you to hold me, Cody."

"I can't."

He knew she was hurt by his rejection, but he made no move to comfort her.

"Why?"

"Because—" his voice was ragged, as if torn from his throat after an uphill climb "—if I do, I won't be able to let you go."

As the realization dawned, Lizzy wrapped her arms around his waist and pressed her lips to his throat. "Then I'll hold you."

He closed his eyes and absorbed the jolt as her mouth moved across his throat. A kick by a mule would have been less shocking.

Of their own volition, his arms came around her, molding her firmly to him. His fingers tangled in her hair as he lifted her head for his kiss.

And then he was lost. Lost in feelings that he had believed dead. Feelings of love, of tenderness. With her he wanted to be gentle. To take care not to hurt her. But even his good intentions dissolved when he took the kiss deeper. Passion, so long denied, churned within him. Needs, so long denied, begged for release.

Framing her face in his hands, he kissed her lips, her cheek, her eyes, pressing light, trembling kisses on her closed lids until he tasted the salt of her tears. Tears?

He put his hands on her shoulders and gently pushed her away. She refused to look at him. Lifting her chin, he studied the tears that squeezed from her eyes.

With his thumbs he gently wiped them away. "Go inside now, Lizzy. Before we do something we'll regret."

Regret? How could she tell him that her only regret would be leaving here without showing him how she felt?

Cursing herself for her cowardliness, she turned and fled.

Up in the loft, as she lay beside the sleeping Widow Purdy, Lizzy swallowed back the tears that burned her eyes and throat. It felt so wonderful to be held in Cody's arms. His kisses awakened feelings she'd never known before. Why, then, she wondered, was she feeling so miserable?

Outside, Cody stormed off to the barn. He wished it were daylight so he could work off his frustration on a cord of wood. Instead, he'd start his chores by the light of the full moon.

In the morning, he'd begin breaking those mustangs to saddle. That ought to be bone-jarring enough to take his mind off one beautiful little female who was eating away at his soul.

Chapter Fourteen

"Think your horse can make it through the drifts, Doc?" Amos bit into a freshly baked biscuit as Anna and Lizzy served a breakfast big enough to feed half the town of Commencement.

"We'll go around them."

"Maybe you ought to stay another day or so," Cody cautioned, "just until the wind comes up and levels some of those drifts."

The set of the doctor's jaw told them he wasn't about to be locked away in this cabin with the widow Purdy for another day and night. "We'll do just fine. That old horse and I have been plowing through drifts for many a year now. And pulling a sleigh is a lot easier on him than pulling a wagon."

"What about the stagecoach?" Sara Jean asked. "Do you think it can get through yet?"

"Lord, how you fuss about that stagecoach, girl." Anna laid a hand on her arm. "The driver can't just take off the wheels and replace them with blades. The stage will have to wait out the storms. But I'll bet, by the time we get back to Commencement, the stage-coach is in."

"You think so?"

Anna nodded and passed a platter of salt pork and biscuits.

"Grandpop," Sara Jean asked in a rush, "do you think I could go to Commencement with Doc Simms and Mrs. Purdy?"

Amos looked stunned. "Sara Jean, you have a brand new baby to think about. Why would you even consider such a thing?"

"Because I..." She struggled to hold back the sting of unexpected tears.

"It's because of little Jobeth that she's asking," Lizzy put in quickly, to cover her sister's tears.

Sara Jean's brows shot up and she cast a grateful look at her sister.

"What are you talking about, girl?"

"If Mrs. Purdy doesn't mind taking her in, Sara Jean would be able to sleep in a real bed, Grandpop. And eat good food, which would be passed along to her baby."

"Oh, Amos," the widow said, feeling a mist of tears herself. "It would be so good to have another woman around the house. I'm so lonely there all by myself. And a baby... Why, I'd be able to fuss over her, over both of them, as much as I wanted. It would almost be like having a granddaughter of my own."

Lizzy could see that her grandfather was relenting. There was nothing he could deny Anna Purdy while her fresh biscuits were melting in his mouth.

"I suppose, as long as you don't mind..."

"Mind? Why, I would take it as a special favor. Oh, thank you, Amos." The widow hugged Sara Jean and the baby in her arms, and for a moment it looked like she might even hug the doctor, who sat beside them. But her happiness hadn't completely robbed her of her senses.

"It's settled, then," Amos said. "Pack your things, girl. You can stay at Mrs. Purdy's until we come by in a couple of days to pick you up."

"A couple of days?" Lizzy felt her stomach suddenly lurch.

"As soon as the wagon can get through those drifts," Amos said firmly, "we'll be on our way. We've imposed on Cody long enough."

Sara Jean hurried to pack her meager belongings.

Within the hour, the sleigh was loaded with a cradle and a bundle of Sara Jean's clothes, and Sara Jean, the doctor and Anna Purdy took their leave.

"You be a good girl now," Amos said, kissing Sara Jean's cheek. "You give Anna as much help as you can, in payment for her hospitality."

"I will, Grandpop."

She drew Lizzy close and hugged her fiercely. "Thanks, Lizzy," she whispered. "I don't know why you came to my rescue, but I'll never forget it. If it hadn't been for you, Grandpop would never have let me go." She sighed long and deep. "You'll never know what it means to me to be able to see for myself if Ned is safe."

"But I do know," Lizzy protested.

Sara Jean shook her head. "Only a woman in love could ever understand what agony I'm going through right now. I think I'll just die if Ned isn't there when we arrive in Commencement."

Lizzy pressed a kiss to her cheek. "I'll be praying for you and Ned."

"Thank you, Lizzy." She found herself thinking that her older sister wasn't the dull old workhorse she'd always found her to be. Still, to Sara Jean's thinking, Lizzy had a long way to go to understand a woman in love.

James sat on a pile of furs, cooing to the baby and rocking her the way Lizzy had taught him. When Sara Jean's shadow fell over him, he kept his gaze averted for a moment, knowing it was the moment when he would have to give up the baby to her mother.

"Goodbye, James," Sara Jean murmured, pressing a kiss to his cheek. "Say goodbye to Jobeth."

He drew the baby close, inhaling the sweet warmth of her, then dutifully passed her to her mother.

Sara Jean tucked the tiny baby close and wrapped her in a fur robe that Cody had given her. Unexpected tears clouded her vision for a moment and she blinked them away. Leaving her family was harder than she'd expected. Ever since the birth of her baby, she found herself getting all weepy and teary eyed at the strangest moments.

As she hugged Cody goodbye, Sara Jean whispered, "I promise you, Cody, if Ned is safe, I'll see that he gets word to you right away."

Cody was surprised at the girl's thoughtfulness. So often she seemed insensitive to the needs of those around her. Maybe he'd judged her too harshly. Maybe she was indeed growing up. "Thank you, Sara Jean. I'd appreciate it very much."

"It's the least I can do after all your kindnesses. Besides, I can see through you, Cody Martin. Even though you talk tough, I know you really love Ned."

His head came up sharply, and he wondered for a moment whether he had given away any other secret feelings. Touching a finger to the baby's cheek, he whispered, "Almost as much as Lizzy loves you and that baby."

"I sure will miss all of you." Sara Jean gave a last lingering look around before being helped onto the sleigh. If Grandpop was as good as his word, it would be her last glimpse of Cody Martin's rough cabin. She didn't mind so much for herself, but James and Lizzy seemed to have taken a shine to it.

With a crack of the whip the horse took off and the sleigh glided across the snow. Cody and Lizzy, Amos and James stood on the porch waving until the sleigh dipped out of sight.

To battle their sudden bout of loneliness, they attacked their chores with a vengeance.

The corral had been divided in two by the addition of more railings. On one side stood the horses. The other side was empty.

Cody's jacket hung over one of the rails. Inside the corral, the horses shifted nervously as he moved among them with a rope. When he'd selected the stallion he wanted, he tossed the rope and stood his ground as the horse began bucking and rearing.

Opening a gate, he coaxed the stallion into the empty end of the corral, then quickly closed the gate behind him. Now it was just Cody and the horse.

It seemed to the woman and little boy who stood outside the rails watching that it took forever for the horse to begin to tire. But Cody never flinched or grew impatient while the animal wore itself out.

When the horse finally stood, breathless and watchful, Cody lay a blanket over its back. Instantly the mustang was wild-eyed and bucking, determined to throw off this strange, flapping thing.

Again Cody stood patiently, speaking soft words meant to soothe. And finally, though the horse quivered, Cody was able to toss a saddle over the animal's back.

This time the reaction was even more violent. The horse bucked and reared against this latest indignity.

As the sun made its lazy arc across the sky, Cody added a bit and bridle until the horse, in full gear, felt the man pull himself into the saddle.

Lizzy and her little brother stood wide-eyed, watching in horror as the mustang took off at a run, heading straight for the fence. When he came to a shuddering stop just inches from the wood railing, Cody stuck to his back as if he'd been strapped on. Then the horse took off around the corral, bucking and rearing fiercely and whirling in dizzying circles.

Lizzy's palms were wet as they closed over the railing. She had never seen a wild horse's reaction to a rider before. It was the most amazing performance she had ever witnessed.

As sleek and stunning as the animal was, it was Cody who held her gaze. He was magnificent. All his concentration was centered on the stallion. Man and beast were in a world apart, learning each other's scents, unlocking each other's secrets.

There was no cruelty in Cody's movements, only kindness. There was no haste in his actions, only extreme patience. Slowly, as if in a primitive dance, he led the stallion through its paces until, almost unnoticed at first, the animal began to respond to his voice, his touch.

By the time the sun was setting behind the distant peaks, the horse was parading smartly around the corral, turning at the touch of a rein, stopping at the slightest signal. The mustang stood still while Cody removed the saddle and bridle and followed him as he strode toward the gate with the saddle slung over his shoulder.

"That was..." Lizzy swallowed, and struggled for a word to describe what she had just witnessed. "Amazing." It was inadequate, but she could come up with nothing better.

Cody stood beside her, gazing at the stallion. "He is a beautiful piece of horseflesh."

"I meant..." Again she found herself reaching for words. "I've never seen a wild horse trained to saddle before. I had no idea how much patience it took. Or how much skill."

"Can I touch him?" James asked.

Cody took his small hand in his and thrust it through the rails. "Let him smell you first. Always let him show you how much he's willing to allow."

The stallion sniffed, then, recognizing Cody's scent, allowed both hands to brush his soft velvet muzzle.

"Well. So he likes to be stroked. Some do. Some shy away. Always let them tell you what they like, James. Pretty soon," Cody said, "he'll be eating out of your hand."

James was clearly enthralled. "Do you think I could ever train mustangs?"

"If you spent enough time around horses. And," Cody added, "if you wanted it badly enough." He carried the saddle to the barn, with James and Lizzy hurrying to keep up with his long strides. "I guess I've always thought that was the key to everything in life, James. Wanting something so much, you just have to reach out and take it."

"Like those bad men who wanted your horses?"

"They wanted to steal them. A good man doesn't want what belongs to another. Thieves aren't willing to work hard like other men. If you really want something, you have to be willing to work, and sweat, and sometimes even die for it."

"That's what I'm going to do when I grow up. I'm going to work as hard as I can. And I'm going to train mustangs like you."

While Cody led the stallion into the barn for its first night in a stall, James ran a hand lovingly over the smooth leather of Cody's saddle and allowed the dreams to play through his mind.

Supper seemed quiet after the excitement of the past few days. But the food was far from plain, thanks to Anna Purdy's generosity. There was a jar of elderberry preserves for the biscuits. And a jug of buttermilk.

"Wind's coming up again." Amos cocked his head to hear it whistle past the roof. "Maybe by morning the drifts will be blown clear away."

Lizzy saw the sad expression on her little brother's face and hoped her own hadn't given her away.

When the meal was over, Amos busied himself at the fire, cleaning his pipe and refilling it. James pulled on his boots and reached for his jacket.

"Where are you going?" Lizzy looked up from the table she was clearing.

"I just want to check on the stallion in the barn."

She glanced at Cody for approval. He gave the boy a smile, remembering the first horse he'd ever fallen in love with. He'd been just about James's age, and he'd checked the stall a dozen times before turning in for the night.

"I was just thinking I'd get another load of wood for the fire," Cody said. "I'll go with you."

As they strode outside, Cody's voice could be heard admonishing, "No sudden moves around him, son."

"I won't."

The door closed, shutting out their voices along with the wind and snow.

Lizzy filled a basin with hot water and began to wash the dishes. Minutes later the door slammed open and James's voice was high and shrill with excitement.

"Grandpop. Lizzy. The mare's foaling. And Cody says, if it's all right with you, I can stay and watch."

With a yelp of excitement Lizzy grabbed up a fur robe while Amos pulled on his sheepskin jacket and wide-brimmed hat.

"Come on, James." Lizzy caught his hand and together they ran all the way to the barn, with Amos trailing more slowly.

Inside, the single lantern cast a dim glow in the stall. The mare's breathing was shallow and strained. Still fighting the pain, she moved restlessly around the stall.

Cody turned as Lizzy and her little brother entered, followed by Amos. It pleased him that they wanted to share this special event.

The old man leaned his weight into the door to close it against the force of the wind.

"Shouldn't she lie down?" James asked.

"She will, son, when she's ready."

"Does it hurt her?"

"I expect it does."

"Can't you do anything to help?"

"I'm afraid she has to do all the work herself, boy," Amos said softly. "But she'll do just fine. You'll see."

"What if she doesn't know what to do?"

"She'll know. Nature sees to it. And if she should get confused, Cody's here to see that she doesn't hurt herself or the foal."

They leaned on the rails of the stall, and later settled themselves in a mound of hay, prepared for a long vigil. Inside the barn, isolated from the snow and wind, caught up in the excitement of the moment, time seemed to stop. It could have been hours later, or perhaps only minutes, when the mare dropped to her knees, then lay down completely, her flesh quivering as the pains rippled through her. Her breathing became more labored.

Cody crooned softly to the agitated animal. She seemed soothed by the sound of his voice. Moving closer, he rubbed her muzzle and continued in that calm, gentle voice.

"Look, James. The foal is coming."

Lizzy lifted the little boy in her arms so that he could have a clear view over the rails of the stall.

It was happening so quickly, he was afraid to blink for fear he would miss something. With his eyes wide he watched as the foal, encased in a sack of fluid, slid easily from its mother.

"It's a colt," Cody announced.

"A boy," James whispered.

"Want to give him a name, James?"

The little boy's mouth dropped open. "You mean I can?"

"Got one in mind?" Cody asked.

For just a moment he forgot his promise to himself. The need to touch her was too great.

And so he allowed his hand to roam her face. His fingers were rough and callused against the incredible softness of her skin.

"You're the one who's perfect, Lizzy." His voice was hardly more than a whisper as he drew her closer and brushed his lips through a tangle of hair at her temple. "You're so warm and vital. So innocent."

She couldn't wait any longer for the touch of his lips on hers. Without a thought to what she was doing, she curled her arms around his neck and lifted her face for his kiss.

Her eyes were closed, her lips pursed invitingly.

His tone suddenly hardened. "You'd better go back to the cabin. Now."

Her eyes blinked open.

He could read her disappointment. But it was best this way. He could bring her nothing but heartache.

"You heard me, Lizzy. Get out of here."

She picked up the fur robe and draped it around herself. As she walked toward the door, she suddenly stopped and turned. In the light of the lantern she could see the pain in his eyes. And the hunger. With fists clenched he turned away.

A moment later he heard her voice directly behind him. "No, Cody. You can't send me away. This may be the last night we'll ever be together. And if it is, I want to spend it here. With you."

"Don't you understand?" His tone was as hard, as cold as he could make it. "If you stay, there'll be no turning back. I don't have the strength to keep turning away from you. And tomorrow, you won't be the same as you are right now. Nothing will be the same. Not you. Not me."

She met his look evenly. Her voice was clear and steady. "I want to stay, Cody. You can't make me leave."

Chapter Fifteen

"I don't want regrets, Lizzy."

Cody needed something to do, to keep from dragging her against him like a savage. And so he turned away from her, hoping to give her a chance to change her mind.

A part of him wanted her to go. His heart silently begged her to stay.

"There won't be any regrets." She tossed the fur robe down on the hay.

"There will be, Lizzy." He turned and caught her roughly by the shoulders, as if to shake her. But the moment his hands touched her, they gentled, moving slowly down her arms. "But not tonight." Even his voice gentled. "Tonight we'll shut out the world. Tonight there will be just us." His strong fingers closed around her upper arms, dragging her closer. "Just this."

His mouth moved slowly, deliberately over hers until her lips parted for him. His tongue tangled with hers, teasing her, tempting her, until she sighed and gave herself up to the pleasure of his kiss.

His lips whispered over her face, seeking, soothing, as he pressed kisses to her closed eyelids, her cheek, her jaw.

"Lizzy. Lizzy." He whispered her name like a benediction.

On his lips, her name sounded beautiful. In his arms, she felt beautiful.

With his tongue he traced the curve of her ear, pausing to nibble and tug at her lobe, then to suddenly dart inside, sending her pulse racing.

She shivered and tried to draw away but he held her close, burning a trail of hot, wet kisses along her throat. Her heart began a painful hammering in her chest, and she thought for a moment her legs might buckle.

With his lips on hers he lowered her to the fur robe.

"There's still time to run, Lizzy."

At the look in his eyes she felt her breath hitch in her throat. Pressing a hand to his chest, she could feel his heartbeat, as thunderous as her own.

"I can't, Cody. I can't leave you." She twined her arms around his neck and drew his head down for another drugging kiss.

"And I don't have the strength to make you leave." The words were spoken against her mouth as he covered her lips with his.

Outside, the wind howled and cried, sending a spray of snow across the log walls. But inside, the sounds were muted. The mare nickered, and her foal made a feeble attempt to reply. The stallion stomped nervously in his stall.

A single lantern hung on a peg, casting a pale yellow glow over the man and woman who could hear nothing except the beating of their own hearts and their shallow breaths mingling.

Cody struggled to hold his own needs at bay. He cautioned himself to go slowly, to make this first time as pleasurable as possible for her. This was, after all, the only thing he could give her.

His kisses were gentle, almost reverent. With lips and fingertips he explored her face, her neck, her soft, sensitive throat. And with each brush of his lips and tongue he felt her body grow more tense, her breathing grow more shallow.

He wouldn't think about tomorrow. There was no future. And for tonight, there was no past. There was only now, this moment. And Lizzy.

As her blood heated and her body pulsed, Lizzy felt the fire seep through her veins. The world outside the door no longer mattered. For now there was only this man, this moment.

Whenever she became alarmed at what she was about to do, whenever her eyes reflected panic, his movements slowed, and with lips and fingertips he soothed, relaxed, eased.

Steeped in pleasure, she sighed and allowed herself to sink into a dreamlike state.

His touch unlocked a million tiny nerve endings, arousing even while it calmed. With exquisite patience he kissed, caressed, touched, allowing her to set her own pace. With soft words and gentle sighs he eased her tension and calmed her fears until she could trust him to lead her to the next step. Trust. She knew, without any doubt, that she would follow his lead. He wouldn't take her where she didn't want to go.

He sensed the change in her and thrilled to it. It wasn't surrender. In all his fantasies about her, he had never been tempted by mere surrender. It was something far more vital to him. It was passion. A passion that had long slumbered within her, waiting for the right touch to awaken it. He saw it in her eyes; tasted it on her lips. Hot, hungry. Pulsing.

With his eyes on hers he began undressing her. He had to curb the urge to tear her dress from her. But she still needed tenderness. And so he would give her whatever she needed.

He unfastened the row of tiny buttons that ran from her neck to her waist, one button at a time. When he slid the gown from her shoulders, he bent to brush his lips across her naked shoulder.

He felt the tremors that rocked her and brought his fingers to the ribbons of her chemise. As the last filmy barrier fell away, he was free to see the body he had only glimpsed before.

She was so beautiful. And more perfect than he had ever dreamed.

He felt his heart thundering as she reached for the buttons of his shirt and slipped it from his shoulders. When her fingers faltered at the fasteners at his waist, he helped her, until his clothes had been tossed aside with hers.

They knelt facing each other on the fur, feeling the cushion of soft hay move and shift beneath them.

Though the wind raged outside, heat poured from their skin as they came together.

His fingers tangled in her hair as he drew her head back and covered her mouth in a savage kiss. For a moment she stiffened, feeling a flash of fear at the change in him. Then the fear was swept away by her own newly awakened passion.

She brought her arms around his waist and felt his muscles contract violently at the first touch of her fingers. With a moan he took the kiss deeper, and his hands moved over her, enticing, arousing.

So this was why he had tried to send her away. This was why he had struggled so long to keep his distance. This was the secret he had held so long. This smoldering passion, this dark, brooding all-consuming sensuality that now struggled to be free.

This dark side of him excited her. Exulting in her power, she brought her lips across his shoulder and down his chest. His low groan made her even bolder. With lips and fingertips she explored his body as he had explored hers.

His body hummed with need. He had wanted to go slowly, to allow her to set the pace. But now, with her own passion unleashed, he was finally free. It was no longer enough to want to please her, to satisfy her. He wanted to show her so much more. Not just passion, though he knew this was her first taste. It was the madness, the insanity of knowing that she was his and his alone. Of knowing that wherever he led, she was willing to follow.

This was what he would give her. More than a taste—a feast. More than a moment's pleasure—a night filled with every delight.

With excruciating tenderness he laid her down and brought his lips to her breast, moving his tongue across her nipple until it hardened. With exquisite care he moved to the other, feasting on her breasts, slowly, patiently, until she writhed and moaned and and clutched at the fur beneath her. Her breathing grew more shallow, and still he held back as his lips and fingertips moved over her, learning her body, drawing out every pleasure.

The cold night air whispered over her flesh, and still her lungs were clogged with the heat that rose between them, around them, as he drove her higher, keeping release just out of her reach.

Lizzy had slipped into a world of touch and taste and feel, where thought no longer existed. There was only Cody. He tasted of windswept mountains and tobacco, and faintly of whiskey. The musky male scent of him mingled with the smell of horses and leather. And the feel of his rough, work-hardened fingers on her flesh was more heavenly than the feel of silk or satin.

She shuddered and strained against him as he slid along her body, damp flesh to damp flesh, and brought his lips to her throat.

He had thought he was teaching her, taking her, but he was the one being led. From the first touch of her he had been imprisoned by needs so primitive they cried out for release. He struggled to hold back his needs, to draw out the moment.

He felt her stiffen as he brought his mouth down her body. But at the exquisite pleasure, bordering on pain, she forgot her fears. And then she gasped as she reached the first crest. He gave her no time to recover before he moved over her, tracing his lips upward until they found hers.

Her lids snapped open. He saw her eyes, dark with passion. It wasn't possible to want more. But she did. His name was torn from her lips as he entered her. Her deeper arousal startled both of them as she wrapped herself around him, wanting to hold him like this forever.

He filled himself with her, breathing in the clean, fresh taste that would always be hers alone. He knew that in the loneliness of winters to come, he would still be warmed by the memories of this.

He whispered her name, or thought he did, as his mouth closed over hers and he raced toward the edge of madness.

And then she was moving with him, climbing toward a distant peak. And as their bodies shuddered, she felt them both break free and begin to soar. It was the most incredible journey of their lives.

They lay, still joined, their breathing slowly returning to normal. He thought he might be too heavy for her, but he couldn't muster the energy to lift himself from her. Besides, she felt so good, so right, here in his arms.

He shifted slightly to kiss away the damp sheen from her forehead. That was when he discovered the tears. Alarmed, he levered himself on his elbows to study her.

"God in heaven, Lizzy. I've hurt you." He touched a finger to the corner of her eye.

"No." She caught his hand and pressed it to her cheek. It was such a tender gesture he found himself incredibly moved.

"I don't usually cry so easily. It's just that—" she struggled to find the words "—it was so much more wonderful than I'd expected."

With his thumbs he wiped away her tears and pressed a kiss to her lips. He wished he were a poet or a man of great words. Instead he said simply, "Sometimes, when a man and a woman are very lucky, they find a special person in this world who fills up all the empty places."

His words moved her and she struggled against letting him see more tears. A special person. He was so special to her. And what they had just shared was something she would remember for a lifetime.

Empty places. She thought of how empty her life had seemed since the war destroyed everything. How much more empty her life would be now, when she was forced to leave him.

He rolled onto his side, cradling her to his chest. She clung to him, loving the way it felt to hear his strong, steady heartbeat against her ear.

She was silent for such a long time he thought she had fallen asleep. He pressed a kiss to her temple and was surprised when her hands moved along his shoulder and down his chest. She felt the raised scar that ran along his side to just beneath his rib cage.

As her fingertips traced it, she sat up suddenly, and her voice was low with passion. "I can't bear that you were wounded in the war."

"Wounds heal, Lizzy. Even hearts, I've learned. And life goes on."

"Oh, Cody. Why are you here, all alone on this mountain?"

He was silent for a long moment, and Lizzy thought he would refuse to answer. She'd had no right to ask such a personal question. His life, his secrets were his own.

In an oddly unemotional voice he said, "I spent the last year of the war as a prisoner of war, with hundreds of wounded and dying men."

She licked lips that had suddenly gone dry. "Where?"

"Andersonville."

He had been held prisoner in her own home state. She had heard about the condition of the prison camp. So many men hadn't survived.

"And when I got home," he said simply, "I found more death. My wife and son, my reason for living, were gone. I couldn't be around people anymore, Lizzy. I just had to find someplace clean and untouched by the madness."

"Oh, Cody." The love she felt for him was so deep. If she could, she would erase all the pain from his life. But she couldn't speak the words. And so she could only show him.

She bent her lips to the scar. Her hair swirled forward, brushing his chest. With incredible tenderness she spoke of love, of healing, of the magic of sharing.

As she slowly moved her lips along the uneven seam of flesh, he caught her by the shoulders and uttered a low moan of pleasure.

It wasn't possible that he could want her again so soon. But he was already thoroughly aroused.

"Woman, do you know what you're doing to me?"

At his reaction she felt a surge of power. This was what she wanted. To know that it was her touch that he craved, her body that he sought. Her love that he wanted.

With a wicked smile she murmured, "The same thing you did to me. As I recall, I was able to resist your advances for almost a full minute."

He chuckled low and deep in his throat. This was a side to Lizzy he'd never seen before. She was shamelessly flirting. And he found that he adored her for it. "I'll see if I can do better."

"You will forgive me. I've had little practice. But I think you might enjoy this...." She brought her lips lower and felt him flinch. "Why, Cody Martin. Are you afraid of me?"

"You scare me to death." He tried to drag her upward but she evaded his touch and continued tormenting him until he moaned again. A slow, sensuous smile curved his lips. "But you certainly do pleasure me."

His smile fled when she suddenly straddled him and wrapped herself around him. And then he was lost in the wonders of the woman in his arms.

Chapter Sixteen

Cody studied the woman who slept so peacefully in his arms. She would never know what a gift she had given him. It wasn't just the touch of her, though it had been a long time since he had been touched like this. And it wasn't just her soft, sultry voice, though he loved listening to her. Her voice reminded him of those long-ago dinners at his grandmother's fine big house. A voice that belonged to lush, velvet ball gowns and French perfume.

No, it wasn't her touch or her voice alone. It was her goodness, her tenderness, her generous spirit. These few hours with Lizzy had healed him. It was as though all the wounds had never happened. What was more important, his shattered heart had mended, as well.

He had hoped, through their long night of love-making, to fill himself with her so that he would never feel empty again. But now, watching her as she lay sleeping, he knew that he had set an impossible task. He could never have enough of her. And now that he had tasted her lovemaking, the loneliness would be even more unbearable when she left.

The thought of asking her to stay tantalized him. Sleep eluded him while he agonized over the thought. But he knew he had no right. He had nothing to offer a woman. Nothing except a life of hardship and loneliness, far away from civilization. He had seen the elegant plantations of Georgia. A woman like Lizzy deserved something better than this. The best thing he could do for her—the only thing he could do for her—was to let her go.

She stirred and he waited, heart pounding, for that moment when her eyes would open and she would realize that their night together was over.

Perhaps, he thought, throat going suddenly dry, she would regret what they had shared. If she had regrets, he'd know. There would be no way for her to hide her emotions in those honest, open eyes.

Her lids flickered and he saw the instant recognition. His heart stopped beating. He forgot to breathe.

Like a contented, lazy cat, she stretched and wrapped her arms around his neck, dragging his face close for a slow, lingering kiss.

"Mmm." She smiled and snuggled closer. "I just had the nicest dream."

"Want to tell me about it?"

She laughed, a warm, rich sound that wrapped itself around his heart like a hug. "Words wouldn't do it justice. But I suppose I could show you."

"Was I in your dream?"

"Oh, yes. You were doing something like this." She pressed her lips to his throat and began running hot, moist kisses across his collarbone.

Cody tried not to squirm, but it was impossible beneath such an assault. His voice was warm with a mixture of passion and laughter. "Did you like it?"

"Oh, it was all right."

"Just all right?"

"Yes. But then you did this...." She brought her lips across his chest, stopping occasionally to nip with her teeth or tickle with her tongue.

His hand fisted in her hair, and he tried to drag her head up, but she continued teasing him.

"This dream is getting serious." His blood was already pounding in his temples. He felt as if he'd just chased an entire herd of mustangs on foot. Grasping her by the shoulders, he muttered, "How did this dream of yours end?"

"It didn't. I woke up just as you..." She moved her head lower and heard him moan.

She was still laughing when he rolled her over and pressed his mouth to hers. "Now let me tell you about my dream."

Her laughter died, replaced by a soft sigh as he took her. Slowly, deliberately, he drew out all the pleasures they had shared through the long, glorious night. And while dawn light began to touch the mountaintops with a pale, pink glow, they slipped into a world of whispered words and murmured phrases. A world of intense feeling. A world of love.

"I can't put it off any longer." Lizzy sat up and pushed the hair from her eyes. "Grandpop and James will be waking soon. I'd better wash up and get breakfast started."

Cody lay in the fur robe, his hands under his head, watching as she sprinted across the barn and began washing herself in a basin of cold water.

"It isn't fair," she said with mock anger, "for you to be all cozy and warm while I'm standing here freezing."

"You could always come over here and let me warm you."

She laughed as she slipped her dress over her head. "No, I can't. I know where that would lead. And then who'd do the cooking?"

"Let them eat cold beans and biscuits. What I have in mind is much more satisfying than food."

He watched as she smoothed the fabric over her hips. Picking up a brush, she began to run it through the tangles. With each movement of the brush his hand tightened until, in a low voice, he muttered, "Lizzy, come over here."

At the urgency of his tone she crossed to him. "Cody, what's wrong?"

"I want to do that." He patted the fur and she knelt beside him. Getting to his knees, he took the brush from her hands and began running it through her long hair.

Delicious tingles of fire and ice snaked along her spine.

"What are you...?"

"Shh." In silence he brushed her hair until it drifted, all shiny and smooth, like a silken veil around her.

Then, handing her the brush, he bent to kiss her cheek. The gesture was so achingly sweet she felt a lump begin to form in her throat.

"It's just something I've always wanted to do." For long minutes he studied the way she looked, as clean as a mountain stream, lovelier than any sunset. She was so perfect he felt his throat go dry just looking at her.

"I'll come in when I've finished my chores." He pulled her close for another kiss and ran his hand possessively along her back. Then he helped her to her feet and drew the fur around her.

Feeling slightly dazed, she slipped the barn door open and ran to the cabin.

Amos spent the day making the final repairs on the wagon. All day long the sound of hammering filled the air as he fitted sturdy new sides to the wagon bed.

With every blow of the hammer, Lizzy felt a blow to her heart. Against her will she was being drawn toward the one terrible, painful thing she had begun to dread—her final parting from Cody.

James sensed it, too. All day he found reasons to trail behind the man who had become his hero.

He stood at the corral fence in the biting cold and watched as Cody broke a second mustang to saddle. He carried food and water to the horses in the barn and spent hours watching the antics of the foal, who was now frolicking around the stall, testing the patience of its mother.

Several times, while Cody wrestled with the mustang, he found his concentration wandering when Lizzy came into view. All he could think about was the way she had looked, all fresh and sweet, as she had allowed him to brush her hair. All he could taste, while he ate a noontime meal of corn bread and rabbit stew, was Lizzy on his tongue. And when he forked fresh hay into the mare's stall, he could think only of lying in that same hay with Lizzy in his arms.

The daylight hours of this last day together seemed to drag on forever. By the time the final chores were finished and he made his way to the cabin for supper, the need for her had become a slow, simmering fire deep inside him.

He barely tasted his food. Minutes after he'd finished, he couldn't say if he'd eaten venison or salt pork. He'd burned his tongue on hot coffee and wasn't even aware of it. The small talk he'd made with Amos made no sense at all. In fact, he couldn't recall a single thing they'd talked about. But he knew everything about Lizzy. How her hair seemed more red in the glow of the lantern. How her eyes crinkled whenever she smiled. How her tone softened whenever she spoke to her little brother. How her hands looked when they passed the food, or folded in prayer, or lifted to an errant strand of hair that fell over one eye. He had to keep himself from reaching out and capturing her hands in his.

After supper he worked on mending a frayed cinch on his saddle. But while he worked, he watched Lizzy wash and dry the dishes and clean off the table. He felt a tug at his heartstrings when she knelt beside James and heard his prayers.

When she was finished, she crossed to where Cody was working and hung the lantern on a peg just over his shoulder, allowing the light to fall on his work. Without a word he smiled his thanks, and she responded with a smile of her own.

Though no words passed between them, they were able to communicate with their hearts.

Lizzy took a seat in the rocker and began to mend a pair of her little brother's torn britches. While her needle flew, she watched Grandpop smoke his pipe and waited, praying his chores had worn him out and hoping he would soon roll himself into his fur and sleep.

The minutes ticked away, feeling like hours. And at last, with a yawn, Amos set his pipe on the mantel and kicked off his boots. Slipping his suspenders from his shoulders, he rolled himself into his fur.

"I'll turn in now. You'd better do the same. We'll want to get an early start in the morning. Good night, Lizzy. Cody," he called.

"'Night, Grandpop." Lizzy kept her head down, concentrating as hard as she could on her mending.

"Good night, Amos." Cody's fingers moved over the leather, doing by rote what he had done a hundred times before. But this time, his mind refused to cooperate.

He glanced at Lizzy, head bent over the cloth in her hand. If she knew what he was thinking, she would surely blush.

Oh, the things he wanted to tell her. But he knew he never would. And the things he yearned to share with her. But he would keep his secrets safely locked in his heart. Tonight, on this, their last night together, there would be little time for words. Tonight he would try, as only a fool could, to hold the morning at bay.

Cody pulled on his jacket and walked to the barn. Scant minutes later he looked up to see Lizzy lean her weight against the door.

As she hurried toward him, he raced halfway to meet her, his arms opened wide. With a half laugh, half sob, she danced into his arms and felt herself being lifted high in the air. As he slowly lowered her, she slid along his lean, hard body and waited, waited, with a hunger that nearly drove her mad, until their lips mated.

Her hands dug into his hair as he held her and kissed her, slowly, thoroughly, like a man starved for the taste of her lips.

Without a word he carried her to the nest of furs he'd prepared in a bed of fresh hay. Still kissing her, he lowered her to the fur and nearly tore her dress in his haste. Her movements were equally frantic as she fumbled with his buttons and tugged his shirt from his shoulders.

Their kisses were hot, urgent, their hands almost bruising in their intensity. The silence of the night was filled with sighs and moans as they struggled to pour a lifetime of love into a single night. Though neither of them spoke, each knew what the other was thinking as they came together in a frenzy that left them both shaken.

* * *

"You'll hit gentler weather in Arizona Territory. From there the passage to California should be easy." Cody cradled Lizzy in his arms. All night they had clung together, loving until they were sated, and then surprising themselves by loving again. The hours were passing quickly. Too quickly. They had a desperate need to hold on to the last remaining hours of darkness.

"Don't let your grandfather give in to the temptation to quit too soon and sink roots in Arizona. You told me he's a man of the soil. Make certain he keeps going. I've heard that some of the valleys in California have soil so rich you can grow two crops a year."

Cody knew he was rambling. But he needed to speak, to fill the silences that screamed at them. And he dared not speak about the things in his heart. These topics were safe. And meaningless.

"And the weather in the southern valleys of California will be more to your liking. You'll never have to see snow or feel cold again."

Lizzy felt the blade of a knife pierce her heart, and she had to press her eyes tightly shut to keep from crying out. How could she live without ever seeing snow again? And the cold. She would miss it. How was that possible? What had happened to her here in this wild, primitive place, that she should have changed so?

She swallowed the lump in her throat.

"You're awfully quiet. Would you like to sleep for a while?"

"No." She spoke quickly, running a hand across his chest as she did. "I'll never be able to sleep tonight."

"I know." He rolled onto his side and drew her firmly against the length of him. "I thought the day would never end. And now that we're together, I waste our time by talking nonsense."

"It isn't nonsense. Grandpop has had it in his head since he left Georgia that California is the promised land."

"I hope—" the words tasted like ashes in his mouth, but he forced himself to go on "—that you find your heart's desire there, Lizzy."

She took another knife thrust to the heart and wondered if he could see her pain. She'd warned herself, over and over, that their lovemaking had merely filled a void in his life. Wouldn't a drowning man cling to any lifeline? That's all she was to Cody. A lifeline. And though it hurt, it would have to be enough. For a little while, at least, she had felt special. In his eyes, she had felt beautiful.

I love you, her heart whispered. I love you as I will never love anyone again. Aloud she said, "And I hope your foal is the beginning of good things in your life, Cody."

She was the only good thing in his life. And if it killed him, he would return her goodness by letting her go as gracefully as he could.

He framed her face with his hands and studied her in the glow of the lantern, memorizing every line and curve. The perfectly arched brows that gave her a haughty look. Her eyes, which could glow amber, as they did now in the light of the lantern, or dance with little green points of flame when she was angry or aroused. The slightly upturned nose, giving her an impish appearance. The lips, beautifully sculpted, with a full lower lip that spoke of sensual delights.

He knew that even when he was very old, and his steps faltered and his vision faded, she would be etched clearly in his heart. He would carry her memory forever.

Very slowly, very deliberately, with a kind of reverence, he kissed her eyes, her cheek, her mouth. And then, with equal care, he took her on a long, slow journey that spoke of his love more eloquently than any words. A love that would survive separation. A love that would warm him through all the long winters of his life, and transcend even death. A love that would carry him through a lifetime and beyond.

Chapter Seventeen

Cody awoke with a start and realized at once that the place beside him was empty. Cursing himself for having dozed, he glanced around the barn, expecting to see Lizzy washing herself by the basin of water. She wasn't there.

He knew then that she had wisely decided to avoid the pain of parting. This way, they would bid a final public farewell in the presence of the others. What words, after all, could they say that would make the parting easier? Still, he felt the sharp pain of regret. He'd wanted, needed these last private moments with her.

He lay a moment, inhaling the scent of her that still lingered in the folds of the fur robe. He knew that, with enough hard work, he could get through the morning, and even their goodbyes. But how could he face the rest of his life, empty and meaningless, looming before him?

He folded the furs and tossed them over the rail of the mare's stall. Striding to the basin, he plunged his arms into the frigid water and was grateful for the icy shock. Clenching his teeth, he splashed himself liberally and scrubbed until his skin tingled. He drew on his shirt and pants, then slipped into his boots and set about his morning chores.

Working carefully, Amos stretched the freshly mended canvas over the frame of the wagon, then hitched up the plow horse and led him around to the cabin. There Amos and James made endless trips from the cabin to the wagon, loading bundles of clothing and the meager household goods they'd managed to salvage from the accident.

When all was in readiness, they tramped inside for breakfast. With a heavy heart Cody trudged past the loaded wagon and followed them inside.

The cabin was filled with the fragrance of apples and spices.

"Something smells wonderful," Amos commented, taking his place at the table.

Lizzy avoided looking at Cody. "I found some wrinkled apples in the cellar. I figured, since they were too old to eat, I'd peel a couple and bake them in the biscuits."

Amos bit into one and closed his eyes, savoring the flavor. "Girl, if I didn't know better, I'd say your grandmother baked these."

Lizzy flushed at the rare compliment. "I thought of Grandma while they were baking. The cabin smells the way I always remember her kitchen smelling."

Cody breathed deeply, filling his lungs with the memories of a happy childhood. When he was a boy,

the kitchen had always smelled like this at Christmas-
time, when his mother and grandmother went into a
frenzy of cooking and baking. From now on it would
remind him of something even more exciting, and more
elusive, than that special day.

"You're not eating," Amos said almost accusingly.

Startled, Cody filled his plate. But though he ate
mechanically, he didn't taste anything.

Lizzy wrapped a towel around her hand and lifted
the blackened coffeepot from the fire. As she moved
around the table, filling their cups, Cody watched with
hungry eyes. Despite her faded, shapeless dress with its
prim rows of buttons, he could still see in his mind her
perfect body and feel the way it had molded and softened beneath his, opening for him like a flower.

When she paused beside him and bent to his cup, he
had to dig deep for all the willpower he had to keep
from reaching his hand to her. He needed to touch her,
to hold her one last time. To feel her lips warm against
his.

There were so many things he still wanted to say.

Amos turned to James, who was eating in silence
beside him. "I'll bet you're eager to leave the wilderness behind and see a town and people again, aren't
you, boy?"

The little boy shrugged. "I guess they won't have
herds of wild mustangs running across the meadows,
will they, Grandpop?"

Cody glanced up in time to see James drop his fork
and raise sad eyes to his grandfather. "Can I please be
excused?"

"If you'd like. But I warn you, boy," Amos admonished, "you're bound to be mighty hungry before we reach Commencement tonight."

The little boy crossed the room and knelt down beside the big dog that lay in front of the fire. Wrapping his arms around Beau's neck, he buried his face in thick fur. He wanted to cry and beg Grandpop to stay here, where the air was sharp as needles in his lungs and the horses roamed right across the front yard while he watched. But he knew that would make Grandpop angry. He swallowed back the tears that scalded his eyes and struggled to remember. What had Lizzy always said, when her heart was heavy? The answer came instantly to his mind. Prayer, Lizzy had been often heard to say, lightened any burden and lifted any heart.

The little boy's trembling lips moved in silent prayer.

"I guess that's the last of it." Amos checked the wagon, then turned to James. "Go fetch your sister, boy."

Reluctantly James returned to the cabin, knowing how his heart would turn over one more time. He found Lizzy standing just inside the door to the cabin, staring around as if memorizing every square inch.

"What are you doing, Lizzy?"

"Nothing." Wrapping her shawl around her shoulders, she took a deep breath and followed him out to the porch.

Cody was shaking hands with Amos. Both men turned as she approached.

"Got everything, girl?"

"Yes, Grandpop."

"Then let's get started. I want to make Commencement by nightfall." He pulled himself up to the wagon seat and picked up the reins.

"Goodbye, Cody," she whispered. "Thank you for—everything."

He was glad that she didn't offer her hand. It wouldn't have been possible to take that small hand in his and not drag her against him and beg her to stay.

She turned away and accepted her grandfather's steadying hand as she pulled herself to the wagon seat.

"I want you to have these for the journey." Cody handed Amos a pile of fur robes.

"I can't take your pelts. You trade them for food and other goods, and I have no way to repay you."

"You've repaid me enough. You helped me rebuild my barn. Besides," he added with a thin smile, "Lizzy's cooking was worth all the pelts I've collected. Take them."

Reluctantly Amos accepted the offering and draped one around his granddaughter's shoulders. She drew it around her and avoided Cody's eyes.

"Goodbye, Cody," James said, offering his hand like he'd seen his grandfather do. He would be a man about this leave-taking if it killed him.

"Goodbye, James." Cody accepted the boy's handshake and felt a lump start to grow in his throat.

"Take good care of Beau and Stormy."

"I will, son."

They looked up at the sound of hoofbeats thundering across the meadow. As a horse came into view,

Cody picked up his rifle and called a low warning to the others. "Get down and go inside."

Grandpop and Lizzy climbed from the wagon and, gathering James to them, stepped inside the cabin, holding the door ajar so they could see and hear.

"Cody Martin?" the rider called when he was close enough to see the rifle pointed at him.

"Yes."

"My name's Owen North. Mrs. Purdy sent me from Commencement to inform you that the stagecoach came back late last night."

Cody gave a sigh of relief, but as his finger relaxed on the trigger, the boy added the words he had most dreaded, causing him to suck in his breath on a thrust of pain.

"The driver and guard didn't return with it."

Lizzy rushed outside, wishing there was some way she could offer Cody comfort. But with the others watching, all she could do was say softly, "Ned will be all right, Cody. I just know he will."

Glancing up, she caught sight of the boy on his horse. The animal's mouth was flecked with foam, and it was plain that the boy had pushed his mount to the limit. They'd probably been on the trail since dawn.

"Take your horse to the barn," she called. "There's food and water there. Then come inside. I'll fix you something to eat before you head back."

"Thank you, ma'am."

As he started toward the barn, Cody's words stopped him. "The coach was empty?"

"Yes, sir."

"Had the gold been delivered?"

The boy shrugged. "Don't know about that. Don't know much about anything right now, except the driver and guard are missing, and Mrs. Purdy and her young guest said you ought to be told right away."

Cody spun on his heel and strode into the cabin. Lizzy followed, fearful of the dark look in his eyes.

Inside, he began pouring bullets into a pouch, which he tied around his neck. Working quickly, he rolled several furs and secured them with leather strips, then began filling a saddlebag with food.

By the time Owen North had been given a quick meal of biscuits and salt pork, Cody had saddled his horse and affixed a blanket behind, then rushed to the barn. Leaving enough food and water for his animals for several days, he secured the barn and returned to the cabin.

"Come on, Beau," he said sternly to the dog.

Immediately Beau set up a wild yelping.

"Looks like I'll be riding with you as far as Commencement," he announced.

He banked the fire in the fireplace and secured the door. Pulling himself into the saddle, he gave a last look at the place he called home and moved out without a word.

James, seated between his grandfather and Lizzy, kept his eyes downcast as the whip cracked and they started off. He'd prayed that he wouldn't have to be separated from the man who had assumed so much importance in his life. But he'd never dreamed that, in order to have his prayers answered, Cody would have to pay such a terrible price. The sin of selfishness weighed heavily upon his young mind.

It was dark long before they reached Commencement. When they crested a hill, Owen North reined in his mount and pointed.

"There's the town." His voice held a note of pride.

"Those lights look mighty inviting," Amos said with a sigh.

By the tone of his voice Lizzy knew her grandfather's knee was paining him. The ride had been a hard one. They'd been forced to stop often along the way, wasting precious time digging the wagon wheels out of the drifts. It had taken all of them, pushing, pulling, straining against the weight of the wagon, to make it through.

Lizzy thought how difficult the journey would have been without Cody and Owen along to help. It would have taken them another day or more on their own. Another day or two in the bitter cold.

All day she had prayed that Cody would find good news awaiting him in Commencement. Now, as they began the descent into the valley, she whispered another prayer.

The town was just as Sara Jean had described it, with a lantern blinking a welcome in the window of the blacksmith's shop, standing beside a darkened stable. Their wagon rolled along a wide dirt path, bordered on either side by wooden buildings. The snow and dirt had been churned up by horses' hooves and the wheels of dozens of wagons, turning the snow to a muddy brown. Beyond the lights in the windows, Lizzy could see men and women moving around; there was smoke pouring from chimneys. Despite the bleakness of the night, it was a cozy scene.

"I'll leave you folks here," Owen announced. "My pa's place is right over there." He pointed to the mercantile.

"Thanks, Owen." Cody offered his hand. "I'm obliged for your help."

"The sheriff's office is just up there." The boy pointed. "He'll be able to tell you whether or not there's any news of your brother."

"Thanks again."

They drew up in front of the sheriff's office and waited while Cody went inside. Scant minutes later he returned. By the grim look on his face they knew that the news hadn't been good.

"Still no sign of him?" Amos called.

Cody shook his head. "Come on. I'll accompany you to Mrs. Purdy's."

The widow's house was the last one in a line of houses just beyond the town. It stood far enough from the road to escape the dust and dirt spewed by horses' hooves and wagon wheels. Clean, fresh snow frosted the roof and windowpanes. Lantern light glowed behind the frilly curtains at the windows.

Cody dismounted and helped James and Lizzy from the wagon. His hands lingered a moment at Lizzy's waist before he released her. She was so clean and warm, and more than ever he wished he could accept the solace offered in her eyes.

At the sound of the wagon the door was thrown open, and Sara Jean and Anna hurried out onto the porch.

"We've been watching for you for hours," Sara Jean said in a scolding tone.

"That's the truth. We expected you earlier," Anna called to Amos.

"We kept getting stuck in the snow. If it hadn't been for Cody and Owen, we'd still be out there."

"Oh, Cody," Sara Jean wailed. "We had to send word of Ned as soon as we heard. Whatever are we going to do?"

Cody had hung back while the others hurried up in greeting. Now he stepped forward. "I'm going to look for him."

"Well, come inside first," Anna said. "There's a pot of stew and a whole platter of biscuits just waiting for hungry travelers." As she held the door for the others, she noticed Cody turn away. "Cody?" She was puzzled. "Aren't you coming?"

"No, ma'am. I just wanted to see the Spooners safely to your place. I can't stay here and fill my stomach while my brother's out there somewhere. It's time I started searching for him. Too many hours have already been wasted."

"Do you have any idea where he might be?" Sara Jean's voice trembled.

"No. But the sheriff mapped out the route they were supposed to take with the stagecoach. All I can do is follow the same trail.'' He turned away and pulled himself into the saddle.

When he had mounted, he paused for a moment while his gaze held Lizzy's.

She thought of all the things she should have said and never would. ''Take care of yourself, Cody. I know you'll find Ned.''

He touched a hand to the brim of his hat.

She watched as he turned his horse and headed down the wide road of town. And when his shadow blended into the night, she glanced at the stars, twinkling in a sky as black as velvet. ''Please,'' she whispered. ''Keep him safe.''

Shivering, she turned and let herself into the warmth of the widow's cozy house.

By the light of the moon Cody knelt and studied the tracks in the snow. The thing about a snowstorm was, it tended to keep people indoors, warm and dry. So the only people who ventured out had compelling reasons. The way he figured it, any people following the trail of the stagecoach probably knew about the gold shipment and decided even a snowstorm wasn't going to keep them from getting rich. That meant they were fools or desperate criminals.

He counted four horses. One of them had a distinctive circular groove in his right front hoof.

It looked like Whit had found a new band of gunmen ready to follow his lead.

With a chilling sense of foreboding, Cody hunched into his parka and urged his horse into a run.

Chapter Eighteen

On the windswept hills overlooking Commencement, the tracks had been obliterated by wind and snow. Cody had no way of knowing if the horsemen had come this way. But an inner sense told him they had.

He lifted his head, catching a faint whiff of wood smoke in the air. A fire meant that someone was nearby. He slid from the saddle and led his mount through the towering evergreens until, cresting a ridge, he spotted the chimney and part of a sagging wall of a deserted cabin. It was nearly buried beneath a drift of snow.

On a far ridge he saw a sudden blur of color. As he watched, a man darted from tree to tree, inching toward the cabin.

Peering through the snow, Cody made out the forms of several horsemen standing in the shelter of a row of trees. He felt the hair at the back of his neck begin to rise and knew that they were poised to attack whoever had taken shelter in that pitiful shack. Ned, he thought.

It had to be Ned. "Let him be alive," he prayed. "Let me be in time."

The men on the far ridge hadn't spotted him yet. That gave him the advantage of surprise. He tied his mount to a tree. Dropping to his stomach, he began to crawl through the snow toward the cabin.

As he slithered over half-buried boulders and crawled under snow-laden branches, he tried not to imagine what he might find. The thought of his brother lying bloodied and half-frozen flitted through his mind. He felt a band tighten around his heart.

His eyes narrowed as he fastened his grip on his rifle and continued forward.

When he reached the wall of the cabin, he crawled alongside until he found an opening. Shimmying through, he found himself staring into the muzzle of a rifle.

"Cody." Ned spoke his name on a rush of air he'd been holding. "Why didn't you announce yourself? I almost pulled this trigger."

"Thank God you're alive." Cody got to his feet and thought about pulling his brother close for a hug. But there was no time. There was never time. There'd been no time to say the things he'd been wanting to say when he left for the war. There was no time now.

"You've got company coming." Cody motioned toward the other wall. "Spotted a man sneaking among the trees. He's got three friends waiting up on the ridge."

Just then Cody noticed a man lying in the shelter of two sagging walls. Ned had wrapped his jacket around the man and was doing his best to stay warm in only a thin shirt. The remains of a fire smoldered in a crumbling fireplace. But it wasn't enough to heat the frosty air that poured through the shattered walls.

Seeing the direction of his gaze, Ned said, "That's Roy Waters, the driver of the stagecoach. When he keeled over, I had no choice but to stay with him. He fell clear out of the stage and landed on his head. I leapt out to save him. I was hoping the stage might make it back to town and alert someone that we were out on the trail." His voice lowered. "I think it's his heart, Cody. It's failing him."

Cody had to admire his brother's courage. Not many men would give up their only chance for safety and shelter to stay with a dying stranger. But Ned had always cared about all men. It was his most endearing virtue. However, at the moment, there was something more pressing than admiring Ned's virtues.

"Can he hold a gun?"

Ned shook his head. "He's barely alive."

"Then it looks like it's up to you and me. Those gunmen out there aren't going to wait."

Cody untied the sack of bullets from around his neck and handed some to Ned. "You take that door, I'll take the window. Hold your fire until they get careless. They think you two are alone here. And maybe wounded or dead. And they certainly don't know you're expecting them. That gives us the edge."

Ned nodded and moved toward the door.

The two brothers watched from their places of concealment as the four gunmen stealthily made their way down the snowy slopes toward the cabin. One of them brought up the rear, leading a horse and cart, to carry away the strongbox of gold that Ned had been hired to guard.

So, Cody thought as he studied the cart. This was what it always came down to with men like Whit. They wanted what other men had. Even at the cost of another man's life.

"Don't let it be Ned's," he prayed. "I'd rather die than see Ned's blood spilled for a box of gold."

At a signal from their leader, one of the gunmen strode forward and kicked in the door, shouting, "We've come for the gold."

As he stepped inside, he was shocked to find two men holding rifles aimed at him.

"Drop it," Ned commanded.

The man tossed down his gun and lifted his hands.

"What are you waiting for?" came a voice from outside. "Are they both dead?"

Cody nudged his rifle against the man's ribs. His voice was an angry hiss. "Answer him."

"It's all clear," the gunman called.

The other three strode confidently into the cabin, only to find two rifles trained on them. What might have been a massacre ended without a scuffle. The four gunmen dropped their weapons and were easily subdued.

A short time later, the four gunmen, hands securely tied, sat astride their horses while Ned and Cody lifted the wounded driver into the cart and wrapped him in Cody's furs.

"All right," Cody said, turning to his brother. "Now, where's the gold?"

Ned smiled. "We weren't carrying the gold shipment on the stage." He enjoyed the look of surprise on Cody's face, as well as the faces of the four gunmen. "I suggested that we send the gold ahead with a shipment of goods from North's Mercantile. I figured nobody would be expecting it, and the shipment would arrive without a hitch."

Cody studied his brother with new respect. "It was a fine idea. So your stagecoach was empty?"

"That's right."

"And you risked your life for nothing?"

Stung by his words, Ned said defensively, "We had to take the stage on its usual route. Otherwise the plan wouldn't have worked. Besides, I wouldn't say it was for nothing. We did catch four criminals."

Cody grabbed his brother by the front of the shirt and dragged him close. He thought about what had almost happened and the fear that still churned through his veins, and his words were harsher than he intended. "You damned fool. You'd risk your life for a shipment of gold? Or worse, for a decoy?" His eyes narrowed and his words sliced like a razor. "You have no business here, Ned. This is no life for you."

Pushing away from him, Ned's hands fisted. "And who are you to tell me about the life I'm leading? Look at you." His voice shook with fury. "Hiding on some mountaintop, afraid to even try to live like a human being again."

"At least I know what I am. I'm not trying to be something I can't be." Seeing his brother's fists, Cody lifted his own. "Come on, Ned. Do you want to fight me? Would that make you feel better?"

"Yes." Ned took a step closer, his fists raised. "I've been itching to fight you since the day you told me you were going off to war and ordered me to stay behind like a little kid with Grandmother."

"You still don't understand, do you? I didn't want to think about someone as fine as you being caught up in the horrors of war. I wanted you safe from that hell."

"What about what I wanted, Cody? Didn't you give any thought to that?"

"You were too young to think clearly about war. You had no idea what you were getting into. And look how you made your decision. Instead of hitting me, you went off and joined up with the Rebs." Cody gave a bitter laugh. "I guess that was one way to get even with me for leaving you."

"I didn't do it to get even, Cody. Don't you see? I had the same rights as you, to fight the same war you fought. I chose my side, you chose yours."

Cody's tone was bleak. "Well, it looks like neither of us won."

A moan from the man in the cart had them both dropping their hands. With a sheepish look Ned said, "I can't believe I'd put my own anger ahead of Roy's safety. We'd better get him back to town."

They mounted and began the slow trek to Commencement. Neither brother spoke during the entire journey. Each was lost in his own private thoughts. It was plain that their shouted words had not eased the hurt between them. If anything, the rift was wider than ever.

It was Owen North who came riding up the lane toward Mrs. Purdy's house, shouting the news.

"Ned and Cody Martin just arrived in town with Roy Waters and four gunmen."

Lizzy's heart nearly stopped as she threw open the front door. "Is anybody wounded?"

"Just Roy Waters. They brought him to Doc Simms's place in a cart. Everybody in town's gathering around to hear the news."

Lizzy felt her heart begin to beat again as her sister and little brother peered out from behind her.

"They're at the sheriff's now, locking up the gunmen," Owen said with a trace of awe. "Can you imagine? Four gunslingers, and the Martin brothers brought 'em in alone."

While Sara Jean and James expressed delight, Lizzy found herself fretting over the ominous term "Martin brothers." It made them sound like famous outlaws.

"Look," James called. "It's Ned and Cody."

Everyone spilled out the front door, watching as the two hitched their horses and stomped through the snow to the front porch.

"Oh, Ned, I just knew your brother would find you," Sara Jean shouted, running down the steps to greet them.

Ned's frown eased a little at the sight of her. But only a little. "I didn't need my big brother to come and save my neck. I was doing just fine without him."

"I didn't mean..." Sara Jean bit her lip. "I'm just so glad you're back." She caught his hand and led him up the steps.

"I've got supper going," Anna Purdy called from the doorway. "Don't either of you men think about leaving until you've joined us. You can tell us all about your adventure while you eat."

"I can't think of anything I'd like more, ma'am." Ned removed his hat and allowed Sara Jean to lead him past the others. As the door slammed behind them, Sara Jean could be heard exclaiming, "Why, you and your brother are heroes."

The tension between the two brothers was thick enough to cut. Sensing it, Lizzy stood silently on the porch, watching as Cody took great pains to tend to his horse.

Seeing the dark scowl on Cody's face and the wary way Lizzy watched him, Amos caught his grandson's hand and pulled him inside. "Come on, James. Let's wash up for supper."

"But I want to hear what Cody—"

"He'll tell us over supper."

When everyone had gone inside, Lizzy stood on the porch and watched as Cody slowly climbed the steps.

"You look tired," she said.

"I am. Or at least I was—" he touched a finger to her cheek "—until I laid eyes on you."

He had the strangest desire to carry her off to his cabin in the mountains and hide with her there, where no one would ever find them. Lord, he was tired. So tired. Only Lizzy could restore him.

"Was it bad?" she whispered.

He shook his head. "Not nearly as bad as I'd feared."

"Then why do you seem so sad?"

He forced a thin smile. "I'm just hungry, Lizzy. Hungry and tired. Come on." He held the door for her. "Time to face the widow Purdy's never-ending tongue."

"So you weren't carrying the gold after all?" Amos said between bites of the finest chicken and dumplings he'd ever tasted.

There was a real linen tablecloth on the table, and fine china and crystal, as well as candles in silver candlesticks.

"No, sir. And we were never really in any trouble. That is," Ned added sheepishly, "until Whit and his men tracked us to that cabin."

"It's a good thing Cody found you first." Sara Jean shot Cody a grateful smile.

Ned ducked his head and took a long time to butter a roll. Now that his temper was cooling, he was beginning to feel sorry for the way he'd reacted to Cody's help. He hadn't thanked him. In fact, he'd scorned his brother for interfering. He was behaving like a spoiled little kid, pretending he could have done it all himself. The truth was, without Cody's warning and Cody's rifle, he'd probably be lying dead at that cabin right now. And Roy Waters along with him.

"Yeah," Ned said softly. "It's a good thing." It was the closest he'd come to acknowledging Cody's help.

Across the table, Cody sat in silence. The thought of nearly coming to blows with his brother still rankled. How had it all come to this? When had they chosen opposing sides? And when had they forgotten how to forgive one another? How to love one another?

Maybe it was the war. Or maybe men just wanted something on which to blame all their shortcomings.

Everyone looked up at a loud knock on the door. Anna Purdy hurried to answer it. A moment later she trailed behind an important-looking man in a fine black suit and hat.

Ned jumped to his feet. "Mr. Wetherby." Remembering his manners, he said to the others, "This is the owner of the stage line." Knowing that Wetherby and Anna were acquainted, he handled the introductions of the others at the table. "Mr. Wetherby, this is the Spooner family. Amos, Sara Jean, Lizzy and James. And this is my brother, Cody."

When the man finished shaking hands with Amos and Cody, Ned asked, "Is something wrong?"

"Wrong? No, Ned. Something is very right. Everyone in town is talking about what you did. In fact, most of them are out in the street, exchanging gossip about you and your brother. It's the most exciting thing that's happened in our town for years. If an outlaw like Whit hadn't been stopped, he might have terrorized our people for years." His voice lowered. "I just talked to Roy Waters."

"How is he?"

"He's a very sick man. Doc Simms says if it wasn't for you, Roy would be dead. He's mighty grateful just to be alive. He told me how you stayed with him, and actually risked your own life for him. I'd like to give you this bonus, Ned, and ask if you'd be willing to take the stage run again tomorrow."

Ned seemed about to refuse when he saw the scowl on Cody's face. Though the thought of going back on the trail made his heart pound, he would never admit it to his brother. Something perverse in his nature made him say, "Why, that would be fine, Mr. Wetherby. I'll be there tomorrow. But you don't need to pay me any bonus."

"I insist." The man pressed a handful of bills into Ned's palm. "Thank you, Ned. I wish I had more brave men like you." He turned to Anna Purdy. "I'm sorry for interrupting your supper, ma'am. I'll just go out now and join the others in the street. They're eager to hear Ned's answer."

He nodded to everyone at the table, then followed Mrs. Purdy to the front door.

When she returned, she was beaming with pride. "Can you imagine? Everyone in town is talking about the men at my supper table."

The others seemed startled when Cody scraped back his chair. "Thanks for supper, ma'am."

"You're leaving? But you've hardly touched your meal."

"I have a long ride ahead of me."

"But it's late. Why don't you spend the night?"

"I've left my animals alone long enough."

Lizzy felt as if her heart had just been trampled. He was leaving. Without a word to her. Without a word to any of them.

"Cody. About the rest of those mustangs..." Ned began, but Cody cut him off.

"They're yours, Ned. You earned them." He barely glanced at his brother as he bid an abrupt goodbye and headed for the front door.

No one spoke as his footsteps sounded across the porch and down the steps.

James pushed away from the table and rushed to the window to watch as Cody pulled himself into the saddle.

Lizzy pretended to fetch her little brother. But it was only an excuse to stand beside him and watch. With every movement Cody made, she felt the knife slowly twist in her heart.

As Cody turned his horse and started down the wide lane, a voice, loud and taunting, broke the stillness.

"Cody Martin." The words were slightly slurred. "I hear you're the Yankee who thinks he's so fast with a gun."

There was muffled laughter, and then another loud voice shouted, "Let's see if this Yankee hero can stand up to a couple of real men."

Chapter Nineteen

Cody sat very still, deliberately keeping his hand away from the gun at his waist. His rifle was in a boot alongside the saddle. There was no way he could slip it out without being seen. And even if he could, there was no way he could win against men who were already holding their rifles aimed at his back.

He felt the icy trickle of sweat along his spine, which he always experienced in battle. Only a fool wouldn't be afraid of facing a madman with a gun. In this case, four madmen. But if there was no way out, he'd face them the same way he'd faced all of life's madness—with quiet dignity.

From the sound of their voices he knew that the men were liquored up and spoiling for a fight. Of course, none of them would be willing to face him alone. But when a group of drunks became a mob, they suddenly found their courage.

Very slowly he turned his mount until he was facing the men. They stood in a semicircle, their faces shadowed by wide-brimmed hats.

One of them was older than Amos. He spat a wad of tobacco and said, "It was some cowardly Yankee who burned my shed and stole my mule."

"Maybe it was him, Pa."

Cody turned his head to study the young man who had spoken. Under his piercing gaze the young man flushed and looked away.

"Got no use for Yankees," spat another. "We came here to get away from them. Let's keep this town pure."

The others muttered their agreement.

"I say we kill him. Fair and square." One man stepped forward, and Cody recognized the taunting voice as the first one who'd called him out. "You draw, Yankee. And if you're fast enough, maybe you'll live."

"Just you and me?" Cody's voice was low, dangerous as he climbed from the saddle.

The man stepped back a pace and glanced left and right to make certain that the others were still with him. "Hell, no. You're the hero, remember? You got to outdraw all of us."

"You call that fair and square?"

"As fair as any Yankee deserves."

They all laughed nervously.

The taunting voice hardened. "We've wasted enough time. You draw now, Yankee, or we'll shoot you anyway."

A voice, low and menacing behind him, caught Cody by surprise. "You're going to have to shoot this Reb, too."

The men whirled.

One of them called, "We got no fight with Rebs."

"You fight my brother, you fight me." Ned strode beyond the circle of men to stand beside Cody.

"Now just a minute..."

"No. No more time." Ned's voice was cold and flat. "My brother and I fought on different sides of the war because we each believed in a cause. But that can never change the way we feel about each other." He glanced toward his brother, who stood unmoving beside him. Then he turned to the men. "I love Cody. He's my brother. I'll stand against any man who threatens him. And if I have to, I'll die beside him."

Ned stunned the onlookers by tossing his rifle into the snow at his feet. "But I won't fight back. You'll have to gun down an unarmed man. I'm through with guns and fighting."

"What are you doing?" Cody asked through gritted teeth.

Ned's voice lowered. "I guess I'd rather die beside my brother than any other place I can think of."

While the men were still trying to decide whether or not to shoot an unarmed man, Amos strode into the circle, holding his rifle.

"Name's Amos Spooner of Georgia," he said with pride. "I gave my land and my only son for the Confederacy. But if I have to die, I'll by God die beside two of the finest men I've ever met." His voice swelled like a tent preacher's, reaching out to all those who stood, watchful and afraid. "And I'll tell you something else. Unless this town, and this whole country, learns that we aren't Yankee and Reb anymore, but just plain men, we won't be worth the powder it takes to blow us all to the hereafter.''

The crowd began to mutter among themselves.

Stirred by his words, Mr. Wetherby stepped forward, holding a small black pistol in his hand. "Well said, Mr. Spooner. I salute you." He turned toward the others who had stood on the fringe of the crowd, watching in silence. "Well, folks, what do you say? Is this a town of Yankee and Reb, or a town of honest, honorable men seeking a better life?"

Owen North stepped forward, followed by a man who could only be his father. They carried identical rifles; wore identical frowns on handsome, square-jawed faces.

"I want my son to grow up in a town of honorable men," Mr. North said. "That's why we named this place Commencement. After seeing this land we love torn apart by war, this was our chance for a new beginning."

Nodding, Doc Simms was joined by the blacksmith, who said firmly, "It's time for every man in this town to take a stand."

Soon, all the men in the town stood on either side of Cody and Ned.

The leader of the four who had taunted them lowered his rifle. "Looks like we made a mistake."

"A big mistake," the sheriff shouted, racing along the street after having been roused from his office by one of the townspeople. "Go home now," he called, "and sleep it off. But I'll expect the four of you in my office in the morning."

"Why?" one of them shouted. "What's the charge?"

"No charge," the sheriff said. "I just think we'll come to an understanding. That is, if you want to continue to make your home in Commencement."

The men nodded and crept away under cover of darkness. By morning, sober and suffering the effects of their whiskey, they would be ashamed of their behavior.

"I'd like to buy a round at the saloon," Mr. Wetherby called.

With shouts of relief and laughter, the men trailed him toward a building in the center of town.

When they were gone, Lizzy and Sara Jean, along with Anna Purdy and James, rushed from the porch where they'd been watching and hurried toward the three men who stood alone.

"It's my turn to thank you, Ned," Cody said softly. "You just saved my life."

"It's about time I did something right. You were always the one who took charge of everything. All I ever had to do was follow along."

"That's not true." Cody turned to stare into his brother's eyes and realized that they stood head to head, shoulder to shoulder. When he hadn't been looking, his brother had grown into manhood.

"You know it is. When Dad died, you became my second father. You were like him, you know," Ned said softly. "Tough, fair, demanding. You always set yourself the hardest tasks. You even followed him to West Point. I just knew I'd never be able to keep up."

Cody placed a hand on his brother's shoulder. "I didn't want you to. I wanted better for you, Ned, than having to live by the sword."

"I know. At least, I know that now. But at the time, I couldn't help being a little resentful."

"You were always—special, Ned. You had the best qualities of both our parents. You've always been kind and gentle and noble. You know how to speak to the heart of people."

Ned looked down. "I haven't been doing such a good job lately."

"It isn't too late."

"No." Ned looked up to meet his brother's eyes. "It isn't, is it?"

He laughed, and Cody's mouth curved into a warm smile. For a moment, while the others watched in puzzlement, the two men merely grinned at each other. Then, with a laugh, they fell into each other's arms and embraced.

"You meant it, didn't you?" Cody whispered. "You weren't going to pick up that rifle."

"I meant all of it. I wasn't going to fight. But I was willing to die beside you."

"You're crazy. You know that?"

"I know. It's another quality we share."

They were still laughing when they turned toward the others.

With his arm around his brother's shoulder, Cody extended a hand to Amos. "I haven't properly thanked you, Amos. That was a fine thing you said, about the country not being Yankee and Reb anymore, but just men."

Amos cleared his throat in agitation. "I meant what I said."

"You mean Cody isn't a Yankee anymore, Grand-pop?"

Amos tousled his grandson's hair and grinned as the others started to laugh. Then he knelt down and said in a serious tone, "I guess I needed to be reminded that the war's over. It's time to start thinking about living in peace. A good man's a good man, no matter what part of the country he comes from. You remember that, boy."

"Yes, sir."

"Do you think we could go back inside and have dessert now?" Anna asked.

"Depends," Amos said, bursting with relief now that the tension was ended. "What did you make?"

"Baked apples with sugar and heavy cream. And there's apple cider to warm us."

"Woman, you sure do know how to spoil a man."

"I know," she said simply. "So come inside and let me do what I do best."

The others needed no coaxing to hurry indoors.

When they were once again seated around the table, Ned surprised everyone by saying, "If you don't mind, I'd like to offer a prayer."

While the others bowed their heads, Cody glanced across the table and watched as his brother closed his eyes and murmured, "Thank You for bringing us all to this place. I guess we needed to be reminded that when we lose our way in the darkness, Your path is there, waiting to lead us home."

The others glanced up, puzzled by his words. But when Ned glanced at Cody, the two men merely smiled.

"So you've found your way?" Cody muttered.

"Yes. And so will you."

"Whatever are you talking about, Ned Martin?" Sara Jean checked her sleeping infant and took the seat beside him.

Ned picked up his spoon and realized that the others at the table deserved an explanation.

"When the war broke out, I had just finished my education. But I decided that, because of the suffering of those around me, I had no right to follow my heart until all men were free to follow theirs."

He refused Mrs. Purdy's offer of cider and sipped strong, hot coffee. Glancing up, he said, "Now, I think, after following so many twisted trails, the Lord led me to Commencement." He turned to Anna Purdy. "You said the people were hoping for a preacher?"

She nodded.

"I'm a graduate of divinity school." He felt a swell of pride and humility as he admitted aloud for the first time, "I'm an ordained minister."

When everyone had recovered from their surprise, Amos chuckled. "Here I was, leading you in prayer, when all the time, you should have been leading me."

"No, sir," Ned said with quiet humility. "I needed to be reminded that there were still men who trusted in the Lord. After all I'd seen in the war, I was beginning to think that guns were the only way to survive. Until tonight, I'm ashamed to say that I was ready to turn my back on all my training and try to live by my wits and wiles alone." He lowered his gaze to his plate, no longer hungry for the sweets that had only moments ago tempted him. "It was your simple faith that restored me. And my love for Cody." He turned to his brother. "When I thought I might lose you without ever telling you how I felt, I knew I had to do something desperate."

"That was about as desperate as I've ever seen." Cody shook his head. "When I saw you toss down that rifle, my heart nearly quit on me."

"Yours." Ned chuckled. "My own was pounding so hard I figured those men could all hear it."

"And I thought I was the only one who was shaking in his boots," Amos admitted with a laugh.

"You mean you were all scared?" James asked with a trace of awe.

Cody's gaze met his across the table. "Son, there's nothing shameful about a healthy dose of fear. Just as long as a man does what he knows is right, no matter how scared he is."

"I was afraid, too," Sara Jean admitted, touching a tentative hand to Ned's sleeve. "Afraid I was going to see you shot down before my very eyes."

"Let's talk about happier things." Anna scraped back her chair and led them toward the parlor, where a cozy fire burned. "I can't wait to tell the rest of the townsfolk that we have a preacher," she added excitedly.

As the others left the room, Lizzy started after them. Cody placed a hand on her arm to stop her.

Startled by the warmth of his touch, she waited, refusing to meet his eyes.

He stood behind her, staring at her bowed head. In the light of the candles her hair was the color of flame. He longed to touch it, but instead, he curled his hands into fists at his sides.

"I have to leave now, Lizzy. But before I say goodbye to the others, I wanted to say goodbye to you here, alone."

Her head came up slowly and she half turned, being careful to keep her gaze averted. She was afraid to look at him, afraid he would read too much emotion in her eyes.

"I'm glad you and Ned have made your peace with each other, Cody."

"I am, too." But it wasn't Ned he wanted to talk about. "You realize that I have to go back now. I can't wait until you leave in the morning, even though I wish we could have this last night together." He'd give anything, anything for one last night in her arms. "The mustangs, the mare and her foal, need me."

"I understand."

She started to walk away, and he caught her by the wrist.

He felt a terrible sense of frustration. Why, when she was being so damnably understanding, did he feel so miserable?

"I have no choice, Lizzy, but to go."

"I know, Cody."

He shocked them both by swearing savagely. Catching her roughly by the shoulders, he turned her into his arms. He wanted to shake her. He wanted to... He wanted to crush her against him and kiss her until she was breathless. Until they were both breathless and weak and clinging. The thought of it had him trembling.

"Lizzy. Guess what!"

James came bursting into the room and skidded to a halt as Lizzy and Cody stepped apart. The blazing look in Cody's eyes startled him. He'd never seen Cody look like this before.

Lizzy took a deep breath to calm her pounding heart. "What is it, James?"

"Grandpop says we're not leaving in the morning."

"But I thought..."

"Remember when you said that Christmas comes even way out here?"

Lizzy nodded. Had it only been weeks ago? It seemed like years.

"Mrs. Purdy says tomorrow is Christmas Eve. And she says every year, Commencement has a dance on Christmas Eve. And Grandpop just said we were going to stay for the dance. Isn't that great, Lizzy?"

"Yes." Christmas Eve. It didn't seem possible. With all that had happened, she had lost track of time.

She glanced at Cody and swallowed back a wave of pain at the thought of him alone on his mountain while everyone else was celebrating at a festive dance.

"Can you come to the dance, Cody?" James asked.

Cody struggled to keep his tone flat. "I don't see how I can, son. I'll be riding half the night just to make it back to my cabin. I'd have to start out again by noon, if I wanted to be here in time. That wouldn't leave much time for my chores."

"But you could do it, Cody." The little boy was embarrassed by the tears that sprang to his eyes. He wiped them away with the backs of his hands. "I know you could."

Feeling calmer now, Cody knelt and touched a hand to the boy's shoulder. "I don't like to make promises I might not be able to keep, James. But I'll tell you this. I'll try to come back."

James met his look and sniffed back his tears. Lizzy always said Christmas was a time of magic. And if he wished hard enough . . .

As Lizzy and Cody made their way to the parlor, James followed more slowly. Walking to the fireplace, he wrapped his arms around Beau's neck. He watched Cody shaking hands with the others and speaking in soft tones about a safe journey. He watched as Cody and Ned came together in a fierce embrace. And then Cody called to Beau, and the dog's tail was thumping furiously as he raced ahead of his master to the door.

James watched as Cody spoke stiffly to Lizzy, and she responded in equally stiff, awkward terms. And as the others watched Cody leave, James continued to study his sister's face.

Were those tears? They couldn't be, James decided. Lizzy never cried. But as he watched, she quickly brushed her hand across her eyes. In the firelight he saw the moisture glistening on her lashes.

His chubby hands tightened into fists. Nobody had the right to make Lizzy cry. Not even the man who'd become his hero. He'd find out what Cody did to make Lizzy cry. And then, even though Cody meant the world to him, he'd make him pay for it. Because, next to Ma and Pa, Lizzy was the most special person in his young life.

Chapter Twenty

There was a quiet, expectant hush in the air as Commencement awoke on Christmas Eve morning.

All day the townspeople buzzed with the news that a preacher was in their midst.

Shortly after breakfast, Mr. Wetherby and the sheriff paid a call on Mrs. Purdy's star boarder.

"We haven't much to offer you," Mr. Wetherby said solemnly. "Without a church, the best we can do is the back room of North's Mercantile. That's where the dance will be held tonight. It's big enough to accommodate the families of Commencement, but we realize it's not a proper house of worship."

Ned smiled. "The Lord was born in a humble place, Mr. Wetherby. But He promised us that wherever two or more are gathered in His name, He'll be among us. I don't think He'd be offended by the back room of North's Mercantile."

Their relief was evident on their faces.

"As soon as the snows melt, we'll start building a real church," the sheriff said. "And a parsonage for you, if you'll agree to stay on as pastor."

"I'd be honored," Ned said.

The men offered their handshakes, then hurried off to tell the townsfolk about their agreement.

As snowflakes danced past the window, Anna Purdy and Lizzy locked themselves in the kitchen, indulging in an orgy of cooking and baking. Lizzy refused to look at the snow. That would be an admission that another storm was blowing in. A storm that would prevent Cody from returning to town for the dance. A storm that would prevent him from seeing her one last time before she was forced to move on.

Each time James tried to sneak into the kitchen, he was gently shooed away. Each time he asked to taste the gingerbread cake, the spicy cookies, the apple muffins, he was rebuked. Disappointed, he went in search of Sara Jean.

Sara Jean, so excited about the dance she could hardly sit still, carried her sleeping infant to her bedroom, where she ripped the seams from one of her mother's old dresses and made it over to fit her newer, slimmer figure. When James tried to watch, she ordered him away.

Then, when the baby was fed and changed, Sara Jean left her in Grandpop's care while she slipped off to the mercantile. For a little while James was content to watch the way Jobeth lifted her tiny fists and made strange little ovals with her mouth as she stretched and yawned.

"She's snagged you, too, hasn't she?" Amos whispered, watching the way James hovered over the blanketed bundle.

James looked up in surprise. "I don't understand."

In a gentler tone Grandpop said, "That's the thing about babies. They're so helpless. And they can't do a gosh darn thing. But somehow, they sneak up on you, and before you know it, you're in love. You love her, don't you?"

"I guess I do."

It was hard to believe he could fall under the spell of such a tiny creature. But each day she drew him into her web, scrunching up her eyes and bleating like a lamb, or smiling that tiny, ethereal smile that Lizzy said was caused by the touch of angels.

"She'll always look up to you, James. To Jobeth, you'll always be her big brave Uncle James."

The little boy's heart swelled with pride. He was no longer the baby of the family. He was somebody's big brave uncle.

By the time the baby had settled down to sleep, Sara Jean had returned. She carried the baby away to the bedroom with orders not to be disturbed until supper.

James followed his grandfather out to the shed behind Mrs. Purdy's house. But when he tried to follow him inside, Amos shoved him away.

"Secrets, boy," he said tersely. "This is a day of secrets. Go on now. I have things to do."

Discouraged, James kicked at a stone and watched as it skimmed across the road and landed in a snowbank. Digging it out with the toe of his boot, he kicked it again, sending it flying through the air until it settled a short distance up the road. Again he kicked it; again it skimmed forward before sinking into fresh snow. He kept this up until, when he looked, he was standing in front of the mercantile. With his nose pressed to the window he studied the rows of shelving filled with every sort of imaginable goods.

Stepping inside, he walked among the rows, allowing his fingers to roam the coarse woolens, slide over the smooth satins. He stared at the fancy bonnets, the high-topped shoes, the bolts of fine fabric. He stopped when he heard Ned's voice.

"This will make a fine place for Sunday services. And you can pass the word tonight at the dance that, tomorrow morning, Christmas morning, I'll conduct the town's first service."

Peering around a corner, James saw Ned shaking hands with Mr. North.

As Ned rounded the corner, he nearly collided with the little boy.

"James." He stooped until their eyes were level. "Were you looking for me?"

James thought about it a minute. Maybe he had been, and just hadn't known. "Do you have time to talk to me?" he asked.

Ned gave him a gentle smile, and the little boy was reminded of Cody's eyes, Cody's smile.

"Let's walk," he said. "Sometimes it's easier for men to talk when they're walking."

Cody awoke in the loft and lay a minute, listening to the wind whistle around the roof. He sat up, pressing a hand to his back. The ride to the cabin had been long and cold. And though he'd started a fire, it must have gone out. The cabin was cold enough to turn his breath to frosty plumes.

He climbed down the ladder and shivered as he waited for the kindling to catch fire. Finally, as a thin line of flame ate along the bark of a fresh log, he placed the blackened pot over the fire and struggled into his clothes.

A short time later he ate a meal of cold meat and biscuits, washed down by bitter coffee, and started his morning chores.

The mare was glad to see him. As he rubbed her nose, he laughed aloud at the antics of the foal. His voice sounded hollow in the big barn and he glanced around, wishing for someone to share the moment. And the laughter.

He mucked out the stalls and spread clean straw, then filled the troughs with food and water and headed out to the corral. When the mustangs had been fed and watered, he bent to the task he had set for himself.

He was a fool, he thought, as he smoothed and shaped the wood and fitted the metal pieces he'd bartered from the blacksmith. What he ought to do was forget his honor and his foolish sense of pride and beg Lizzy to stay. Yes, beg. Or plead, or whatever it would take to convince her that he needed her more than her family needed her.

He thought of the Spooners. With a new baby, Sara Jean certainly couldn't be much help on a journey to California. And Amos wouldn't admit it, but his energy was flagging along with his eyesight. And James was just a little boy. Hell, he thought angrily. Who was he kidding? The only one who'd get them all the way to California was Lizzy. Without her they had no chance. To ask her to stay, when he had nothing to offer her except a life of hardship, was worse than selfish. It would destroy an entire family.

When he stepped from the barn hours later, he was surprised to see that darkness had descended early. And with it, another blizzard.

It was just as well, he consoled himself as he made his way to the cabin for a supper of more cold meat and biscuits. Now the decision had been taken out of his hands. He would get no more chances to see the Spooners before they left Commencement. And someday, if he was lucky, Lizzy would become just a dim memory. And the pain of his loss would fade to a dull ache.

Anna Purdy had produced a round wooden tub, which she set up in a corner of the kitchen. When it was filled with warm water, she and Sara Jean and Lizzy took turns bathing.

Lizzy thought she'd never felt anything so wonderful as she dipped a cup into the water and let it flow over her soap-covered hair. She had forgotten the pure luxury of warm water, soap and a steamy room.

Here in this pleasant oasis, she could pretend that there was no snowstorm outside. There was no cold. There was only this room, and the fragrance of perfumed soaps.

She wouldn't let herself think about a snow-covered mountain, and a barn that smelled of new wood, and a cabin tucked away among the snowdrifts.

Wrapped in towels and sheets, the three women turned the kitchen over to Amos and James, while they hurried up the stairs to Anna's big bedroom.

They took turns combing each other's hair and fussing with fancy hairstyles. With strips of torn rags Lizzy coaxed Sara Jean's fine blond hair into fat ringlets held back from her face with pretty blue ribbons.

The two sisters combed Anna's long, white hair and plaited it into a neat braid, which they twisted around her head like a coronet.

"You look as regal as a queen," Lizzy said.

The older woman studied her reflection in the mirror and gave a smile of approval. "It's very pretty. I think I like it better than my old style."

"It's your turn, Lizzy."

When Sara Jean and Anna began fussing over Lizzy's hair, she felt a sudden sharp, searing pain around her heart as a vision of Cody brushing her hair slipped unbidden into her mind.

"Hold still," Sara Jean commanded. "Lizzy, what's wrong with you?"

"Nothing." She took a deep breath and forced the image aside. It was Christmas Eve. She would not allow anything to spoil this day for the others.

"Oh, Lizzy," Anna sighed. "It would be a shame to hide this hair in a simple knot. You must wear it long and loose tonight." She had a sudden thought. "And I have the perfect combs." Rummaging through her bureau, she turned with a triumphant smile. "These were my mother's." The two girls gave a gasp of appreciation at the two combs, inlaid with mother-of-pearl.

"I couldn't wear these, Anna. They're far too lovely."

"Don't be silly. They're just a loan. Besides, I can't wear them since my hair went gray. They're lost among all those silver threads. But against these burnished tresses..." Her voice trailed off as she positioned them and stood back to admire her work.

"Oh, Lizzy," Sara Jean whispered. "You have to wear them. They'll be so perfect with the dress I made you."

"Dress?" Lizzy was mystified.

Sara Jean hurried across the hall to her room and returned with a long, green velvet gown.

"But this was destroyed in the fire," Lizzy said, her eyes wide with disbelief.

"I salvaged it," Sara Jean admitted. "Along with several other gowns I thought I might be able to sell." She brought a second gown from behind her back.

Lizzy caught her breath at the midnight blue gown. "That was Ma's."

Sara Jean nodded. "I made it over to fit me."

"And you kept it a secret all this time?"

Sara Jean blushed and stared at the floor. "I know I haven't been much help on this journey. You had to do the work for both of us. But I thought, after I had the baby and we found a new home, that I could set up a little business making over other women's clothes."

"If this is an example of your work," Anna said, "you could certainly please every woman in Commencement."

"You think so? Did you hear that, Lizzy?" The younger woman's eyes sparkled with pleasure.

Lizzy hugged her sister. "You've always been a marvel with needle and thread. But, Sara Jean, I want you to know I never minded doing your work. You were having a baby. That was more important than chopping wood or fixing a wagon."

"Maybe. But I felt like I was a burden because I couldn't help." She felt her cheeks redden. "Do you like your present?"

"I love it." With help from Sara Jean and Anna, Lizzy slipped into the gown. When she turned to look at herself in the looking glass, she was astonished at the beautiful woman looking back at her.

Lizzy and Anna helped Sara Jean into the blue gown and then the sisters helped Anna into her best dress, a black and silver gown with a little black jacket.

When they were all ready, Anna drew the two young women into her embrace and whispered, "You'll never know what this has meant to me. I've been alone for such a long time. I feel like the Lord has suddenly blessed me with two wonderful daughters. And a little granddaughter." She laughed, picking up Jobeth from the middle of the big bed.

With Anna cradling the baby to her heart, the three women made their way downstairs to the parlor. Amos and Ned, wearing dark frock coats, turned from the window where they had been carrying on an earnest conversation.

"Oh, my" was all Amos could manage to say when he caught sight of Anna and his two granddaughters.

"Sara Jean." Ned started forward, then seemed to catch himself. "All of you ladies look lovely."

Lizzy glanced at her sister, whose cheeks were bright with two round spots of color.

"Here, Lizzy," Anna said. "You hold Jobeth while I fetch some elderberry wine. Amos, I think this calls for a celebration. Would you like to help me?"

As the two headed for the kitchen, Lizzy caught sight of James standing in the doorway.

"Why, James, don't you look fine."

The little boy looked uncomfortable in his long-sleeved white shirt of fine lawn and a pair of short pants. "Mrs. Purdy said these once belonged to her son." He tugged on the shorts and nearly stumbled in the stiff, high-topped shoes. "I'd rather have my old britches."

Lizzy swallowed her laughter. She figured it wouldn't do to tell him how adorable he looked. Little boys didn't think much of cute or adorable. James was already trying so hard to be manly. He glanced at Sara Jean and Ned, who were smiling into each other's eyes without saying a word. "What's wrong with them?"

"Nothing," Lizzy said softly. "Nothing at all."

Anna and Amos returned with a tray of crystal glasses and a bottle of dark wine.

"I haven't tasted this wine since my husband passed on," Anna said, offering a glass to each of them. "But

I want you to know what it's meant to me to have you folks here. This big old house has never felt more alive, more like a home, than it does tonight." She lifted her glass and said, "If God directs all our footsteps, then I'm grateful that He brought you here to me. I was feeling old and tired and useless. And look at me now. Why, I feel young and alive again." She laughed and said, "I'd better stop talking, or we'll never get to taste this wine. So here's to the Spooner family. You've become like my own. And to Ned Martin, who's bringing the word of God to Commencement."

She touched her glass and drank, and the others did the same.

"Now we'd better go," Amos said when he'd drained his glass. "We don't want to miss any of that good food."

While Amos brought the wagon around to the door, the others went to the kitchen, where a table was piled high with trays of food wrapped in linens. Even James carried a tray to the wagon. Then they all piled into the back, while Anna sat up front with Amos for the short ride to North's Mercantile.

The street was crowded with carts and wagons and sleighs. From miles around people came for the rare opportunity to eat and dance and visit with neighbors they might not see again for many months.

Though she knew better, Lizzy found herself scanning the horses for a glimpse of Cody's mount. She warned herself not to allow the disappointment to spoil her evening. When she saw that Cody's horse was not at the hitching rail, she scolded herself for such foolishness. Snow hung like a thick veil over the countryside. This fresh snowfall would add hours to an already difficult journey. Only a fool would attempt such a trip in the darkness.

Inside the back room of the mercantile, Anna Purdy knew everyone. And everyone knew about her guests. While they clucked over the new baby and fussed over Amos's fine family, their greatest enthusiasm and their greatest curiosity was reserved for Ned Martin.

"So you're the new preacher."

"I hear there's going to be a Christmas service."

"Will you be staying with the widow Purdy until the new parsonage is built?"

"Is there a Mrs. Martin yet?"

Ned was especially pleased to see the stagecoach driver, Roy Waters, sitting beside Doc Simms.

"I've been waiting to thank you," Roy Waters said loudly, causing heads to turn.

The two men shook hands and Roy added, "I never thought I'd live to see another day. And here I am at a Christmas dance."

"Will you be able to go back to work?"

"Doc says I can take a desk job in a few weeks. But it looks like I won't be driving a stage anymore." The older man shook his head. "You could have knocked me over with a feather when Doc told me the young man who rode shotgun on my run was an ordained minister. You sure had me fooled."

"I guess I had myself fooled, too," Ned admitted.

"Now I want you to meet my wife and sons," Roy said.

When the introductions had been made, and Lizzy's head was swimming from all the new names and faces, she took the baby from Sara Jean's arms and found a quiet corner where she could sit and watch.

After so many months on the trail, she had forgotten how much noise a crowd of this size could make. Though she had lived in a big city, she had been away too long. She found herself yearning for the pristine wilderness of Cody's land, then scolded herself for such foolish fantasies.

She watched as the men and women moved along the tables groaning under the weight of all that food. And though she knew it would only cause more disappointment, she found herself studying every tall figure for the one she most wanted to see. Each time a dark head turned, she felt the sudden tug at her heart until she realized it wasn't Cody.

In no time it looked like a swarm of locusts had gone through the food, devouring everything in its path.

A bearded gentleman picked up a fiddle. A plump lady played a guitar with one string missing. A thin young boy began to play a mouth organ.

As soon as the music started, couples moved onto the floor and began circling. Lizzy tapped her toes and smiled as Amos and Anna moved easily to the music. It was plain that Grandpop's knee wasn't paining him. At least, for tonight.

Ned bowed before Sara Jean and led her to the dance floor. When he took her in his arms and began to move with her, the look on her face said more than any words. Their faces were close together, their lips almost touching as they whispered and smiled. When the music ended, they continued waltzing until, faces aflame, they suddenly moved apart. But moments later, when another song started, they came together and began dancing once more.

Halfway through the evening, Sara Jean took a squalling Jobeth to a quiet corner where she could feed her. Relieved of her burden for the moment, Lizzy walked to the table and accepted a cup of punch.

"Are you having fun?" Anna asked.

"Oh, yes." Lizzy sipped her punch and watched the parade of sight and sound and color.

Many of the men, she noted, stepped outside every so often, where, it was rumored, there was a jug of liquor. Out of deference to the ladies and to the new reverend, they were discreet.

James had made friends with a boy and girl who looked to be close in age to him. The boy was a head taller and not at all shy. The girl, with long glossy dark curls and a sweet smile, trailed James like a shadow.

When the music started up again James hurried over to Lizzy. "Will you dance with me?"

She couldn't help but smile at his sweet gesture. "Of course I will."

Placing her left hand on his shoulder and her right hand in his, she moved with him in a slow circular pattern around the floor.

"Do you think Cody will come to the dance?" James asked.

"No, James." Lizzy tried to keep her smile in place. She hadn't expected it to hurt this much. "It's just too far for Cody to ride."

"But he said he'd try."

"And you know he would if he could. But with this new storm..."

At the look on her little brother's face she stopped. "James, what's wrong?"

"It's..." He swallowed, unable to speak.

Concerned, Lizzy turned. And found herself staring into the dark, piercing eyes of Cody Martin.

Chapter Twenty-One

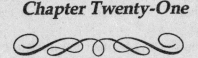

Lizzy wondered how her heart could beat this fast and not leap clear out of her throat.

"You look—different." She wanted to add how handsome he looked, but she couldn't find the words.

He had shaved his beard. Now, for the first time, she could see the firm chin, the perfectly chiseled nose, the slightly sensuous lips. If he had been ruggedly handsome before, he was now even more so. She thought her chest might explode from the pounding going on inside.

His dark, perfectly tailored jacket and pants would have been suitable for any important big-city gala. Here in Commencement, he was the best-dressed man in the room, attesting to the fact that he had once lived the life of a wealthy gentleman. But all the fine clothes in the world couldn't camouflage the muscles of his arms or the calluses on his hands, the signs that he was now a man who pitted himself against the forces of nature. There was still the look of a rugged mountain man about him.

"And you look—beautiful." She was so dazzling she took his breath away. But he had never been a man of words. He'd always left such things to his younger brother. The poets of the Bible would have called her a vision of perfection, a feast for the eyes, a song written on his heart. Cody could only call her beautiful. And mean it.

He studied the way her hair fell forward over one shoulder and spilled down the bodice of the green velvet gown. Glints of green sparkled in her eyes. Eyes that held him so that he couldn't see anyone else in the room.

The couples swirled around them, but they stood, staring at each other, unable to move, unable to hear the music.

"I thought—with the snow..." All the things she was thinking, all the things she was feeling, churned inside her. But all that came out were a few babbling phrases. "I didn't expect to see you tonight."

"When I saw the snow, I didn't plan on coming. But I knew it would be our last chance..." He opened his arms as if awakening from a deep sleep. "Lizzy, will you dance with me?"

She moved into his arms and had to fight a desire to weep. Though she had tried so hard to deny it, this was what she wanted. Cody was all she ever wanted.

Together they began to circle the floor.

"I was afraid you wouldn't know me without my beard."

Tentatively she touched a finger to his clean-shaven chin. "I would know you anywhere."

At her touch he felt a slow, simmering flame begin to flicker along his spine. All day he'd felt so alone, so empty. And now, holding her, touching her, he was alive again.

This was what had driven him to leave the warmth of his cabin and brave the blizzard. This one last chance to be with her, to hear her voice, to bask in the warmth of her smile.

He had to pull himself back each time someone from town stopped him to offer a greeting. With Lizzy in his arms he paused, made small talk, then moved on, eager to lose himself in her again.

They greeted Amos and Anna and grinned at James, who abruptly ducked away to rejoin his little friends.

They greeted Sara Jean and Ned, and the two brothers took a moment to embrace. But it was clear that Ned was just as eager to return his attentions to Sara Jean as Cody was to return to Lizzy. After all, it was Christmas Eve, and for this one night, the cares of the world could be forgotten.

And so they returned to the dance floor and began to move, eyes staring into eyes, lips curved into warm smiles.

Cody felt the tap on his shoulder and was pulled from his fantasies as Amos said, "I haven't danced with my granddaughter yet. Do you mind if we switch partners?"

Reluctantly, Cody and Lizzy moved apart. As Lizzy whirled off in her grandfather's arms, she nearly laughed aloud when she saw Anna Purdy take Cody's hand and heard the widow's voice.

"Why, Cody Martin, I declare I hardly knew you. If the women of Commencement knew what a handsome man was hiding beneath all those bushy whiskers, they'd have been out to your place with sheep shears."

Cody found himself staring across the room at the long column of Lizzy's throat revealed by the modest neckline, and the swell of her breasts beneath the lush green velvet. Her waist was so tiny, his hands itched to circle it. He watched her hips sway as she moved to the music and felt his throat grow tight. He knew intimately the body beneath that gown. The thought tormented him.

"You're awfully quiet tonight, Cody." Anna followed the direction of his gaze. In a low voice she said, "She is beautiful, isn't she?"

He shifted his gaze to her, and Anna smiled. "I'd have to be blind not to notice the way you feel about Lizzy Spooner."

"She's a fine woman." He met her look squarely. "She deserves a fine life."

"I see." Anna, always so talkative, found herself at a loss for words. But her mind was working overtime. From the tone of his voice, she surmised that Cody thought it would somehow be dishonorable to ask Lizzy to share his humble life in the wilderness. And being a man of honor, Cody Martin would let her go without a word before he would speak of the things in his heart.

Life could be so complicated. Anna thought back to her own youth and was swamped by memories of painful bouts of shyness and uncertainty. If only there were some way to ease young people through the maze. Unfortunately, everyone had to find his own way. As for herself, she had no desire to be young again. She much preferred the life she had now. But there were things she could still wish for.

If she could have but one wish this Christmas, she thought, it would be that these lively people could continue to share her life. Commencement would be poorer without the Spooner family.

Amos and Lizzy stopped beside them, interrupting Anna's thoughts, and Amos handed his granddaughter over to Cody.

"I'd like to finish the dance with this lovely lady," Amos said, taking Anna into his arms. With a peal of laughter they whirled away.

The instant Cody's arms were around her, Lizzy felt the flare of heat.

"Did you miss me?"

He looked into her eyes and she could read the surprise there. "Are you flirting, Miss Spooner?"

"I believe I am." She surprised even herself. "Do you mind?"

"Not at all." He drew her close and executed a perfect waltz turn. "In fact, I think I like it. It's a side of you I haven't seen often enough."

"It's a side of me I didn't know I had until I met you."

Lizzy wondered if her feet even touched the floor as she moved and dipped and whirled. She knew only that she had never been happier in her whole life. She was wrapped in Cody's arms, and they moved in perfect rhythm. The night had taken on a special glow.

She wouldn't think about tomorrow, or where their journey would finally take them. Tonight, held firmly against Cody's chest, his lips just inches from hers, she moved with him and allowed herself to imagine that the night, and the magic, would never end.

"This will be the last dance, folks."

Lizzy wondered if her disappointment was revealed on her face.

As the fiddler began to play a slow waltz, Cody caught Lizzy's hand and whirled her onto the dance floor. But before they had taken more than five steps, he waltzed her through a darkened doorway. When her eyes adjusted to the dim light, she was surprised to find that they were in the mercantile, standing between a shelf loaded with bolts of fabric and a shelf lined with jars and cans of food.

"Cody, we're missing the last dance."

"No, we aren't." He gathered her close and began to move, slowly, slowly, his lips pressed to her temple.

She felt a tiny ribbon of pleasure curl along her spine at the intimacy of their setting. Or was it the nearness of him?

She knew he could feel the wild, unsteady rhythm of her pulse. And though she didn't want any words to spoil this moment, there was so much she still wanted to tell him. If she didn't speak now, he would be gone. And all the things she'd wanted to say would be lost forever.

"I'm glad you came to the dance, Cody."

"I couldn't stay away. Lord knows I tried. But I had to come."

"You tried—" she pushed a little away, so that she could see his face "—to stay away?"

He was frowning.

With an angry hiss he drew her close again and began to move to the music.

Once more she pushed away. "Cody?"

"Let it go, Lizzy." His voice was low, angry.

"I don't understand."

"There's nothing to understand. I didn't want to come tonight. I thought we'd both be better off if we didn't have to put ourselves through this again."

"I see." She started to turn away.

He caught her roughly by the arm. "No, you don't see."

She lifted her head and met his gaze. "Why did you come, then?"

"I decided that, no matter what the pain later, I needed to see you this one last time." He brought both hands to her shoulders and dragged her close. Lowering his mouth to hers, he muttered against her lips, "To have this last taste of you to carry with me."

His kiss spoke of hunger and need as his lips devoured her. He wanted to be gentle, but his mouth ravaged hers and his hands were almost bruising as they moved over her.

He had thought of nothing but Lizzy on the long ride through treacherous snowbanks. And now that she was here in his arms, he felt half-crazy with the need for her.

"Lizzy, how I've missed you." He held her a little away, allowing his gaze to burn over her. Was this the ragged little waif he'd rescued from wolves? "Who would have ever thought," he whispered, "that the heavens would deposit an angel in the middle of a blizzard?"

He dragged her close and covered her mouth in a searing kiss. When he ran moist kisses along her throat, she sighed and arched herself in his arms.

She had dabbed rose water at her throat, and the fragrance was intoxicating. Like a long, hot summer night. He allowed his lips to linger, filling himself with a scent he knew he would remember for a lifetime.

The mercantile was dark, with only a thin sliver of light drifting through the doorway. Moonlight slanted in through the front windows and spilled at their feet in a pool of liquid gold.

When he looked at her, she seemed touched by magic. His hands roamed over her shoulders, and his fingertips moved from the lush velvet to the smooth texture of her skin.

Intrigued, he slipped his fingers beneath the fabric and found heat. He felt her fingers tighten at his shoulders and knew that she was as aroused as he.

He captured her mouth again and dived into the kiss, trying to tell her all the things he could never say.

Her response was instantaneous, her surrender complete. She tangled her fingers in his hair and clung to him as if desperate to get inside his skin.

With sighs and soft moans they moved together, needing fulfillment, seeking release.

The need for her was so great he thought about taking her here on the cold hard floor of the mercantile. At the same moment he chided himself for such thoughts. This was madness. And yet he needed her, wanted her.

"Dear God, Lizzy, I love you," he muttered against her lips. "I will always love you."

She thought her heart would explode with happiness. He loved her. Truly loved her. And though he had not asked her to stay with him, it would have to be enough to sustain her for a lifetime.

She touched a hand to his face and committed every craggy line, every curve to memory. "And I love you, Cody."

With a moan they came together in a kiss so hungry, so filled with longing, it spoke of the needs hidden deep in their hearts.

They heard the rush of footsteps, the rustling of skirts, a moment before a tiny, feminine voice broke the stillness.

"James, I know you're hiding in here. Come on, our wagon's leaving. My papa's waiting."

A small figure in a dainty gown darted through the darkened doorway and nearly collided with the couple standing in the shadows. The little girl skidded to a halt then backed up.

"I was playing hide-and-seek with James and Robbie. I—I found Robbie, and I thought James might be in here."

Before either of them could speak, she turned and fled.

With the moment shattered, Lizzy took a step back, smoothing her skirts as she did.

Cody clenched his hands at his sides and struggled to calm his ragged breathing.

For the first time they became aware of what was going on in the next room. The music had ended, and the sounds of the crowd grew louder as women sought wraps and men stomped outside to load empty dishes and sleeping babies into wagons.

"Grandpop will be waiting for me." Lizzy was surprised at how difficult it was to speak. She glanced up, meeting his dark eyes. "Will you ride with us as far as Mrs. Purdy's?"

It wasn't possible to face the final parting yet. Without a word he nodded.

Being careful not to touch, they walked slowly into the other room and forced themselves to say all the right things as friends and neighbors bade them goodnight.

"Don't forget the Christmas service tomorrow," Anna Purdy called to those who were leaving.

Cody watched as Lizzy picked up her shawl and followed her grandfather and sister to their wagon.

Lizzy was achingly aware of Cody as he pulled himself into the saddle and waited stiffly beside his brother's mount, while Ned took a moment to speak to each family that was leaving.

Neither of them was aware of the little boy who slunk out of his hiding place among the shelves of the mercantile. With his arms around Beau's neck, he gave the dog a quick hug, then climbed into the wagon and drew a fur robe around his trembling shoulders.

Chapter Twenty-Two

The sharp night air was filled with the sounds of voices raised in greeting, and laughter, and the jingling of sleigh bells. The snowstorm had swept past, leaving a clean white frosting over the land.

"It's past midnight," Amos said, checking his pocket watch.

"That means it's Christmas." Sara Jean's eyes glowed as she stared down at the tiny bundle in her arms. "Your first Christmas, Jobeth."

Lizzy thought how beautiful her sister looked, with snowflakes sparkling in her golden hair like a million tiny diamonds. It wasn't just her eyes that glowed. Everything about her seemed soft and golden tonight. She looked, Lizzy realized, like a woman in love.

She glanced at Ned and saw how his gaze fastened on Sara Jean's. They were sitting close together in the back of the wagon, their thighs brushing, their arms grazing. When the wagon came to a halt in front of Anna's house, Ned stepped down and took the baby from Sara Jean's arms before helping her to the ground.

"You're coming in, Cody," Anna said firmly. "You missed supper and the food at the dance, as well. But you're not missing all the wonderful things Lizzy and I baked today."

"Can I taste them, too?" James asked.

Lizzy realized it was the first time she'd heard him speak in hours. But then, she'd been too busy dancing with Cody to notice her little brother.

"Of course," Amos said. "Didn't you hear, boy? It's Christmas. This is a special time. You can stay up as late as you please and sample all your sister's fine cookies."

Suddenly, as the fact sank in, the night seemed to become even more festive. The little boy, who had been frowning, broke into a wide grin.

The house smelled of apples and spices. Cody breathed deeply as Anna went from room to room lighting the lanterns until the house was ablaze with light.

Amos and Cody carried logs into the parlor and busied themselves preparing a roaring fire. The dry evergreen boughs they used for kindling added their perfume to the air.

Lizzy and Anna hurried to the kitchen. While Lizzy made coffee and arranged cakes and cookies on a platter, Anna set glasses and a bottle of wine on a silver tray.

Sara Jean carried Jobeth upstairs to her bedroom. Ned trailed behind, carrying the cradle.

When he placed the cradle in the corner of the room, she laid the baby down. Ned handed her the blanket, and together they tucked it around the sleeping infant.

As they stood together gazing at the tiny figure, Sara Jean felt Ned's arm slip around her shoulders. It seemed so right, so natural, as though they'd always stood like this, gazing down at the baby.

Sara Jean looked up quickly and met his smile. "Jobeth was so good at the dance tonight."

He nodded.

"I felt so proud when everyone made such a fuss over her."

"So did I." Ned flushed. "I mean, she almost feels like my own."

"Does she?" Sara Jean didn't know why, but his admission made her happier than almost anything he could have said.

He turned her into his arms and touched a hand to her cheek. "Sara Jean, I've never been afraid of public speaking. At divinity school I found out I had a real talent for it." He swallowed. "But here, alone with you, I'm so afraid I'll say the wrong thing."

"What did you want to say, Ned?"

He took a deep breath. "I know it hasn't been so long since you lost your husband. There are those who think it's only right and proper for a woman to grieve for at least a year. So if you think I'm speaking out of turn, just tell me and I'll apologize."

She waited, feeling her heart begin to race.

When she made no protest, he said, "I don't have anything. No home, no money. And if the good people of Commencement don't want me to stay, I'll be forced to move on until I find another town looking for a minister, because I've decided that's what I have to be. There'll be no more turning my back on my calling. Without a gun or a trade, it isn't much of a life to share with a woman and her child. And I know I'm presuming a whole lot by asking..."

In her whole life, Sara Jean had never had an ounce of patience. But though these few moments were the longest of her life, she forced herself to remain silent, even though her heart was already shouting for joy.

"Sara Jean, I'll always do the best I can for you and Jobeth, and I swear I'll love her like my own, if only you'll say that—that you'll marry me."

Laughing and crying, Sara Jean threw her arms around his neck. "Oh, Ned. Oh, Ned," she began. But the rest of the words were lost as she hugged him fiercely.

"Does that mean I can go downstairs and ask your grandfather for your hand?" he whispered against her temple.

"Yes. Oh, yes." She moaned with pleasure as he finally brought his lips to hers.

He tasted the salt of her tears and thought his heart would surely burst from all the love he had locked inside.

"I love you, Sara Jean. More than I've ever loved anyone in my whole life. And I promise I'll go downstairs and ask Amos in just a minute," he breathed against her lips. "But first, I need a few minutes more to hold you."

* * *

Amos cleared his throat. Several times. "I have some very happy news."

Anna looked up from the candle she was lighting. James, rolling around on the floor with Beau, sat up. Lizzy entered the room carrying a platter of goodies and set them on a table, then gave him her attention.

It occurred to Amos that it should have been his son making this announcement. Who would have thought he'd outlive a fine, strapping man like Jonathan? Hadn't life dealt him a strange hand? But there was no sense thinking about something that would only make him sad. This was, after all, a happy occasion. And it had never been his way to question the Lord. There was some rhyme or reason for all this. And in time, it would be revealed.

"Ned has asked for Sara Jean's hand in marriage."

There was an audible gasp from Anna, who almost burned her fingers.

Lizzy raced across the room and hugged her sister. "Oh, Sara Jean, I'm so happy for you."

Sara Jean felt fresh tears and brushed them away as Lizzy turned to press a kiss to Ned's cheek.

Cody glanced toward his brother, standing beside Sara Jean. The two of them shared secret smiles. Then he glanced at Lizzy. She looked so right in her velvet gown, in an elegant, genteel house, surrounded by beautiful things. Whatever temptation he felt to carry her off to his mountaintop was swept away by the knowledge that, like her sister, this was the sort of life she deserved. He felt the knife twist in his heart as he crossed the room to his brother.

"Looks like you're making all kinds of important decisions," Cody said, shaking his brother's hand.

"Do you approve?"

"Absolutely. I can see that Sara Jean's already made you a happy man."

Anna was crying as she embraced first Sara Jean and then Ned. "Now at least I know some of you will be staying on." She dabbed a handkerchief to her eyes. "It was the only thing I wanted for Christmas. That my house wouldn't be empty ever again. Promise me you'll stay here with me until the parsonage is built."

Sara Jean threw her arms around Anna's neck. "You've been so good to me. I feel like I'm already home."

"Well." Amos cleared his throat again and began to pour elderberry wine into glasses. "It looks like we have to drink another toast."

He lifted his glass and said, "To Ned Martin and my granddaughter, Sara Jean. May you find the riches of life together."

Everyone drank.

"And may you help Jobeth remember her past, and forge a better future."

They drank again, more slowly, and Lizzy wondered if it was the wine or Grandpop's words that warmed her.

"Now we'll eat," Anna said firmly. "Lizzy, will you pour the coffee?"

James was the first one at the table. All day the wonderful aroma of spices and apples had driven the little boy half-crazy. Now he would get to sample every one of Lizzy's special Christmas cookies. When he reached for a fourth one, he waited to hear a scolding. But when no one said a word, he realized it was indeed a magic night. He slid his hand under the table and handed a sugar cookie to Beau. After all, it was Christmas. And Lizzy said Beau was one of God's creatures, too.

"That was a fine meal, Anna." Cody drained his cup. "But I suppose I'd better get started if I'm going to get back to my cabin in time to get my horses fed."

"It seems a shame that you won't be here for your brother's first Christmas service. Especially since it will also be his wedding day."

Cody ignored the shaft of pain that twisted in his heart. He was good at ignoring pain. He'd been doing it a long time now.

"It can't be helped. I have no one to see to the animals when I leave." He turned to Amos, carefully avoiding Lizzy. "I brought a present. It's for the whole family. I hid it behind the shed."

He strode from the house and was gone for so long the others had begun to twitch with anticipation. Then at last, hearing the sound of sleigh bells, they rushed to the door.

He had hitched their horse to a brand-new sleigh.

"But that was supposed to be your sleigh," Amos protested. "You said you were making it to haul lumber down the mountain."

"I'll make another one. But you need it more than I do. I started worrying about you traveling in that old wagon. You still have a long way to go in snow before you reach California. And I hated the thought of Lizzy...of all of you," he corrected, "trying to dig those wheels out of snowdrifts."

"But what about when the snow is gone?" Ned asked. "What will they do then?"

"The runners can be exchanged for wheels, which will fit in the back of the sleigh with their household items."

"Now, how did you think of that?"

Cody grinned. "It was something Anna said up at my cabin, when she was remarking that the stage couldn't exchange its wheels for runners to get through the snow."

Amos was impressed. He walked slowly around the sleigh, running his hands over the smooth wood. "It appears you've thought of everything. You do mighty fine work, Cody. If you decide not to breed horses, you can always earn your keep by working with wood."

"Thank you, sir." Cody glanced at Amos's gnarled old hands. One day his hands would be as leathery as those. Old and alone, with nothing to show for his life. Not children. Not grandchildren. Not Lizzy. The thought hurt more than he cared to admit.

"Well." Amos glanced at the others, standing in a cluster on the porch. "I guess now I'll have to show you my present."

With a chuckle he walked to the shed and threw open the door. Inside was the beginning of a sleigh, much like the one Cody had just presented them.

"Grandpop, it's another sleigh."

Amos laughed. "That it is, boy. But I'm a much slower worker than Cody. I figured we'd have to hang around Commencement for weeks while I completed our sleigh." He closed the shed door and tried not to think about the fact that he'd been looking forward to hanging around Anna Purdy's for a few more weeks while he worked on the sleigh. If he was lucky, he might have stretched out the work until spring.

"Thanks to Cody, it looks like we'll be able to leave right after Sara Jean's wedding."

No one said a word. It was as if they had all been struck mute.

Sara Jean glanced at the older sister she had always been able to count on. What would she do when Lizzy left? And James? And Grandpop?

Anna glanced at the man who clenched a pipe in his teeth while he walked slowly around the new sleigh. She had hoped and prayed that Amos would be persuaded to stay, at least until the snows melted. But now...

Lizzy studied the man who stood beside her grandfather. How many hours had Cody slaved over that wood to make a gift from the heart? A gift that, ironically, would seal their fates by hastening their separation.

Amos shot a quick glance at Lizzy and James. And though he said nothing, his look spoke volumes. He expected them to show the proper gratitude.

"Thank you, Cody," Lizzy began, feeling as if her heart was shattering into a million pieces. "That was kind of you."

"Well, James?" Amos challenged. "Don't you have something to say to Cody?"

The little boy hung his head and dropped a hand on Beau's neck.

"It's all right, Amos," Cody said quickly.

He walked to where his horse stood saddled and waiting, wishing he could have found a private moment with Lizzy. "It's time I took my leave." He pulled himself into the saddle and tried not to look at her. It would be too painful. "I wish you all a safe journey. I hope you find your heart's desire in California."

James glanced at Lizzy's face and saw the tear that squeezed from the corner of her eye and rolled down her cheek.

The little boy knew that his beloved sister had just lost all hope. Then he thought about the talk he'd had with Ned, when he'd confessed his worries about his family. After losing Ma and Pa, the little boy had kept his fears locked deep inside.

"Christmas," Ned had said, "is all about new beginnings. A tiny babe brought light into a world of darkness. This war we went through has extinguished the light in our land, James. Maybe this one magical day can light a new candle. A candle of hope. That's why our hearts will be light on Christmas. That's why we'll smile through our tears.''

James wanted desperately to bring a smile to Lizzy's face. It nearly broke his heart to see her cry. But how could he defy Cody, his hero? A man who had become, in his child's mind, larger than life.

He lifted his head, searching the heavens for a miracle. Lizzy had said that if you could find the Christmas star, you could ask for a miracle. But there were so many stars winking down at him. And then he spotted it, brighter than all the others. This time he wouldn't ask for anything for himself. This time his request was purely unselfish. His lips moved in simple prayer. And in that moment, he remembered what Cody had told him.

As Cody wheeled his mount and started down the lane, James swallowed hard and dug for courage.

''Cody.'' His high little voice was nearly carried away by the sigh of the wind, but he saw Cody turn his head. Cupping his hands to his mouth, he shouted, ''Cody, wait.''

Cody reined in his mount and turned in the saddle.

The others could only watch as the little boy jumped off the porch and began running after his horse.

''What is it, James?''

''You said, it's all right for a man to be afraid, as long as he does what's right.''

''Yes, son.''

The little boy's eyes flashed. He was doing this for Lizzy. He wouldn't let fear paralyze him. ''And you

said, if a man wants something badly enough, he has
to be willing to risk everything for it.''

''That's right.''

James struggled to find the words. Defiantly he
shouted, ''I was in the mercantile. I know about you
and Lizzy.''

Except for a narrowing of his eyes, Cody showed no
emotion.

Lizzy felt the others staring at her as she started
down the steps, then stopped and lowered her head.

Cody slipped from the saddle. This was too important a discussion not to speak face-to-face. Kneeling so
that his eyes were level with the boy's, he said softly,
''You heard what I said to Lizzy?''

The little boy lifted his head and met Cody's look.
''Yes, sir. You love her. And she loves you.''

On the porch, Ned and Sara Jean exchanged surprised glances.

Amos made a move to interrupt his grandson but
Anna caught his arm. ''Don't, Amos.''

''But the boy...''

She shook her head.

''So why are you sending her away?'' James demanded.

''I'm not sending her away.''

''You gave us a sleigh.''

''To make your journey safer. It's because I love her
that I want to keep her safe.''

''If you really love her, why don't you ask her to stay
here with you?''

"I have nothing to offer a woman as fine as Lizzy, son. Look around you. Look at Anna's house. This is where Lizzy belongs. In a town with friendly people. In a house with curtains at the windows, and soft feather beds. You saw how I live. How can I ask her to share a life of hardship in the wilderness?"

"You should at least ask."

"Then what would become of your grandfather?" Cody touched a hand to James's shoulder, but the little boy pulled away, determined to remain defiant. "Without Lizzy, how could your grandfather ever realize his dream of reaching California?"

Hearing that, Amos felt a tug at his heartstrings. Was it possible that Cody was actually sacrificing his own love because of an old man's dream?

"About California." Amos cleared his throat and glanced nervously at Anna, who was standing beside him. "I've been thinking that Commencement is a fine little town. A good place for a man to put down roots and start a new life."

Anna turned to stare at him with wide, shining eyes. "Are you saying you'll stay, Amos?"

"I might. That is, I'd like to. If you wouldn't think me an old fool."

She lifted a hand to his weathered cheek. "It was my fondest wish."

He caught her hand in his and their fingers laced as they turned to study Cody and the little boy.

"So," James prodded, "are you going to ask her?"

"You really think I have a chance?"

"She loves you," the little boy said firmly. "I heard her tell you. And she was really happy in your cabin." His voice lowered wistfully. "Who wouldn't be, with wild horses running right past the barn, and the prettiest little mare and foal in the world waiting for you every morning?"

"You make it sound like heaven, son."

"Yes, sir. I guess it is."

Cody stood, and though his words were directed at the little boy beside him, his gaze fastened on the woman who stood a little apart from the others. "If I was to ask her, and she agreed, would you be willing to come and live with us? After all, she is like your mother. Oh, I know I could never take your father's place," he added quickly, "but I'd do my best to be like a father to you."

James looked across to his sister and felt his heart nearly explode with longing. "Will you, Lizzy? Will you marry Cody and take me with you to live in his cabin?"

Lizzy knew that tears were streaming down her cheeks, but she couldn't stop them. Besides, they were happy tears. Ma always said happy tears didn't count.

Lifting her skirts, she raced the distance that separated them and flew into Cody's arms. With her lips pressed to his throat she murmured, "That's just about the most unromantic proposal I've ever heard."

"I warned you I wasn't much good with words."

"You don't have to be. James just said them for you."

The little boy seemed amazed as he looked around. "I did, didn't I?" He glanced toward his grandfather, standing beside a smiling Anna.

The little boy dropped to the ground and buried his face in Beau's neck. It might be all right for Lizzy to cry happy tears, but it wouldn't do for anyone to see him crying.

Years from now he would be able to recall this moment with exact clarity. And no one would ever be able to convince him that it wasn't the hand of God that had touched him, giving him the courage he needed to confront Cody.

"I guess we'll be having three weddings at the Christmas service instead of one." Ned's voice was warm with laughter. "I think it's safe to say this is one Christmas the town of Commencement is never going to forget."

"I know it's one I'll never want to forget." Cody drew Lizzy into his embrace and stared into her eyes. "I love you, Lizzy Spooner. And I can't imagine spending another night without you."

"Then you'll have your wish. It will be morning soon. And we can be married at the Christmas service."

"You won't mind living in a rough cabin miles from your family?"

She gave him a smile that melted the last of his fears. "I thought maybe we could get started on a family of our own. Do you think you could build an addition to the cabin?"

"I'll get started on it as soon as we get back."

"The addition?"

"The family," he growled against her ear.

With a laugh she flung her arms around his neck and he lifted her high in the air. Overhead, one star, brighter than all the others, winked in a black velvet sky. It was the dawn of Christmas, a time of magic.

Slowly, slowly, he lowered her until her lips met his. With a sigh she fitted against him as if made for him alone.

She had set out hoping only to find a safe haven in a world gone mad. Instead she had found so much more. A family that had learned they could withstand anything, as long as they stood together. A land of primitive beauty. A rugged man who touched her heart as no other man ever could. And a love to last a lifetime and beyond. Christmas was truly a time of miracles.

* * * * *

HISTORY IN
THE MAKING!

Join Harlequin Historicals as we celebrate our 5th anniversary of exciting historical romance stories! Watch for our 5th anniversary promotion in July. And in addition, to mark this special occasion, we have another year full of great reading.

- A 1993 March Madness promotion with titles by promising newcomers Laurel Ames, Mary McBride, Susan Amarillas and Claire Delacroix.

- The July release of UNTAMED!—a Western Historical short story collection by award-winning authors Heather Graham Pozzessere, Joan Johnston and Patricia Potter.

- In-book series by Maura Seger, Julie Tetel, Margaret Moore and Suzanne Barclay.

- And in November, keep an eye out for next year's *Harlequin Historical Christmas Stories* collection, featuring Marianne Willman, Curtiss Ann Matlock and Victoria Pade.

Watch for details on our Anniversary events wherever Harlequin Historicals are sold.

HARLEQUIN HISTORICALS . . .
A touch of magic!

HARLEQUIN®

Temptation®

Rebels & Rogues

Jared: He'd had the courage to fight in Vietnam. But did he have the courage to fight for the woman he loved?

THE SOLDIER OF FORTUNE
By Kelly Street
Temptation #421, December

All men are not created equal. Some are rough around the edges. Tough-minded but tenderhearted. Incredibly sexy. The tempting fulfillment of every woman's fantasy.

When it's time to fight for what they believe in, to win that special woman, our Rebels and Rogues are heroes at heart. Twelve Rebels and Rogues, one each month in 1992, only from Harlequin Temptation.

HARLEQUIN®

Temptation®

the **Fortune Boys**

A funny, sexy miniseries from bestselling
author Elise Title!

LOSING THEIR HEARTS MEANT
LOSING THEIR FORTUNES....

If any of the four Fortune brothers were unfortunate enough to
wed, they'd be permanently divorced from the Fortune
millions—thanks to their father's last will and testament.

BUT CUPID HAD OTHER PLANS!
Meet Adam in #412 **ADAM & EVE** (Sept. 1992)
Meet Peter #416 **FOR THE LOVE OF PETE**
(Oct. 1992)
Meet Truman in #420 **TRUE LOVE** (Nov. 1992)
Meet Taylor in #424 **TAYLOR MADE** (Dec. 1992)

WATCH THESE FOUR MEN TRY TO WIN
AT LOVE AND NOT FORFEIT $$$

HE CROSSED TIME FOR HER

Captain Richard Colter rode the high seas, brandished a sword and pillaged treasure ships. A swashbuckling privateer, he was a man with voracious appetites and a lust for living. And in the eighteenth century, any woman swooned at his feet for the favor of his wild passion. History had it that Captain Richard Colter went down with his ship, the *Black Cutter,* in a dazzling sea battle off the Florida coast in 1792.

Then what was he doing washed ashore on a Key West beach in 1992—alive?

MARGARET ST. GEORGE brings you an extraspecial love story this month, about an extraordinary man who would do anything for the woman he loved:

#462 THE PIRATE AND HIS LADY
by Margaret St. George

When love is meant to be, nothing can stand in its way . . . not even time.

Don't miss American Romance
#462 THE PIRATE AND HIS LADY.
It's a love story you'll never forget.

HARLEQUIN ◆ PRESENTS®

A Year Down Under

Beginning in January 1993, some of Harlequin
Presents's most exciting authors will join us as we
celebrate the land down under by featuring one title
per month set in Australia or New Zealand.

Intense, passionate romances, these stories will take
you from the heart of the Australian outback to the
wilds of New Zealand, from the sprawling cattle and
sheep stations to the sophistication of cities like
Sydney and Auckland.

Share the adventure—and the romance—
of A Year Down Under!

Don't miss our first visit in
HEART OF THE OUTBACK by Emma Darcy,
Harlequin Presents #1519, available in January
wherever Harlequin Books are sold.   YDU-G